MURDER AT MAR A LAGO

D1364015

D W Leber

PART ONE

CHAPTER ONE

M y wife, Audrey, and I had first been introduced to Palm Beach about twenty years earlier. We had had the pleasure of attending a business conference at the world-famous Breakers Palm Beach. We were quite taken by the beauty and conspicuous wealth of the hotel and even more so by Palm Beach in general.

The hotel, we learned, was literally the epicenter of the town of Palm Beach. Its address spoke volumes—One County Road. Every building to the north was numbered and listed as North County Road, and any property south of the hotel had a number followed by South County Road. The Breakers also sat on over one hundred acres in the middle of what was likely the most expensive real estate in the world. And the hotel ownership apparently thought nothing of dedicating the majority of those precious acres to a full eighteen-hole golf course, enabling their guests to tee off no more than a fifty-yard walk from the hotel lobby.

We enjoyed our luxurious accommodations in the Breakers, complete with beautiful ocean views. Audrey and I spent hours sunbathing at the hotel's private beach and pools. We also relished the lunches and dinners we shared in the many Palm Beach restaurants. Palm Beach restaurants were naturally places of elegance and superb cuisine, but they were more about character and tradition. We found them ideal for people watching, and we wondered what their lives were really like. It was a bit overwhelming.

We were instantly hooked on Palm Beach and after repeating the Breakers Hotel experience many times over the next five years or so, and after our youngest began her college years, we dared to investigate the possibility of renting an apartment for an extended period of time—that is, for the *season*.

The season extended from Christmas through March. It was a tradition started in the early nineteen hundreds by the developer of all of South Florida, Henry Flagler. In the brief few weeks of the season, all high society and socially significant events were scheduled—the Heart Ball, the Red Cross Ball, and the Emerald Society Ball, to name a few. Also scheduled were other, smaller events too numerous to mention: dinners, cocktail parties, and charitable events to support causes from housing the homeless to feeding the cats.

A real estate agent who had been highly recommended to us turned out to be a real Palm Beach dowager. Elenore Huggens was a Palm Beach fixture who had been selling real estate for literally decades and whose friendship we gained and have cherished ever since. She preferred to be addressed as Ellie.

She escorted us to a number of potential rentals from the northern end of Palm Beach to the south strip of the island over a period of several days, all to no avail. Audrey politely explained to Elenore, "You have shown us many lovely and acceptable units. However, we're not crazy about their location."

The northern end of Palm Beach was a family-oriented community, mixing modest, single-story homes with grand mansions. Several of the more modest homes were in our price range, but we were not interested in accepting the added responsibilities of maintaining a house. My wife and I agreed to eliminate that section of the island as a potential seasonal rental.

The Southern Strip of Palm Beach Island is just as its description implies: it is the southern portion of Palm Beach. As for the term "Strip," the island narrows to no more than four or five blocks wide at its southernmost border. The real estate in this area was comprised almost exclusively of multi-unit buildings on the oceanfront, and there were several apartments available for rent. The apartments there were larger and our options far more plentiful than in town, but we agreed that we would prefer to spend less time in Palm Beach and continue to frequent the Breakers Hotel rather than be that far removed from the excitement of central Palm Beach.

To give some additional feedback, my wife further explained to Elenore, "We don't wish to waste your time, and we are well aware that the options are limited, but we would prefer to be in town and have the ability to walk to shops and restaurants rather than have to drive thirty minutes. Quite candidly, Ellie, we enjoy a few cocktails and prefer not to drive."

Ellie got the message, but the problem was that there were precious few apartments available in our price range in our preferred location.

As fate would have it, and in what must have been desperation on Ellie's part, we entered an in-town condo on Chilean Avenue that had suffered substantial damage due to a water leak. It seemed that a fifty-cent plastic coupling in the hall powder room cracked, and since the owner was out of town for two months, and the apartment was a ground-floor unit, the leak was not discovered until the hardwood floors and wall-to-wall carpeting in the entire place were soaked and ruined.

When we inspected the apartment, it was under restoration. The furniture was covered in plastic, but dust covered the plastic and everything else. Ellie and Audrey were heading to the door, and they were surprised to hear me say "How much?" Then they were further shocked to hear me add, "Not to rent. To buy."

Elenore shrieked, "Nate, are you nuts?"

Through the dust and disarray, I could see the pecky cypress ceilings, the coral-stone fireplace, and the beautifully refurbished bathrooms. Once the floors were finished, all that would be needed were elbow grease and paint. Little did we realize that the purchase of our new condo would set us aside from the tourists and renters of Palm Beach. It mattered little how grand our accommodations were. What mattered was that we were now permanent Palm Beachers. It certainly had that effect on Vincent Xavier Houten.

One evening, shortly after our purchase, we headed to the popular Taboo Restaurant on Worth Avenue for dinner. As we left our complex, we noticed a party on the terrace of a large penthouse apartment directly across South County Road from our building. The terrace railings were decorated with white string lights, and the laughter and music wafted down onto us as we passed. All in all, it appeared to be a very chic, fun event. I joked to my wife that although we weren't in Palm Beach for more than a few weeks, we were social outcasts. "There's another party we weren't invited to."

Fate once again prevailed because the very next day, while enjoying the sun on the Chilean Avenue public beach, only one long block walk from our new condo, we observed a man walking along the sand with a long stick, or maybe it was a staff.

Audrey commented, "How odd. Nate, do you think he is a derelict or an eccentric?"

A few hours later, we were enjoying oysters and a beer at the bar in Charlie's Crab Restaurant, and to our surprise, the odd man entered accompanied by a significantly tall and even more significantly beautiful woman. The pair sat next to us.

Charlie's Crab was the only non-hotel ocean front restaurant in Palm Beach. In the few short weeks since we had purchased, cleaned, and decorated our new acquisition, the restaurant bar had become part of our new ritual. We would spend as much time on the beach as possible, clean up as best as we could, and go to Charlie's for afternoon cocktails and a snack with a tasteful seafood flair.

It took no time at all for Audrey to strike up a conversation with the odd man, and little more time to discover that he used his staff to turn over dry seaweed in search of sea beans. Surprisingly, it was true. He'd learned this hobby as a child from his uncle Bob, and he had thousands of beans: Brazilian from the Amazon, Cuban hearts from Cuba obviously, and the most elusive Sea Pearl, a milky white bean from the East African coast. He was not a derelict, but Vincent Xavier Houten was definitely an eccentric.

As we chatted and enjoyed a few more beers, we informed them that we had recently purchased and just completed decorating a condo in town. "Congratulations! Where is your apartment?" Vincent now had a heightened interest.

Audrey proudly responded, "Casa Two Fourteen." Then to give Vincent and his lovely companion additional detail, she added, "Just off the corner of Chilean and South County."

Almost interrupting my wife, Vincent stated, "I know Casa Two Fourteen."

The eccentric's lady companion joined in the conversation with a hearty laugh and an accent that I could not quite identify. "Vincent's penthouse is across the street on South County, and I live around the block on Australian Avenue. We are all neighbors."

My wife and I instantly came to the realization that it was Vincent's party that we had observed the night before. As Audrey relayed my comment of not being invited to another Palm Beach party, his face lit up like a boy's on Christmas Day. "Not to worry! I'm having another tonight, and you're invited. Come between six-thirty and seven for cocktails, and then we all are going to Nando's Restaurant for dinner at eight. Please join us."

We didn't know who the "all" were but couldn't care less. There was no trepidation or hesitation. We, the Stevens, were going to our first private party in Palm Beach and excited was an inadequate term to describe how we were feeling.

Not to appear to be overly anxious, we purposely aimed at the latter end of the suggested time frame, arriving at seven. The doorman quickly checked our names against the guest list in hand and motioned to the elevator saying, "Go right up. You're expected. Penthouse number two."

What we encountered was a vastly different Vincent X. Houten from the odd eccentric we had observed that very afternoon. His hair, complete with graying temples, was loosely brushed straight back. He wore a blue blazer over gray linen slacks, a starched white shirt adorned by a blue-and-gold striped bow tie with matching pocket-handkerchief. Sockless, in alligator loafers, he observed our entrance and moved quickly to greet us.

Vincent's attire could not be described as elegant but was rather aristocratic. His horn-rimmed tortoiseshell glasses gave him the added air of an intellectual. Both were in stark contrast to the bean hunter we had encountered over beer and oysters.

Our host doted over us. He graciously introduced us to the other guests as his new friends, making us feel as though we truly belonged. He escorted us to the bar station manned by Marco to oversee our cocktail request, and once we all had drinks in hand, he leaned toward us and quietly predicted, "We are going to be great friends. I can feel it."

That was the beginning of a fifteen-year friendship. It was more like a fifteen-year amusement ride that was almost addictive, and each year, my wife and I stole more and more time away from our New Jersey home and business to get our fix.

Until Monday morning, January first, when Vincent Xavier Houten was found slumped over the console of his 1956 Jaguar XK 140 convertible. The bullet, it was confirmed, entered slightly behind his left ear and since it was from a small-caliber Saturday night special, it lodged in his head and left no exit wound.

His car was parked in the employee parking area at Donald Trump's Mar-A-Lago Club. Due to the exquisite condition of his favorite classic auto, one of fourteen, Vincent would not let valets park for him. As he was a prominent and regular member of the club, the employees were accustomed to seeing Vincent's vintage cars in the more secluded parking area. Therefore they did not take notice that it was there when they left for home after serving a New Year's Eve extravaganza, complete with a fireworks finale provided by the Grucci family.

His body was discovered just before 9:00 a.m. on New Year's Day. The fifteen-year amusement-park ride had come to a screeching halt. A new ride was about to begin, one that would prove to be anything but amusing.

CHAPTER TWO

On New Year's Day, due to our evening of celebrating, Audrey and I were barely able to drag ourselves to the ten thirty mass at St. Edward's Church on North County Road. Although we were surely not very attentive, we both found the church to be an oasis, an escape from the isle of excess upon which we lived. On that particular morning, we enjoyed the serenity and solemnity of the service and the message of a new year and a new beginning. With the help of our friend Elenore Huggens, some years back we had traded our original apartment for one in an oceanfront building one block's walk from St. Edward's.

January first was a holy day of obligation for us Roman Catholics, and after the service, Audrey and I took a leisurely stroll toward Royal Poinciana Way and Testa's Restaurant for their Sunday and holiday brunch. Testa's Restaurant is another Palm Beach institution. Established in 1921, it has a wonderful following for both lunch and dinner, but the Sunday brunch has a religiously faithful following.

Although a few spicy bloody marys helped, our energy levels were still pretty low, so we finished our brunch and opted to head back to our apartment for a restful afternoon. I was thinking of the couch and some football. Audrey usually took the bed, a novel, and a nap. We approached the building at about 12:45 p.m. and couldn't help but notice the police vehicles parked at the front entrance. One was a painted patrol car and the other, a dark, unmarked sedan that had police written all over it.

It was not terribly surprising to see police or fire department activity at our building, although past activities were more often the result of a frying pan left on the stove for a few hours. My wife and I weren't expecting anything unusual. What surprised us was being addressed by name by a Palm Beach detective as soon as we entered the lobby. We had most likely been identified to the detective by our doorman, Judas—or was his name John?

Detective Edward Gerity was professional, and that, when translated, meant direct and callous. He spent little time informing us that our friend was dead—that he had, in fact, been murdered. I could not completely recall the conversation, but it went something like this.

"I'm sorry to have to inform you that Vincent Houten was found dead this morning. I believe you knew him."

I didn't know how to respond. I simply asked, "What happened?"

His less-than-compassionate response to my question went directly to the point. "Murdered." And without so much as pausing to take a breath, the detective stated, "A gunshot, at close range, to the head."

I was truly overwhelmed by the shock at having to face the sudden reality of such a gruesome act perpetrated on someone I knew so intimately. After all, how many people knew someone who had been murdered? Shock is a strange sensation. Your eyes are working, but you don't see anything, not anything that registers in your brain anyway. You start breathing in short, rapid breaths like mild hypertension, at least I did. Audrey, on the other hand, nearly collapsed. In hindsight, she was most likely already overcome by grief at the loss of her friend and our constant companion. As it has been said, men are from Mars, and women are from Venus.

Detective Edward Gerity, who informed us that he preferred being called Chuck (I don't know how you get *Chuck* out of *Edward*), gave us a minute or two to gather ourselves, then asked us to come to the police headquarters to assist in the investigation. His tone indicated he was all business, and I had the feeling that "assist" might not have been an accurate term for what was to come.

"Officer Charles will drive you to the station and bring you back when we are finished." He stated this as if he were describing the accommodations one would expect at the Breakers Hotel, except he wasn't offering. He was telling.

We were transported to the Palm Beach police station in the patrol car, not in Detective Chuck's sedan. There was a plexiglass divider separating us from Officer Charles. When we arrived at our destination, I realized that the rear doors could only be opened from the outside. That had a very chilling effect on me. The initial shock must have been wearing off because I was coming to the realization that my wife and I were actually suspects in our friend's murder.

Oh, maybe I should mention—we were the last people to have seen Vincent Xavier Houten alive.

CHAPTER THREE

T he plan for New Year's Eve was to meet at Vincent Houten's house at seven thirty for cocktails, then attend the Mar-A-Lago celebration, arriving fashionably late at 9:00 p.m. Vince's companion for the evening was his current live-in girlfriend, Megan Kelly. Meg was a stunning, thirty-five-year-old, five-foot-eleven-inch, Worth Avenue, Palm Beach model.

Megan agreed to move in with Vince after their second date. She obviously recognized a good deal when she saw one. As for Vincent, at sixty-six, he was in love with the deal, at least most of the time. But for V. X. Houten, as he liked to refer to himself, a live-in arrangement did not mean a monogamous relationship. That was the root of many confrontations between them.

Mar-A-Lago, "Sea to Lake," was designed and built in 1927 by Marjorie Merriweather Post, who used it as her private winter estate. Currently, it was owned by Donald Trump and operated as a private beach, tennis, and dinner club. Its ballroom was large enough to host more than five hundred guests, but even that was not large enough for The Donald. Mr. Trump's variance application for a larger venue was just one of a number of legal battles he waged with Palm Beach. Most of the legal challenges initiated by Mr. Trump had been decided in The Donald's favor, causing great frustration to the "don't change my Palm Beach" crowd.

Subsequent to the purchase of Mar-A-Lago, in short order, The Donald was able to become the bane of the old Palm Beach establishment. He dared to accept the nouveau riche not accepted by the old establishment. He provided a spectacular alternative for those for whom society and ethnicity meant little and the ability to pay the fare meant everything.

Vincent was not from old money, but he had built a very successful business in Kansas City, was prep-school educated, and had very sophisticated tastes, as evidenced not only by his exquisite classic car collection but also by the museum-quality antiques that decorated his homes in Palm Beach and Kansas City. Lastly and more importantly Vince had the charm of the Great Gatsby. Audrey and I often wondered why he had joined Mar-A-Lago and not one of the more established Palm Beach social clubs.

Some years prior to all of this, and as guests of our friend Eleanor Huggens, we had lunch at the Everglades Country Club, a quiet celebration of the purchase of our latest condo. The Everglades is one of the most exclusive and least inclusive clubs in the country. We had enjoyed lunch there after a round of golf on a few previous occasions but had not had the pleasure of touring the extensive interior of the clubhouse. After lunch, Ellie rectified that lack completely with a historical-architectural review of the building's array of interconnecting venues, able to accommodate events of various sizes.

The club was quite unique, combining a Moorish exterior with a spattering of Swiss-painted ceiling beams in its large foyer and a main ballroom equipped with a retractable ceiling so that revelers could literally dance under the stars.

My wife and I were grateful for the special treatment, but before departing, Audrey couldn't help but ask Ellie, "Wouldn't Vincent Houten be better suited as a member here rather than the Mar-A-Lago Club?"

Eleanor might be described as a dowager because her better years were behind her, but she was not ready to give up any time soon. Many years ago, she had married (and shortly after, divorced) James Francis Huggens. Mr. Huggens was one of the founders of the First Bank of Palm Beach. He subsequently died, as she said "quite prematurely." I wondered what a more appropriate time to die might have been.

Due to the brevity of their marriage and his untimely death, Ellie did not significantly gain from either event. He hadn't left her financially well off, but he had introduced her to Palm Beach society, where she had gained acceptance and a sense of belonging. She would not let go of that.

Ellie Huggens' social acceptance greatly benefited her career. She was not unfamiliar with the sale or purchase of properties in the eight-figure range, but she also was not above helping a friend or the friend of a friend find an inexpensive apartment or even a seasonal rental, even if it meant little or no financial reward for her. People like her were hard to find in Palm Beach.

To Audrey's inquiry, Ellie replied in her gravelly voice, "Vincent Houten?" After a pause, she repeated, "Vincent Houten?" She needed a minute to collect herself. "You don't understand. Everyone loves Vince. Everyone loves to attend his Super Bowl party or his Oscar Night party or even invite him to their parties, but he could never become a member of Everglades." For emphasis she added, "Or the Bath and Tennis."

The Bath and Tennis Club was the other less-inclusive club in Palm Beach. It was located on the sands of the Atlantic, immediately adjacent to The Donald's Mar-A-Lago and far less grand than its neighbor—a true thorn in the side of Palm Beach's old money.

The membership of the B and T, as the Palm Beach Bath and Tennis Club is known, argued that the club's drab, aged interior was a reflection of tradition and understated elegance, but when Mr. Trump obtained final approval for the construction of his breathtaking, oceanfront pool and cabana, the old guard was green with envy. In short order, they erected No Trespassing signs on the beach between the two clubs. A not- so- subtle message to the Mar A Lago riff-raff that there was a line in the sand, physically and figuratively, that they could never cross.

Ellie Huggens' comments were so definite that all we could do was wait for her to elaborate—or not. After all, we were her guests. She finally ended the conversation with the simplest of explanations. "It's the girlfriends." Then for emphasis, she slowly shook her head and said, "So many girlfriends."

Vincent's lady friend at that time was one Joan Olsen. She was well accepted in most Palm Beach social circles and served on many committees, both civic and charitable. She had once been honored as a Distinguished South Florida Leading Business Women of 1999. We thought that she could be the difference for Vincent, but there were many lady friends before her and, as time would show, many to follow. We came to understand that neither Vince nor his potential sponsors, members of these bastions of Palm Beach society, would risk the humiliation of a rejected application.

Vincent X. Houten was most interested in enjoying the moment. Maybe he was experiencing a midlife crisis, or maybe he just craved being loved, or maybe he didn't enjoy his own company, or maybe he wasn't properly toilet trained—the bottom line was our friend just wanted to have fun, and we were along for the ride.

His relationship with Joan Olsen was based on her ability to gain him entry into those social circles that would otherwise have been closed to him. He might have been a successful wealthy businessman, but he was still from Kansas City, after all.

Mrs. Olsen did gain him an entrée into appropriate events and also guidance as to the size of the obligatory donations, but their romantic relationship did not last very long because she was just not exciting enough for Vincent. And in Vincent Houten's world, that was unforgivable. He would have liked to be more socially accepted but not at the price of boredom.

When their romantic relationship was obviously over, Joanie moved to Aspen to start a new business venture and a new societal experience, but she never let her relationship with Vincent completely wither. In fact, she made sure to return for the appropriate balls, exhibits, and even a few car shows, to all of which Vincent would arrange invitations, transportation, and even serve as her escort, as long as his current girlfriend, Megan Kelly, was out of sight. Such engagements when exposed were the source of great consternation for Miss Kelly.

CHAPTER FOUR

The Megan Kelly/Vincent Houten relationship had begun almost three years before his murder. Vincent had seen Megan several times modeling on Worth Avenue and was obviously attracted to her. One day, on a whim, he extended an invitation to his Super Bowl party, never expecting she would accept. That party was the start of Vince and Meg and everything that came after. I remember Vincent telling me about their first encounter in great detail.

As I recalled, it was February three years prior to his New Year's Eve murder. The morning following his annual Super Bowl party, I decided to once again take advantage of my friend's hospitality. I drove to his Chilean Avenue house on the ruse that maybe Vince could use my assistance in the cleanup and reorganization of his home after the revelry of the previous evening. I was pleasantly relieved when he greeted me enthusiastically, invited me into an immaculately clean house, and offered me a Vincent Houten custom-made bloody mary.

Vincent's special added ingredients to Mr. T's Bloody Mary mix were simply a generous splash of beef bullion, a half teaspoon of horseradish, complemented by approximately four ounces of vodka. The result was a libation designed to right the ship.

Over drinks, we shared some amusing events that we recalled from the night before such as who got quite drunk, who was hitting on whom, who won the gambling pool, which I perennially conducted, and a few other inane happenings. We enjoyed reminiscing for a while but then pondered the appropriate venue for an enjoyable lunch.

We settled upon the Bice Restaurant on Peruvian Avenue, but not the inner dinning area. We liked the courtyard, which extends south from the main restaurant into the Via Mizner. The tables were always elegantly set and adorned with large, bright yellow umbrellas. The Via Mizner's architecture allowed you to imagine that you were dining not in Florida but somewhere in the Mediterranean.

A bottle or two of Chianti, a salad, and a half order of one of Bice's authentic Italian pasta dishes were always reliable ingredients for a wonderful afternoon. Vincent and I had just finished our salads and were still laughing at some of our recollections of his annual Super Bowl party and the fact that we did not actually recall who had played in the game, much less who won, when the very attractive Megan Kelly entered the Via Mizner.

Vincent was the first to notice her as I was sitting with my back to the entrance of the Via Mizner. His face brightened, and with his gaze fixed over my shoulder, he said, "Nate, you have got to see this."

I wasn't the least bit embarrassed by turning completely around to observe Megan's entrance and admire her ensemble. It was a very pleasant scene, and I did not feel the need to abbreviate the experience, so I did the only logical thing. I adjusted my chair to face in her direction and took hold of my glass of wine.

Megan was wearing a skirt, midthigh in length and tight enough to accentuate the form of her upper thighs and well-proportioned posterior. Her blouse was a loose-fitting, full-sleeved model, like something from the *Pirates of Penzance*, and fashionably unbuttoned to just above the navel. The scene was about to get even better.

Megan very professionally stopped at every table, described her outfit to the patrons seated there, left the boutique of the day's business card, and then moved onto the next table. When she reached our table, she approached from over my right shoulder and proceeded directly to where Vincent was seated. She made her approach slowly but deliberately until, for maximum effect, her thighs were pressed against the top of our table.

Looking down on us as from on high, staring straight into Vincent's eyes, she asked, "Do you see anything you like?"

"Everything" was all Vince could conjure up in response.

She slowly turned and glided in the direction of the main dining area to continue fulfilling her obligation to her employer who, for this day, was the famous fashion designer Fiadanca. But before leaving our sight, Megan gracefully came to a stop, turned around to face us once more, and addressed Vincent quite directly. "Call me," she said.

You couldn't describe her comment as an invitation. It definitely wasn't a request. It wasn't even a suggestion. It was more like a command. Vincent's laughter filled the Via Mizner.

Slightly mesmerized, I watched Megan move through the terrace doors of the restaurant and into the interior dining room. Once she was out of sight, I turned to my friend and asked, "Would you care to explain?"

His laughter had subsided, but his smile seemed painted on his face. He did not quickly offer an explanation, but I remained silent, confident in the knowledge that if he were withholding any information of substance, he could not keep it to himself for long.

Vincent was not someone you could expect to keep your confidences, especially if the secrets shared with him included sex, and more importantly, if he deemed that the dissemination of such knowledge might serve to enhance his image. What information he was presently withholding fit into both categories.

It didn't take more than a minute or two before V. X. Houten began recanting some events at the Super Bowl party that related to the latest object of his affection. He described how annoyed his weekend date, Jaycee from Kansas City, had grown due to the attention he was paying Ms. Megan Kelly (and therefore not paying her). He humbly acknowledged that he was a cad to have embarrassed Jaycee, but he admitted that he was completely carried away by Megan.

Vincent was between live-ins at the time. Joanie was in Aspen, and Megan was not yet in the picture. He dated numerous ladies— tall, short, blond, brunette, he was indiscriminate. Some were attractive, and quite frankly, a few were less than beautiful. Audrey once asked me, "As a man, what characteristics do you think Vincent looks for in a woman?"

My answer was simple. "They have to wear a skirt and have a pulse."

Jaycee was different. First of all she was age appropriate, which could not be said of most other companions. She had a wonderful sense of humor and was a down-to-earth, midwestern lady. She was quite attractive and apparently well liked in Kansas City where my wife and I had the pleasure to meet her on more than one occasion.

Impatiently, I said, "Vincent, cut to the chase."

I knew my friend was willing and longing to spill his guts, and predictably, he responded to my request immediately and in great detail. He explained how he, in a flirtatious conversation with Ms.

Kelly the evening before, had expressed his admiration of her beauty, statuesque figure, and most specifically, her breasts.

"Well, 'Would you mind if I felt them?' is what I actually said," he confessed to me.

Incredulously, I asked, "How do you ask a woman to feel her breasts? A woman you met only once? Why didn't she just slap you?"

He explained that after lavishing her with compliments, he suggested to Megan Kelly that she was most likely the type of woman who would take such a request as a compliment rather than an insult. He queried her as to why a women would respond to such a suggestion with a "how dare you" rather than a "thank you for your keen observation."

All I could say was "Please go on."

Vincent and Megan's conversation took place at the service bar near the loggia that separated the house from the pool area. An aging gay bartender named Marvin, who plied his trade at many private events, year in and year out, all over the island, was tending the bar. He might have overheard what the pair was saying, but no doubt he had heard far more scandalous conversations.

Megan obviously thought Vincent's request was very amusing. Without a pause, she straightened her spine, rolled her shoulders back, shook out her hair, and said, "OK."

Vincent told her, "Not here." Then he took Megan by the hand and led her out the side door of his house, which was just a few steps behind the service bar. They left their cocktails on the bar with Marvin and exited into the covered parking area that housed the overflow of his vintage cars.

The cars were on their right, and to their left was a garden wall and wooden gate that separated the parking area from the pool. The DJ's station was immediately on the poolside of the garden wall, providing them with the protection of a noise filter and eliminating the possibility of an unwelcome intruder accessing the gate.

In the questionable privacy of their surroundings, Vincent wasted no time in attending to the agreed-upon task. As soon as Megan turned to face him, he reached out to caress her. It didn't take long for Megan to respond and become aroused by the outrageousness of the event. She asked Vincent a ridiculously obvious question. "Would you like to see what you are feeling?"

She was wearing a simple, straight-fitting, one-piece Bebe dress that fell to four inches above the knee. Megan reached down and in one fell swoop, pulled the dress over her head with no more effort than removing a T-shirt, revealing the fact that she was wearing absolutely nothing else.

Vincent told me that he couldn't move. He didn't resume caressing her. He had no idea how far this would go or where it might end. He said he just kept looking and waited to see what Megan would do next.

Megan theatrically "let a tender moment alone" and for a few seconds, simply allowed Vincent to absorb the image in front of him. She finally stepped closer and engaged him in a lingering and passionate kiss. Continuing to stare into his eyes, she unzipped his trousers, assured herself of his readiness, and then turned her back to him.

Her palms on the hood of his 1957 Mercedes Benz 300, they consummated the beginning of their relationship, a very rocky relationship. As they returned to the party, they retrieved the drinks they had left in Marvin's care. Marvin didn't even have to refresh their ice.

CHAPTER FIVE

The Palm Beach police station was another unique feature of our exclusive island. We all, Vincent, Audrey, and I, had observed its construction some twelve years ago or so. Vince, who as well as being a gracious and generous host, was also a frugal man, and he took great exception to the cost of such an opulent facility to house a garrison in this virtually crime-free community.

If exquisite architecture were not enough, it was also located on County Avenue, two short blocks north of Worth Avenue and immediately adjacent to Café Europe, one of the finest restaurants in all of Florida, much less Palm Beach. Additionally, as required by the Architectural Review Board of the same City of Palm Beach, the exterior design had to be compatible with the Mizner style that dominated the immediate neighborhood. The result was a structure that looked more suited to hosting a state dinner than dealing with the underbelly of society. Taxpayers be dammed. This was Palm Beach.

I understood that in the early stages of a murder investigation, everyone was a suspect, but I don't care how many detective novels you read: being treated as a suspect is not an experience easily described. When we arrived at the Palm Beach police station, the patrolman escorted us to a small conference room. I suspected that it wasn't the interrogation room because there were six chairs instead of two, and instead of one light bulb hanging from the ceiling as portrayed in countless movies, there was a long fluorescent light fixture, which frankly had a very similar effect.

Detective Gerity was nowhere to be seen. I guessed that was for effect. So while we waited, Audrey and I talked intermittently about the unimaginable horror of Vincent's murder. We talked about some of the great times we had shared but spoke more of the immediate plans we had had with Vince for tomorrow and the next day and the day after that. When we were all in town, we did everything together. Strangely enough, we didn't broach the subject of who might have done such a thing.

After what seemed like an hour or more (but was probably closer to fifteen minutes), Detective Gerity entered the room and began the inquisition. Foolish of us to think that we were only there to provide assistance. He began by informing us that he would be recording the interview, then went onto basic information: name, address, and the like. He next asked questions about our relationship with Mr. Vincent Houten. How long had we known him, when did we meet, how often were we in his company? That being sufficiently settled, he moved onto the events of the previous night.

Detective Gerity was now focused on the timeline of the evening. "What time did you arrive at the Houten house for the cocktails before going to the ball? Who was there when you arrived? Who came next? What time was that?"

It was obvious that the line of questioning was intended to determine the chronological details of who arrived at what time and who left the table during the course of the evening, for how long and for what purpose? As you can imagine, at a New Year's party, you can probably with accuracy remember what time you arrived and maybe with less accuracy what time you left, but to recall the details of events in the middle was really stretching it.

Audrey and I were guessing at a number of answers, and I for one could not see how our responses could possibly help the investigation. This was getting tedious. Then one question shocked us out of our boredom and back to reality.

"Was Mr. Houten involved in any type of an altercation last evening?"

The question was simple, but our answers were a bit complicated, mine especially. "No, well maybe, well, I don't know if you could call it an altercation."

Audrey's response was better but not by much. She tried to explain that it was more like an argument rather than an altercation. "I mean there was no violence, physical, I mean, well, not much anyway."

Audrey had had a front row seat at the altercation (or argument) and what led up to it. She was seated next to Megan Kelly at Meg's then mysterious insistence (although the reason Megan wanted to be next to Audrey was later clear to me). My wife began to explain the events that had resulted in Vincent and Megan arriving together but leaving separately. The more she explained, the more explaining was necessary. As I listened to Audrey's account, I kept repeating two questions in my mind. *Did Megan really do this? Could Megan really have done this?* My conclusion was a pretty emphatic no, but in my mind, there was a little too much emphasis on the qualifying word "pretty."

Detective Gerity's question—"Was there an altercation?"—addressed to both my wife and me, naturally caused me to reflect on Vincent and Megan's relationship.

To describe the Kelly-Houten relationship as volatile would be accurate but not complete. It was not terribly violent. There had been a rare incident or two of Megan slapping Vincent, but more often the volatility took the form of a verbal tirade. Vincent's habit of maintaining "platonic" relationship with old girlfriends, and his proclivity for extending a welcome to any attractive female new to Palm Beach, left Miss Kelly furiously jealous. This was the source of the volcanic reaction now under question, whether it was an altercation or an argument.

The New Year's Eve evening started out as planned at Villa V, the residence of Vincent Xavier Houten. We arrived pretty much on schedule. Another couple had already arrived and were enjoying a cocktail with Vincent, who as always was looking elegant in his tuxedo and black patent-leather shoes. He was sockless, of course. He raised a glass of Cabernet toward us in greeting.

Audrey and I had not met our fellow guests but knew that they were Vincent's friends from Kansas City who were in town for the holidays. Megan was in her normal routine, which meant she was not even close to being dressed. She put down her vodka on the rocks, welcomed us with a kiss, and ascended the stairs to prepare herself for the festivities.

Once we were introduced to the Reynolds and had our beverages in hand, my wife and I settled in. We found their company to be extremely pleasant. Vincent served light hors d'oeuvres, direct from Publix's supermarket refrigerator to his cocktail table. The atmosphere was relaxed, and time passed quickly. I mentioned to Vincent that maybe we should consider moving onto Mar-A-Lago, and at that moment, Megan made her entrance in grand fashion. In all honesty, the woman looked absolutely stunning.

As Megan started descending the stairs, she stopped after the third or fourth stair and offered an apology for being so tardy to all who could hear. She was not looking for forgiveness but for attention, and her technique worked to perfection. Now with everyone's attention upon her, she continued her descent pausing at every step, exhibiting the grace that her modeling career had instilled in her.

Her dress clung to her as if it were another layer of skin. As she stood several feet above us on the staircase, she had our undivided attention. Therefore the first thing that drew my attention was the slit in her full-length dress that exposed the majority of her impressively long and beautifully shaped right leg. When she reached floor level, and in her four-inch heels, she was still inches taller than the men and almost a foot taller than the women, her plunging neckline was my next point of interest. Braless as always, and uninhibited by modesty, Megan left little to the imagination. Vince was in his glory.

Audrey informed me that the dress was a Vera Wang and that I should wipe the drool from my mouth.

We caravanned to Mar-A-Lago in separate cars because we all had different plans for after midnight. Once there, we were separated due to the volume of vehicles arriving at the same time, but after our cars were taken care of, we reconnected on the terrace, where cocktails were being served overlooking the West Pool, which was lighted especially for the evening. It started slowly, but it started there.

Vincent shared a few Happy New Year greetings with some fellow members as he entered the club. After finishing his first wine at the club (but who knows how many he had had already that evening), he decided to locate and extend greetings to some other members. He excused himself to get another glass of wine, and according to Megan, he took an unacceptable amount of time to return. Vince knew how to work a room, or as he expressed it, he liked to "check the traps," always looking for some new talent.

Upon his return, Meg expressed her displeasure to Vincent for leaving her alone to entertain his guests, with the emphasis on "his." Her admonition was cut short because we were told that it was now time to move into the ballroom. As we started drifting that way, we found ourselves elbow to elbow with the multitude of revelers funneling through the narrow passage that led to the main event. We shuffled rather than walked and in short order realized that Vincent was again among the missing.

We located our table, and we all took our seats, all except Megan. Six feet three in her heels, she remained standing, searching the crowd for Mr. Houten. She finally spotted him entering the ballroom through the same entrance we had used some ten minutes earlier. Her annoyance was already showing, but when she noticed that Vince was at the very most a step or two behind a quite attractive brunette, she physically stiffened.

As he joined us at our table, Vincent calmly deflected Megan's accusation of his evil intention by insisting he merely took the opportunity to enjoy a cigarette, and he certainly had no idea which young lady Megan was referring to.

That defused the tension a bit, but only for a while because about forty-five minutes later, as Megan was finishing her third vodka, Vincent was obviously focusing his attention on the entrance. He suddenly rose and excused himself, saying he was off to have another cigarette, which seemed innocent enough, except that we all couldn't help but observe that the same brunette was exiting just in front of him, apparently for her own nicotine fix.

Megan ordered another vodka, and we all tried to carry on as if no one noticed the steam coming out of her ears. She waited a minute or two longer and then headed for the door where Vince and the brunette had exited.

Before she reached her destination, the brunette in question reentered the ballroom on her way back to her table. Upon seeing the young lady, Megan came to a halt and stared in her direction for a second while deciding her next move. Having witnessed Meg's Irish temper first hand, Audrey and I both held our breath. Megan then turned and continued her pursuit of Vincent. We immediately thought that that lady would never know how fortunate she was.

A short time later, our host and his companion returned to the table, Megan in the lead, Vincent following, somewhat embarrassed and looking like a scolded child. Meg took her seat in dramatic fashion, brushed her hair off her shoulders with the back of her hand and, leaning toward my wife, said, "If he goes near that slut again, I'll kill him." She then proceeded to consume her forth vodka.

You know the expression, "Three's a charm"? Well, I don't know what he was thinking, but it didn't take long for Vincent to actually go to the slut's table and ask her for a dance. Maybe he thought Megan was too drunk to care. He was certainly too drunk to think at all, but that was definitely the last straw.

Megan stormed, or more accurately, staggered toward Vincent and the unsuspecting guests at the brunette's table. When she reached Vince, she grabbed him by the shoulder, spun him around to face her, and then slapped his face with enough force to nearly cause him to fall. Megan then leaned over the brunette, who was still seated, having innocently refused Vincent's request for a dance, and addressed her, index finger jabbing her chest, calling her a part of the female anatomy that begins with the letter "C," thus striking terror in the hearts of the other innocent guests seated at her table.

Having accomplished her mission, Megan pulled herself up to her full six-foot-plus height, straightened her dress, and headed for the exit as if nothing had happened.

Vincent mumbled something that we could not hear to the horrified guests at the brunette's table and then sought a bit of refuge in the men's room. The Kansas City friends decided that this was as good a time as any to return to the peace and quiet of their hotel, and without apologies, they abruptly left. My wife and I were committed to stay the course and support our wounded friend.

It wasn't long before Vincent returned to our table. Fortunately for the three of us, the ballroom segment of the evening was coming to an end, and the multitudes were beginning to proceed to the West Pool for more cocktails and to secure a preferred seat from which to enjoy the Grucci family fireworks, scheduled to soon begin. We were hoping that we could dissolve into a crowd whose tables had been far enough away from our own to not have witnessed the events of the last few minutes.

Fresh cocktails in hand, we walked to the western end of the Mar-A-Lago's property and stood near the bulkhead on Lake Worth for the best vantage point to watch the pyrotechnics. Audrey told Vincent of his friend's departure and added that the only comment made was Mrs. Reynolds's remark: "I knew this was a mistake." Again showing her female intuition, she stated, "It sounds like there's some history there."

Vincent reluctantly admitted that the Reynolds were friends of Jaycee and had not talked to him for two years after he slighted their friend at his Super Bowl party. For the last year, Vincent had been attempting to mend fences, so to speak, and this evening's invitation was part of that conscious effort.

"The best laid plans of mice and men, huh, Vince?" He just looked at me and shook his head.

Well, that explained the need for Megan to keep Audrey next to her as a buffer and conversational partner, averting the need to speak across the table and therefore include the Reynolds in the discussion.

The fireworks display, not surprisingly, proved to be awesome, maybe a little less spectacular than the emotional fireworks display of a short while ago, but having endured the events of the evening, we were left with little New Year cheer.

We finished our last drink, expressed our concerns about Vincent's safe drive home, and wished him good luck in reconciling with Miss Kelly when he returned home. He responded, "That can wait," and he then invited us to accompany him to the Chesterfield Hotel's Leopard Lounge for end-of-the-evening cocktails, an invitation we quickly refused.

We were emotionally drained, but V. X. Houten had a very different attitude. "Shake it off, and move on." Audrey and I wanted to be there to support our friend, but enough was enough.

We three walked back toward the main house of Mar-A-Lago in the direction of the West Pool, and there we said our good-byes. Vince went to the right, around the south side of the ballroom, heading toward the employee parking area, and we went left, back up to the terrace where the event had begun, and then to the valet station, never to meet again.

Having explained all this to Detective Chuck, we realized that we had put Megan Kelly in the unenviable position of being prime suspect number one.

CHAPTER SIX

The Palm Beach police didn't wait to hear from Audrey and me. They had already started an extensive search for Megan Kelly. It began shortly after the body of Vincent X. Houten was discovered. Her responsibility as a Worth Avenue model was to walk from restaurant to restaurant, wearing the latest designs of a particular designer in an effort to entice patrons to visit some particular boutique. She was therefore very recognizable and known to many of the six hundred guests at the Mar-A-Lago gala and quickly identified to the police as Mr. Houten's date for the evening.

However, by Wednesday morning, more than forty-eight hours after the body of Vincent Houten had been discovered, Megan Kelly was nowhere to be found.

Audrey and I were pretty busy during that forty-eight-hour period. My profession happened be that of funeral director, and Vincent had listed me as the designated undertaker in his will. I know he did it in jest, never contemplating needing my services sooner rather than later. He had no offspring, but he did have two siblings and a few nieces and nephews, all of whom had a keen interest in Vincent Houten's final arrangements—in other words, the distribution of his estate.

Our thoughts and efforts were focused on informing all interested parties of the circumstances as far as we knew. Since our funeral home was located in New Jersey, I had to coordinate the services of a local funeral home in the Palm Beach area and another firm in Vincent's hometown of Kansas City for the final services. We worked closely with George Cavallas, Vincent's attorney, long-time advisor, and friend, whom Audrey and I had met on various occasions in Palm Beach and KC.

George relayed the instructions contained in Vincent's will, which were simple but, knowing Vince, surprisingly detailed. His directive was to have a brief graveside service, without religious content, followed by a party on the grounds of his Kansas City home complete with a jazz band, who were to begin the festivities with the song "Going to Kansas City" and end with "When the Saints Go Marching In."

Although we thought about and discussed Megan Kelly frequently over those two days, other than leaving a message or two on her cell phone, we made no other effort to reach her. We were focused on the job at hand, and it was not a pleasant one. Contacting his relatives, informing them that Vincent was dead, and then having to describe the details of his murder again and again and again was exhausting and emotionally draining. It was even more difficult to inform his close friends who, unlike most of his family, really cared for him.

Sometime before noon on Wednesday, Detective Chuck notified us that the Palm Beach police had still been unable to locate a nearly six-foot-tall, red-haired model whom half of Palm Beach had seen modeling live on Worth Avenue, and the other half had regularly seen photographed in several of the social news or fashion magazines. It concerned me, and a number of possibilities went through my mind. *Did Meg flee? Did she flee because she was guilty? Did she flee because she was scared? Is she in real danger? Could she already be dead as well?*

The revelation that Megan had disappeared or was in hiding was relayed to us late Wednesday morning during our second meeting with our favorite detective, this time in our condo. He had called to say he was in the neighborhood. Thankfully, it was in our apartment because at least we were spared the police station with its "extended delay with intent to disturb" and the "overly bright florescent lighting with the intent to agitate" tactics.

Detective Gerity had given us the impression that he knew who the murderer was and that it was just a matter of time before she would be apprehended, so it was a surprise when he began by saying, "Could you help?"

That was a startling indication that the self-assuredness of our one and only Detective Edward "Chuck" Gerity was actually beginning to diminish, despite only being in the earliest stage of the investigation.

In addition to their local surveillance efforts, the Palm Beach police included the services of the West Palm Beach police department in the investigation. West Palm Beach PD was to stake out Megan's Wellington rental (which she had insisted Vincent maintain for her so she could retain a sense of independence) as well as the many after-hour clubs she was known to frequent with both male and female companions of dubious character.

The Wellington apartment was a small price for Vincent to pay for the independence he gained whenever Megan needed her space. He cared little what she did while they were separated because that just gave him free range to "check the traps."

Incidentally, Wellington is Palm Beach society west. It is South Florida's horse country—not the rope 'em, break 'em, brand 'em type of horse country, but the dressage, jumping, and polo pony type of horse country. As with Palm Beach, Wellington had its collection of billionaires and millionaires, and the scammers, gold diggers, and fraudsters who follow them. Megan had the uncanny ability to be able to blend with all five types.

Detective Gerity's request for our input made me think that Megan could have been in more than a half dozen states and fifty different cities. Detective Chuck asked us to speculate where she might be. I couldn't imagine where to start, or how we could be of any assistance. But it was obvious to Audrey that the authorities had not completed an in-depth review of Megan's local contacts.

I could remember some names of Megan's associates from different parties we had attended, as well as a few events or encounters with the eclectic group. But Audrey remembered names, relationships, ex-boyfriends, the wives of ex-boyfriends, the boyfriends of boyfriends. In addition to Megan's past romantic relationships, as a model, she had developed an expansive network of associates within the Palm Beach gay community.

"Detective Gerity, have you interviewed Roberto Wesson?" Leaning forward with her elbow on her knee and her chin on her fist, my wife patiently waited for the detective to respond. I hate when she does that to me, but I loved watching her do it to Gerity.

Detective Chuck flipped through a few pages of his pocket-size note pad, attempting to appear as though he had collected so much information that he could not possibly recall it all, but after a minute or two, he admitted, "I don't seem to have any background on Mr. Wesson." A moment of awkward silence followed before he asked, "What is his involvement?"

"Rob Wesson is Megan's makeup artist and has been for years. He works out of Salon Marie on the corner of South County and Brazilian Avenue. He owns a home in the El Cid section of West Palm Beach." My wife, Audrey, was showing Chuck up, and I was enjoying every minute of it.

El Cid section of West Palm Beach was a historic area that had deteriorated over the years and was now bordering on total depression. The effort to revitalize downtown West Palm Beach in the mid-nineties, now known as City Center, along with the town's dedication to reducing one of the country's worst crime records, had transformed El Cid and many other old communities into trendy neighborhoods. Roberto, to his credit, bought a depressed house in a depressed area for a depressed price and completely renovated it—resulting in a financial home run.

As the detective took notes, Audrey mercilessly continued. "Do you have anything on Marla Philips?"

The detective started the same routine of fumbling through his note pad, but then he must have realized how ridiculous his dissembling appeared and stopped. "Mrs. Stevens, please enlighten me."

"Marla is one of Megan's neighbors in Wellington. She is a jewelry designer, and Meg sometimes does her the favor of wearing her jewelry on Worth Avenue, if it does not conflict with the products of her designer of the day. She is also a fellow dressage rider. They often go clubbing together, and she most likely is a user, as I'm sure you are aware that Megan is."

Before Gerity could interject a question or comment, Audrey rapidly added several other names. "Her colorist is Salvatore Liguria of New York. He has a seasonal rental on Brazilian Avenue and flies to Palm Beach a few days a month to cater to his New York City women—society clients who winter here and couldn't possibly do without his services for that long a period, considering all of their social obligations. He also most likely is having an affair with Megan, since he is one of the few straight men in her fashion community circle, and frankly, how else could she afford his fees?"

Without taking a breath, my wife continued, and Chuck frantically scrawled notes. "Then there's her hairdresser, Martin Goldstein, who does not work out of a salon but makes house calls, often with Salvatore. He lives with his considerably older and quite wealthy partner on El Brillo Street in the Estate section of Palm Beach, just north of the Mar-A-Lago Club."

The Estate section of Palm Beach was a fairly long strip of the island that began just south of the in-town area and reached almost to the southern strip of the island. It was a narrow section of the island, and therefore several estates extended from sea to ocean. Included in that sea-to-ocean section was an area referred to as Billionaire's Row. The only negative for the billionaires in residence was that their tranquility was periodically disturbed by the take-off and landing patterns at the West Palm Beach airport immediately over their casas.

"Lastly, Detective, you might want to include Paul Ostrow, Megan's self-described personal trainer. He lives in West Palm Beach North." This was a blossoming gay community, just south of Rivera Beach. Houses needing considerable work were extremely reasonable—just don't walk two blocks in the wrong direction or you could find yourself in serious danger.

"I suspect Paul is more like Megan's drug supplier rather than her trainer," she concluded.

With confidence, Audrey speculated aloud to Chuck. "Those are the most likely accomplices and the most likely places to find her."

The detective began to question how my wife could be so confident in her conclusion but stopped in mid-sentence, excused himself, and stepped out onto our balcony to make a call on his cell phone. Detective Chuck Gerity was either frustrated or very embarrassed not to have discovered these leads by now, so I assumed he had decided to see if the lady, my wife, knew what she was talking about. In those few minutes on our balcony, he redirected the police efforts of both forces, Palm Beach as well as West Palm Beach.

Chuck Gerity reentered the apartment and further questioned Audrey about other individuals who might be assisting Megan, in case her conclusion was wrong, but he wasn't getting very far. My wife was not backing down from her original assertion.

"No, Detective. Remember that we are focusing on who might be available and willing to assist an intoxicated Megan Kelly at approximately eleven thirty on New Year's Eve. Consider who would find that task more entertaining then watching the ball drop while singing 'Auld Lang Syne.' I am more than certain you will find the answer in that group of acquaintances."

He revisited the events of the Mar-A-Lago Ball and attempted to further question my wife as to who sat where and who might have seen what, but my wife refused to speculate any further than the five individuals she had already offered.

Finally she stated, "If she is still in the state of Florida, those friends will know. If she is not, you have a lot of work ahead of you, and I don't think I can help you with that."

The detective rose to leave, and at that moment, his cell phone rang. He excused himself and turned away from us to answer it, keeping his voice low so we could not hear. The conversation ended quickly, and he slowly turned back to face us. He thanked us for our time and started for the door, but he must have had misgivings about not sharing the news he had just received. He hesitated and finally gave my wife her well-earned due. "Megan Kelly has been found. The hairdresser knows nothing about the murder. His partner is furious."

Audrey had identified Megan's five possible enablers, and she was right that one of them was Megan's helper. Martin Goldstein, Megan's hairdresser, was the most likely candidate only because he was living with his wealthy lover not more than half a mile from Mar-A-Lago, and as it turned out, he happened to be home New Year's Eve.

It had taken more than forty-eight hours to locate Miss Megan Kelly, but less than forty-eight minutes after my wife's input. The next task would not be so easy. It would take more than twelve hours to dry her out.

As Audrey instinctively perceived, Megan implored the help of one of her fashion-industry associates, who was more motivated by the drama of it all rather than by Megan's well-being. It wasn't the first time that she had curled up for a few days with a jug of Gray Goose (and some Vicodin and who knows what else) to dull her memory of some unpleasant event, usually involving Vincent Houten.

Our relationship with Detective Chuck Gerity had now become a concern to me. Was this guy a competent investigator, or was he in over his head?

CHAPTER SEVEN

It was late Wednesday afternoon when we had our second conversation of the day with Detective Gerity. He apparently thought that we might again have something to add to the information that he had been able to gather from his interrogation of Megan Kelly. While she had appeared to be somewhat sober during her interview, her erratic responses left the detective believing that she might need more time to dry out. He was however particularly interested in some assertions she had vehemently made during her interrogation.

Upon hearing the detective's detailed summary of Megan's interview, our conclusion was that her account of the evening matched the one we had given on New Year's Day. She insisted that the alleged slap was a harmless push and that she never would use the C-word, but aside from that, the other events and the approximate timing of those events were consistent with our recollection. We were all in agreement, meaning Audrey, me, Chuck, and whoever else in the PBPD had been invited to listen in on our phone conversation without our knowledge.

Even though Megan had already had more than twelve hours to sober up, she still seemed somewhat incoherent to the detective. He explained that one minute Miss Kelly would answer his questions, sounding completely lucid, and then the next minute, she would begin to rant, "It was Joanie. It had to be Joanie. Joanie did it."

Gerity wanted our insight, or to be honest my wife's insight, as to why Megan Kelly would think that Joanie Olsen, who was fifteen hundred miles away in Aspen, Colorado, at the time of the murder, could have anything to do with Vincent's death. Her relationship with Vincent Houten had ended years earlier.

In my opinion, my wife explained it perfectly well. She calmly began. "Having known Vincent and Joanie for many years, it is obvious to me that they have been enjoying a platonic relationship for some time." The relationship was complicated nonetheless. She continued, "Although their romantic relationship had faded, Vince valued her business acumen enough to appoint her to his company's board of directors and sought her advice on many manners, both business and personal."

Megan could not possibly accept or tolerate this lingering relationship with a past lover. As demonstrated at the New Year's Eve ball, Miss Kelly had to be the center of attention, and woe to anyone who might outshine her. Her physical stature and beauty were not enough to overcome her personal demons.

"Detective, the poor woman is hopelessly insecure and insanely jealous." Audrey added, "I can't imagine how you could give anything she has to say any credibility."

I thoroughly agreed and so did Detective Gerity, I thought.

Megan's timeline of events on New Year's Eve more or less matched our account, and after the hairdresser, Goldstein, confirmed the time he had picked up a shoeless Megan walking north on South County Road, heading away from Mar-A-Lago, Chuck had no reason to doubt that she had left long before the murder.

He was not eliminating Megan Kelly as a suspect with rage as the motive, considering how volatile their relationship and how it was exposed the night of the murder, but given the size of the Houten estate, it was even harder to overlook money as the motive, that greatly expanded the list of suspects. Enter Vincent Xavier Houten's last will and testament.

Audrey and I might have been the last individuals to see Vincent Houten alive, but we were not mentioned in his will, except of course as those who should coordinate his final arrangements. That fact moved us down the detective's list of suspects. Chuck had recently received a copy of the Houten will from attorney George Cavallas, and his work suddenly became considerably more complicated. His original and very simple assumption was that when they found Megan Kelly, they would find the murderer. This was no longer a certainty. Now nothing appeared simple.

That night we ordered dinner from our in-condominium restaurant, had a few belts while rehashing the day's events, and crashed by ten.

CHAPTER EIGHT

Thursday began, as did Wednesday, with a call from our beloved detective. I was beginning to feel like we were acting in the Bill Murray movie *Groundhog Day*. The Houten last will and testament in hand, the good detective stated, not asked, "I would like to come by to address Joan Olsen's relationship with Vincent Houten."

We agreed to meet Chuck Gerity that morning. The detective entered our apartment, and he began his questioning before he even reached his seat. "Do you know that Mrs. Olsen is the executrix and a major benefactor of Mr. Houten's estate?" His tone of voice was intentionally affected to induce a sense of shock and surprise.

I think Audrey just rolled her eyes at a question with such an obvious answer. I responded with a little New Jersey attitude in my voice, "Hey Chuck, who do you think we have been arranging the funeral plans with for the last two days?"

Chuck continued with his absurd line of questioning. "Does that not surprise you?" Then he added, "Considering that she is not blood and only a past lover?"

I began to attempt to explain to our beloved detective that Joanie was not "only" a past lover but a current and trusted advisor. I was relieved to be politely interrupted by my current and trusted advisor, my wife. Audrey has this wonderful ability to see through the fog and cut to the chase, as she had demonstrated in previous encounters with Detective Chuck Gerity.

Leaning forward with her hand on my knee in a not-so-subtle signal for me to shut up, she began. "Detective, once you interview the blood relatives, you may get a better insight as to why Vincent selected someone outside of the family to administer his affairs."

In all fairness, Detective Gerity was in the dark as to the Houten family circus and was looking at the facts as they came to him chronologically. So he must have realized that his line of questioning was based on his uninformed assumptions and decided that instead of continuing to lead the interview, he would let Mrs. Stevens have the floor. "Mrs. Stevens," he asked, "would you kindly elaborate?"

With all of her feminine intuition and insight at her disposal, my wife confidently began. "Vincent Houten was obviously a very successful man and his success unfortunately resulted in feelings of jealousy and resentment in his siblings. His sister and I feel even more so his brother thought that his success was the result of good luck rather than intelligence and hard work. They both on various occasions expressed to me that his opulent lifestyle, cars, and antique collections were a clear demonstration of his self-centeredness. They expressed without restrain their view that Vincent could have been more 'giving.'"

Chuck wanted to keep Audrey rolling, so he asked her another open-ended question. "Was the same opinion held by the rest of the family?"

My wife leaned back in her chair hesitated for a moment and began her response. "Although I have never discussed that issue with Vincent's nieces and nephews, in any family I know, the feelings and opinions of the parents are more often than not passed to the children, especially views held so strongly and for so long."

At this time, the detective felt it appropriate to inform us that all eight blood relatives were to receive a full and equal share of Mr. Houten's estate, once liquidated. His attorney, George Cavallas, had acted professionally with me over the last few days. He had only disclosed our friend's final wishes and said nothing about the distribution of Vincent's estate. It surprised me that Vince was so generous to his jealous and bitter family.

Vincent didn't see his relatives but every two or three years. His bequest gave further credence to the adage, "Blood is thicker than water."

Audrey was quiet, pondering the confusing relatives' relationships, and before Chuck could relay some additional contents of Vincent's will, she interrupted with a comment that seemed to come out of left field. "Detective, you might want to consider Mr. Houten's mother."

Chuck incredulously replied, "Mrs. Stevens, are you telling me that Mrs. Houten is still alive and is somehow involved in his murder?"

Still deep in thought and ignoring Gerity's last comment, my wife, the psychic, proceeded to explain her latest insight in a trancelike state. "Mrs. Houten, by all accounts, was a very difficult woman. She went from rags to riches and back to rags many times. Her children's childhood was anything but peaceful. Vincent had speculated to me that she most likely had a mental illness. Today, you might call it a chemical imbalance, which often contributes to anxiety, depression, and substance addiction."

Chuck interrupted. "This is very interesting, Mrs. Stevens, but what does this have to do with the subject at hand?"

Audrey, coming out of her thought-invoked stupor, concluded. "As the opinions of the parents are often passed to the children, so are genes passed to the children and the grandchildren as well."

I didn't think Gerity knew where this was going until Audrey wrapped it up. "I was told that of the six nieces and nephews, two have been in rehab for substance abuse, and his brother, Samuel, has in the past been institutionalized for some form of depression." There was no need for Audrey to remind Chuck what he had just told us. They all were beneficiaries in Vincent's will, and the inference was obvious.

Detective Gerity was not yet finished with us. He must have realized, however, that we would appreciate a break, and he retreated to our balcony for several minutes to use his cell phone. I on the other hand took the opportunity to pour myself a double vodka on the rocks. Was there any other kind? After all, it was five o'clock somewhere. Audrey, still in deep thought, opted for ice water. How non–Palm Beach.

I didn't like the way things were proceeding. I especially did not appreciate Chuck's attitude toward us, but particularly his demeanor toward my wife. He seemed to think we should be at his beck and call, as if we were his underlings.

When Chuck reentered our living room, his attention was focused again on the executrix, Joan Olsen. He began with detailing Mrs. Olsen's financial compensation for administrating the estate, and before he could ask another question, I insisted he stop the interview.

Much to my wife's surprise, I told the detective, "Unless you start sharing information you receive regarding this case with us, we are no longer inclined to answer any of your questions." I added that, as a gesture of good faith, he could start by telling us what had just transpired during his balcony phone call. The vodka was definitely helping.

I was not solidifying a long-term friendship with Chuck Gerity. His first reaction was an attempt to intimidate me by using a tone I could only describe as, well as, intimidating. "Are your refusing to cooperate in this investigation?" I immediately thought, *Why does this man continue to ask questions to which he already knows the answers?*

"Chuck, let's cut the shit. You spent fifteen minutes on your phone on our balcony, and we want to know what you know." I think that was a yes to his intimidating question.

"Mr. and Mrs. Stevens, this is a murder investigation. I have no intention of accepting your conditions as to the method of disseminating information with you or any other party involved, even less so with a party so closely connected to the events surrounding the murder."

I don't think my friend Chuck was accustomed to being so directly confronted, certainly not by the Palm Beach gentry.

Detective Gerity had just taken the proverbial bait. I was hoping I could get him to address this point, but I was surprised he did so with such little effort on my part. I paused to let Chuck enjoy the feeling of his puffed-up chest and then began to set the hook. "I see, Detective. Are you reminding me and my wife that we are still suspects in this investigation?"

I employed my best Columbo impersonation and continued. "As suspects, all the information we have provided to you this past week was done so without the protection or presence of legal counsel." I was not going to let this opportunity pass. I wanted to paint Chuck into a corner.

I looked toward my wife and posed the hypothetical question. "Darling what were we thinking? Consider all the conversations we have willingly had with Detective Gerity, do you think we would have been so open if we knew we were prime suspects? Doesn't it if feel as though our new friend Detective Gerity deceived us into thinking we were merely being asked to assist in solving our old friend's murder?"

I let that sit for a while, and when the detective began to reply, I sternly shut him down. "If you consider us suspects, I think you should get the hell out of our apartment. If you consider us a source of information in the investigation, then give us a reason to cooperate."

"Mr. Stevens," he began in a soft but deliberate voice, "I did not intend to imply that you and Mrs. Stevens are suspects in this case." We waited while the good detective seemed to contemplate a solution to the dilemma.

With his chin on his chest, Chuck finally offered an olive branch. "Mr. Stevens, I can share the information that I have just received, but that should not be interpreted as an agreement to share all other information now in my possession or what I might learn in the future."

I was not thrilled with his caveat, but I did not think that I would get much more by pressing the issue. I felt that we had provided a lot of helpful information that, along with Audrey's insights, proved that we were valuable assets. My initial objective was to make sure Chuck would not take us for granted any longer. That, I felt, was pretty much accomplished.

More importantly, I wanted Audrey and me deeply involved in the case. I felt that if I overly pressured the detective, we could find ourselves on the outside looking in. That would be a terrible outcome. Someone murdered our good friend, and it was most likely someone we knew. I wanted to continue to be a part of finding out who, and the sooner the better.

In a gesture of conciliation, I said to Detective Gerity, "Chuck, why don't you call me Nate, and I'm sure Mrs. Stevens would prefer to be addressed as Audrey."

CHAPTER NINE

The information for which I had just negotiated, at the risk of severing our relationship with Detective Gerity, was very mundane—with one exception. In his private balcony conversation, Detective Gerity had received an update about the travel plans of the Houten relatives.

Detective Chuck was planning to be in Kansas City when the array of potential suspects converged for Vincent's funeral service. All interested parties were expected to arrive between late Monday afternoon and midday Tuesday—with the notable exception of Vincent's brother, Samuel, who had not finalized his plans and one nephew, Christopher, who had not yet been reached.

Audrey speculated that Samuel was most likely attempting to raise the airline fare since his older brother had been the reliable source of his past travel funding.

Aloud, she questioned the detective. "I'm surprised about Christopher. I was under the impression that he was back working at Vincent's company, Tri-State Tape?"

Chuck informed us that Christopher hadn't returned to work since December twenty-second, and that the Kansas City PD was running down some leads. He further informed us that Christopher's mother, Vincent's sister, told the investigating police officers that it was not uncommon for her son to be out of contact for weeks at a time. However, she assured them that she and his siblings were making every effort to locate him and would contact the authorities as soon as they had something to report.

Of course, the Christopher circumstances couldn't help but cause Audrey and me to raise our eyebrows since, you guessed it, he was the nephew in and out of rehab. It quickly occurred to me that he was an unlikely suspect because his drug and alcohol problem was not his only flaw; he was in fact quite simple.

Vincent often expressed his concern for his nephew because, as he put it, "Christopher has the attention span of a six-year-old." At times, he gave Christopher financial assistance, but he wisely refused to serve as his nephew's personal ATM machine. Instead he, on more than one occasion, gave him a job at the company. However, a work schedule and his nephew simply were not very compatible.

I couldn't imagine how he could have successfully plotted anything, much less murder. Audrey made no comment, but it was apparent that she was deep in thought. Her wheels were turning. The detective did not dwell on the issue, nor did he seem overly concerned. Christopher would turn up sooner or later. I was sure, however, that we were all in agreement. His disappearance was a development that would require watching.

Detective Gerity finally was able to redirect our attention to Joan Olsen and Mr. Houten's excessive generosity. He would not be content until he understood in detail the financial windfall she was about to enjoy. In addition to a generous administrator's stipend of fifteen thousand dollars a month, she was the only beneficiary of a full share of the Houten estate who was not a blood relation. Moreover, Vincent had bequeathed to her his Palm Beach home, the Villa V, complete with its impressive contents.

Good for Joanie, I thought. It was Vincent's money. He could do with it as he pleased. After all, the administration of an estate of this magnitude was a full-time endeavor. Why not provide her with a substantial stipend, and why should Vincent be any more generous to his blood relatives then he already was? Excluding Joanie would only result in more financial reward for the ungrateful bunch of eight. The Villa V? Well, that might have been a little over the top.

My wife began to explain Joanie's involvement in the purchase, design, and supervision of the extensive renovations to what had been a very ordinary house when purchased. I became a little melancholy and drifted off down memory lane recalling the history and happenings that we were a part of Vincent Houten's infamous Villa V.

It was in our second year in Palm Beach and only Vincent's third in his penthouse apartment when it became apparent to us that he felt the urge for his own space. Vincent was in no particular hurry to purchase, but his desire to do so was obvious. He understood and identified to us his motivation to have a house rather than having to live in the confines of a condo. He quickly became consumed by the search.

The house he was searching for needed to have ample grounds for entertaining but secluded enough for his personal recreation, prestigious enough for his need to uphold his image, but not at a cost that would restrict his lifestyle. He was cautious. He wanted to be sure to make a wise choice.

He and Joanie Olsen spent a portion of every weekend reviewing the local newspapers for properties that fit his criteria, and they attended many open house listings. I thought at that time that it was really Joanie who was pushing Vince to move to a more impressive residence than his penthouse. However, it was my wife, Audrey, who made it clear to me that it was Vincent who was determined to find a house more similar to the type of home he had liked in KC that would still provide the social acceptance he desired in PB.

When the property was finally selected and purchased Vincent further used the assistance of his live-in lady friend, Joan Olsen, who more than adequately handled the more tedious chores. She worked closely with the architect and painstakingly forwarded the necessary applications and permit requirements to the onerous Palm Beach Architectural Review Board.

Vincent dotingly examined every detail of the restoration of his new home. He insisted on numerous modifications and alternatives to ensure that he would not overlook something that could take his creation to the next level. His involvement made Joanie's job far more difficult.

It took a year and a half and consumed two full seasons to complete the project, but the results were unmistakable. Together Vincent and Joan transformed a modest house into an eloquently causal home suitable for lounging in front of the TV or hosting a wonderful dinner party. I had enjoyed both experiences several times, in addition to many others, like his annual Super Bowl and Oscar Night parties.

The Villa V was certainly conducive to any type of occasion, but it was Vincent's presence that brought it to life. His open-door policy was as special as the owner himself. When he was in residence, he would park one of his classic cars on his front lawn as an invitation to anyone familiar with the ritual to join him for a libation appropriate to that time of day.

As I began to return to the present, I could hear Audrey midsentence, still speculating with Detective Chuck as to Vince's motivation. "And it was as much Joanie's creation as Vincent's. After she had devoted two years of constant effort to the project with extraordinary results, he ended their relationship within the next six months."

She then concluded, "So it seems perfectly reasonable that Vincent, probably out of guilt or maybe out of a sense of simple fairness, left Villa V to Joanie."

Detective Gerity remained mystified. I think he understood my wife's premise and probably even accepted her conclusion, but the fact that Joanie was to receive an incredibly large sum of money was not to be taken lightly. To explain away that fact based on my wife's suppositions would most likely remove Joan Olsen from Chuck's list of possible suspects, but that was a step Chuck was not yet ready to take.

The inquisition in our condo was approaching its second hour. Chuck, however, felt the uncontrollable desire to inform us of the fact that there was a second bequest. We were weary but realized that it was important to conclude the review of the estate only after we addressed all aspects of the will that could be relevant to the investigation. That in mind, we wearily but willingly listened to the detective's next account. What he was about to tell us was certainly worth our time.

Contained in the Houten last will and testament was a codicil concerning Vincent's favorite classic car, his 1956 Jaguar XK 140, and a cash award of approximately equal value, two hundred and fifty thousand dollars. The fortunate recipient of this half-million dollar adjustment to the Houten estate plan was one Peter Kunz.

We certainly knew who Peter Kunz was. He was our friend. He was an extension of our friendship with Vincent Houten. Vince introduced us to him weeks after our first encounter at Charlie's Crab some fifteen years ago.

We were therefore able to provide the detective extensive background on Mr. Kunz beginning with the fact that he met Vincent thirty-five years ago when Vince first landed in Kansas City from Philadelphia.

At that time, Vincent Houten was in quest of a small Midwest company that specifically needed to introduce a more sophisticated sales organization and business approach. That was his forte. He was young and desperate to make a success of himself. Tri-State Tape became the opportune target.

Coincidentally, Peter was a close friend of the then-object of Vincent's attention, who just happened to be the daughter of the owners of Tri-State Tape. That object of his affection soon became the second Mrs. Vincent Houten. Peter, who was on his own number two, and Vince established a bond of commonality and remained friends ever since.

It was a fact that Megan, most likely Joanie, and many of the women in his life used Vincent for their own array of purposes, but Vincent was not completely above the practice himself. He wasted little time in divorcing his college sweetheart and seducing the married daughter of the owners of the company he would eventually acquire. He also found nothing wrong in maintaining a relationship with Joanie Olsen until he made a sufficient number of the right social acquaintances and until she had completed the renovation of Villa V before ending that convenient relationship.

However, his generosity to both Joan Olsen and Peter Kunz, as well as his practice of maintaining friendly relationships with his past paramours, often providing financial assistance when needed or invitations to exclusive parties or Mar-A-Lago events, spoke well of Vince's good nature. Or maybe his conscience.

That aside and more significantly, it was not easy to inform Detective Gerity of the fact that Peter Kunz now was basically broke. We had fond feelings for Peter but had firsthand knowledge of him unknowingly investing in a Bernie Madoff feeder fund that was now worthless. Additionally, the general collapse of the market hit the remaining portion of his portfolio especially hard.

As difficult as it was to talk to Chuck about our friend Peter's financial reversal, it was harder to have witnessed its effect on his personality. Over the last few months, it was apparent that stress had taken its toll. He tried to keep up his outgoing persona and good humor, but he would often lose interest in the group's conversation and drift off in thought. He was becoming an old man in front of our eyes.

Vincent must have felt the same way, and since Peter was definitely too proud to accept charity, the only thing Vincent thought he could do for his good friend was to include Peter in his will.

Most interesting to Detective Gerity was the fact that the bequest had been added to the will in late November, less than two months prior to the murder, which occurred in the very same car bequeathed to Peter Kunz.

CHAPTER TEN

M y wife and I were quite worn out by the time we completed our conversation with Chuck Gerity about Peter Kunz, and his personal financial woes. It was approaching six o'clock when Detective Gerity mercifully made his exit. It was time for cocktails and something to eat.

It took little debate to agree to a change of scenery. We decided to dine at the bar in Taboo on Worth Avenue. Taboo is one of the oldest restaurants in Palm Beach. It has been in the same location since it originally opened in 1941. From the avenue, the restaurant looked a bit like a storefront-size local bar, no more than twenty feet wide. A bay window that is always open except in extreme weather is to the left of a matching natural wood-stained french-door entrance. Together they gave off a welcome but upscale feel.

When entering under the intentionally crooked palm tree-styled lettering of the Taboo sign, you immediately sensed the energy. On the left was the first and most-prized seating area. It was a relatively small area with accommodations for maybe two dozen, in two- and four-seat tables and banquettes. Here diners could enjoy the fresh air from the open bay window and the live piano music, all while taking note of the envious diners who entered too late to have a chance at a table in the preferred front dining area. People watching has always been the greatest pastime in Palm Beach.

A long bar extends from the piano to a stand where the hostess arranges for the seating in the three additional dining areas in the expansive rear of the restaurant. All three have a similar design, but all have their own character.

We often ate at Taboo, but we particularly enjoyed the bar because more often than not, we would find ourselves in a conversation with a fellow Palm Beacher or a tourist staying in one of the many hotels on the island. The menu also had something for everyone. We thought that would be the perfect way to take our minds off our friend Vincent and his murder investigation.

Taboo was owned in part by Franklin DeMarco, a fellow New Jersey transplant, although he is now a permanent Floridian. When in attendance, Franklin always takes the last seat at the bar to be able to observe and greet all those coming and leaving.

As we entered, Audrey and I took the first two barstools that were available. They, however, were closer to the front of the restaurant and quite a distance from Franklin. We settled into our space, ordered our first cocktail, and when we felt it appropriate, waved our acknowledgement of the owner's presence.

Even before our cocktails could arrive, Franklin approached us, expressing how shocked and saddened the whole of Palm Beach was over Vincent's murder. He acknowledged that he was well aware of our close relationship to Vincent and then stated, "Vince was more than a customer. He brought energy into this restaurant every time he came in."

Audrey nodded in agreement. "He lit up the room wherever he went. That was what made him so special. "

"He made everyone feel special. He made us all feel as if we were his very close friends."

It was a little out of character for Franklin to be so expressive. Although a restaurateur, he was always quite reserved. I therefore accepted his overture as a genuine and moving gesture. What followed, however, was overwhelming.

Franklin must have told a number of the other patrons of our close friendship to Vincent Houten because in short order there was a stream of Vincent Houten acquaintances lining up behind us to express their sympathy, relay their fond memories, and ask for the latest update.

I felt that some were just caught up in the most scandalous story of the last few years, hoping to get some inside information to be able to gossip. The murder was the biggest news in Palm Beach in the last decade, with maybe the exception of Bernie Madoff's Ponzi scheme that wiped out a quarter of the wealth in the Palm Beach Jewish community. However, there were those who had met and were seduced by Vincent's personality and now truly needed to know what was up. Many of those we had met through our relationship with Vince.

Who could have done this? Do the police have a suspect? I felt that those who really cared harbored a combination of anger and curiosity that they did not want to let loose. It was a combination of emotions that in some strange way allowed them to feel that they were still connected to Vincent. I admit, I was a member of that group.

So the idea that we could somehow get our minds off our newly departed friend, even if for only an hour or two, was now trash. The outpouring of emotions we just experienced was not what we planned but was quite moving. Frankly, we had to make every effort to maintain our composure.

The lady tending the bar that night was the very affable Cindy whom we had known for many years. She did not wait for us to complete the Vincent Houten receiving line but made sure our cocktails were constantly freshened. After a few light beers for

Audrey and several vodkas for me, we somehow were able to order and actually consume a meal. However, what it consisted of, I honestly have no recollection.

My wife was the more rational of the two of us and asked Cindy, "Could we please have our check. We must go home."

Cindy informed us, "There will be no check for the Stevenses tonight."

I slurred in response, "To whom do we owe our gratitude?"

Frustratingly, no one would take credit for the generosity. Not Franklin, nor any of the many acquaintances of Vincent who spoke to us earlier. Our friendly bartender Cindy said she was sworn to secrecy. All we could do was as to ask Cindy to thank whomever it was for the kind gesture.

My loving wife also made a kind gesture: she insisted on driving home. I was in no condition to master the task. I'm sure her decision was based more on self-preservation than consideration for her husband. When we returned to our apartment, however, we were in complete agreement as to what was the only logical thing to do and poured ourselves a nightcap.

It was an emotional night. We recalled some of the conversations we had with Vincent's friends. The ones that meant the most were those with the people we had actually met in Vince's company. We had a commonality with them. One nightcap was enough, and then it was time to call it a night.

As we retired to our bedroom, Audrey noticed the house phone message light blinking. I, drunk and disinterested, moved directly to the bathroom to prepare for bed. As I brushed my teeth, my wife called to me, "Nate, you should hear this."

The voice message was from a very upset Peter Kunz. Audrey hit play. "Thanks a lot. I just got a phone call from a half-wit Palm Beach detective. Did you have to tell him I was broke? Which by the way isn't true, not that it's any business of yours."

He wasn't finished yet and continued. "I thought you were my friends and would keep my confidence." He raised his voice. "Well thanks to you, now I'm a fucking suspect. I didn't even know I was in Vince's will." He ended by informing us, "I'm not going to just sit here and trust some clueless Florida dick to solve my best friend's murder. I'm going to get to the bottom of this." There was a click.

We sat silently for a moment. Audrey then posed the question, "Were we fulfilling our civic responsibilities, or were we in fact doing what we accused the hairdresser of doing?"

I was not following my wife's line of questioning and asked her to explain. Audrey said more directly, "When Detective Gerity questioned us about our friend Peter, did we just get caught up in the drama of the moment, like Megan's friend Martin Goldstein, and ignore Peter's best interests? Did we tell Detective Gerity too much?"

I had no response.

We contemplated returning Peter Kunz's call, but more sober minds prevailed. I guessed that was must have been Audrey's more sober mind than mine that prevailed.

My wife reasoned, "Nate, if we give Peter some time to calm down, then he can't help but come to the realization that we are all suspects."

I countered, "But some are more prime suspects than others."

"Nevertheless, any detective, clueless or not, would eventually discover Kunz's financial circumstances with or without our input." She was right again, but would Peter see things the same way?

We went to bed feeling a little guilty for having given up what we knew about our friend so readily. It had been a long day.

CHAPTER ELEVEN

I awoke Friday to a sun-filled sky and a pleasant breeze. I took a walk to buy a local paper and a New York newspaper, which was my normal morning routine. I made a pot of coffee and poured cups for Audrey and me. I took them to our balcony overlooking the Atlantic.

The move from our in-town apartment to one by the ocean wasn't a hard decision. We gave up a little space, and the original unit had some unique features, but our view was something else. A view of dark-blue almost purple water, a white sandy beach, and a few palm trees thrown in for good measure didn't take much getting used to. Being a couple of beach bums to enjoy it all didn't hurt either.

Audrey soon joined me. She was in her bathrobe and had a request. "Can we please not talk about yesterday until I wake up?"

"That's fine with me, but do yourself a favor and don't read the *Shiny Sheet* until you wake up."

"Front page again?"

"Naturally. But today they ran it with a big picture of Vincent next to his Aston Martin with the '007' license plate that the paper must have had on file. The headline asked, 'Who Shot 007?'"

The *Shiny Sheet* is really the *Palm Beach Daily News* but is referred to as the *Shiny Sheet* by all the locals because of the paper on which it is printed—a crisp white paper with a sheen, not the usual newsprint.

It was upsetting to read about the murder again and again not only because it heightened our grief but also because the stories were not terribly accurate and were becoming increasingly critical of our friend's lifestyle.

The articles first depicted Vincent Houten as a Kansas—not a Kansas City, Missouri, but a Kansas—businessman. It exaggerated the extent of his holdings, and the latest story implied that he was some wealthy alcoholic hick and a mannerless skirt chaser. Nothing could be further from the truth—well, at least the hick and mannerless parts.

"Audrey, how about an onion-and-cheese omelet?" Omelets were my specialty.

"That sounds fine. Would you mind doing a few pieces of bacon?"

"No problem." And I headed for the kitchen.

As I was retrieving the necessary ingredients from the refrigerator, our ringing phone interrupted me. I didn't feel like answering it, but we don't have caller ID on our landline and considering all that was happening, I thought it best that I not ignore it. Wrong choice.

The call was from a reporter for the same *Shiny Sheet*. After identifying herself as Robin White, she said, "May I ask you a few questions for the record?"

I had once attended a business seminar that advised funeral home owners how best to deal with the media in cases of high profile funerals. Well, this was as high profile as it got, and I was beginning to wish I had paid more attention.

One suggestion I remembered was not to answer too quickly but to give your brain five or six seconds to register the question and formulate a response. So the first thing I decided was to ask, "Would you mind holding for a moment?" I needed more than five or six seconds.

That gave me the necessary time to summon Audrey and think strategically. "I hope you are now awake because it's show time."

"What are you talking about?"

"I have a reporter on the phone from the *Palm Beach Daily News*. Would you care to take this call, or should I?"

"No, no, you take it, but let me listen in." Why did I always get the dirty work?

The *Shiny Sheet* is the Palm Beach social newspaper, known more for its paparazzi-type photos of who attended which ball and what celebrity ate at which restaurant, and for its real estate listings of estates for sale at eye-popping prices, rather than for investigative reporting. It therefore was understandable that the editor would want to run this sensational story as long as possible. It was real news.

It was bigger than real news. It was the biggest news Palm Beach had had in years. After all, the *New York Post* and the *New York Daily News* have five murder stories every edition. The *Palm Beach Daily News* has one every five years. That fact made it understandable why it took the reporter three days to locate us.

When I returned to the phone, I calmly stated, "Thank you for holding. How may I assist you?"

She began with a question. "Is it true that you and your wife were with Mr. Houten on New Year's Eve and were most likely the last to see him alive?"

Here we go again, with someone asking a question to which she already knew the answer. I also remembered from my media seminar that "No comment" or a smart-ass answer could alienate a reporter, and then that reporter could take liberties with your remarks that could make you look less than charming in the final article.

I answered in the affirmative, a polite tone of total honesty in my voice. I responded to her further inquires, remaining purposely vague. She was just doing her job, attempting to dig up something scandalous or getting an inside scoop on who the prime suspects could be. Who could have done such a thing?

She went to the skirt-chasing angle. "Is it possible that a jealous husband or boyfriend could be involved?"

That made me uncomfortable, and I did my best to dissuade her from printing such a notion. Audrey was sitting closely by my side and could hear the majority of the conversation. She wrote some suggestions for my reply, which I truly appreciated, especially considering how critical Peter Kunz was of our loose lips. Hearing the latest line of questions, she wrote, "Tell her how elegantly everyone was dressed."

That worked like a charm. Robin instinctively reverted to what she did best, social reporting, and began to ask for details that I could not possibly know. So I handed the phone to my reluctant wife and returned to the kitchen. The omelets and bacon were finished just about the time Audrey finished her fashion review of everything she could remember.

"How did you think to do that?" I asked, mystified.

"I don't know. I just pictured how horrible the story would be in tomorrow's paper and then remembered an article she wrote a couple of years ago about a high-society lawsuit. It began listing the particulars of the case and ended describing the wardrobe of the combatants and their attorneys."

"Brilliant, darling." That was all I could say.

CHAPTER TWELVE

The remainder of Friday was quite uneventful, especially in contrast to our activities over the previous three days. We had a brief conversation with Joanie Olsen to confirm our travel arrangements and the plan to meet her for dinner Sunday night after we arrived in Kansas City. Other than that, we took in some sun and another early dinner, but this time, to avoid a repeat of our Taboo Restaurant experience the previous evening, we selected a steak house in West Palm Beach that we had never been to with Vincent.

We arrived purposely early to avoid the dinner rush. Audrey and I thought we had accomplished our intention to be inconspicuous. There were few diners in the restaurant, and our entrance was uneventful. As the hostess escorted us to a table, and we were about to be seated, we heard, "Hey, Audrey. Hey, Nate."

It was the voice of Skip Walker, who was already seated merely a few tables away with his very congenial wife, Marney. The Walkers were from New Jersey, but we had met and developed our relationship here in South Florida. They wintered here in the elegant Trump Towers on Flagler Boulevard in West Palm Beach. We often golfed with them and dined with them and genuinely enjoyed their company.

Their three-bedroom condo was on a high floor, providing a view of Lake Worth and the whole island of Palm Beach with the Atlantic as its backdrop. It was tastefully decorated and quite spacious. We could fit our entire unit in their west wing. It was also a short walk from the Morton Steak House where we had mistakenly sought anonymity.

We made our way toward their table to be polite but had no desire to chat about what we knew. "What's the latest?"

"We are so sorry to hear about your friend. I know how close you were," Skip remarked.

Marney stood and gave us both a kiss on the cheek and a lingering hug. She didn't say anything at first because tears were welling up in her eyes. It was enough to make a grown man cry.

She finally said, "You must join us for dinner. We just sat down."

Audrey politely but firmly said, "We have had a very trying week, so please don't be offended, but we would like a quiet dinner alone. I promise I'll call you as soon as we get back from Kansas City at the end of next week."

"We understand, but you have to tell us everything when you get back," Marney insisted.

Skip chimed in. "We're thinking about you. Keep in touch. We really want to know how you both are doing."

"You can read about it again tomorrow in the *Shiny Sheet*," I told them and briefly described the Robin White interview.

The restaurant quickly filled, and it was now bustling, full of chatter and laughter. Thankfully, we had arrived early enough to avoid the line forming at the reception desk, and by the time our steak dinner was served, the line extended out the door.

"Marney's reaction was moving to me. What did you think?" I asked.

"Well, I was a little surprised," my wife said, appearing to be struggle to formulate her own opinion. "After all, they were only in Vince's company when we invited them to join us. She and Skip were more like acquaintances of Vincent's rather than friends."

"That's what was so moving to me." My wife looked puzzled, so I explained. "Her tears were for us, not for Vincent."

We finished our meal in silence, and I was thankful for the restaurant noise. It helped relieve the uncomfortable feeling that the lack of conversation usually causes, even to longtime married couples.

When we arrived back at our apartment, Audrey asked, "Are you having a cocktail or going to bed?" That was Audrey's customary question, which she ritually asked every evening as we reentered our apartment.

I gave her my ritual response to her customary question. "Of course I'll have one."

We still were not full of conversation, but over a nightcap, we speculated what tomorrow could possibly bring.

"I'll get the papers early so we can get that drama over with. We'll see what Robin Wright has wrought." I was trying to think of some action plan to help us get through the day. "And maybe get an update from Chuck."

"Oh, Nate." Something struck her memory. "We have to call Peter. We should have called him today."

"I know. I thought of it earlier today, but I just couldn't bring myself to deal with him being so angry with us." I continued soberly, "I am afraid that we may lose another friend, and I am in no rush to confront that. I'll call around eleven tomorrow morning. KC is an hour earlier, and maybe Peter will have had his coffee and by ten o'clock be a little more congenial." I could only hope.

"Do you think that could really happen?" she asked with heightened concern. "Nate, could we really lose Peter as well?"

"Did you think we would ever be involved in a murder?" On that unpleasant note, we went to bed.

CHAPTER THIRTEEN

he Saturday edition of the *Palm Beach Daily News* is typically
five or six pages in total. If it were priced by the ounce, it
would have to go out of business.

Following my regular morning routine, I walked to Green's
Pharmacy, one long block west on Sunrise Avenue to the corner
of North County Avenue. As usual, I bought the *Shiny Sheet* and
the *New York Post*. Since the *Shiny Sheet* was so skimpy, the Robin
White story about the latest development in the sensational Palm
Beach murder case was not edited to save space. It dominated the
front page and most of the third. I was too anxious to wait until I
returned to our apartment to read the news, so I read the entire
story as I slowly walked toward our building, stopping a time or two
to concentrate on the details.

A large photo adorned the front page, approximately four inches by six inches. It was the view of Mar-A-Lago from South County
Road, the scene of the murder. The photo was enhanced with two
inset photos: one of our friend Vincent looking elegant and holding a cigarette in his always-present three-inch cigarette extender;

the other was of Megan Kelly, which I recognized as her professional headshot. Under their photographs were two simple captions: "Vincent Houten, Victim" and "Megan Kelly, Companion."

More shocking was the bold lettered headline for this Saturday's feature, which stated, "Companion: I Know Who Shot VXH," followed by a somewhat ominous subheading: "Murderer Still At Large."

Audrey was sitting at our dining table as I entered. I dropped the *Shiny Sheet* in front of her and remarked, "Well, Ms. Robin White got her big scoop after all."

She immediately picked up the paper and, after a few-second review of the photos and headline, lowered it and asked rhetorically, "What was she thinking?"

I went to the kitchen to make myself a cup of coffee and leave my wife to read the rest of the story. Megan had wisely refused to name whom she suspected but unwisely insisted she had proof. "If only those assholes would listen." That was an obvious reference to the PBPD. It was apparent that she hadn't attended a "Best Techniques in Dealing with the Media" seminar.

"Nate," my wife began, "both of these photographs are quite recent, and therefore the only way the *Shiny Sheet* could have obtained them was from Megan." Audrey then said, "Her allegation is the same as that she made to Chuck on Thursday, but now she has gone public."

"Audrey, the girl is definitely out of control." I continued, "I only hope she doesn't loudmouth herself into more trouble."

"She'll do anything to be in any paper. And she will do back flips to get a feature in the *Shiny Sheet*, of all papers. It's quite pathetic."

The central theme of the report was, as Audrey and I had hoped, more about fashion than murder. It described Megan's Vera Wang dress, her Chanel handbag, and the emerald jewelry that set off her red hair, which was the creation of her renowned colorist Salvatore Ligoria of New York. It also listed the revelers of note, such as The Donald, his wife Melania, two of his children, and then a few of the also-rans: Rush Limbaugh; New York's ex-mayor, now being referred to as America's mayor, Rudy Giuliani, and his wife, Judith; Mr. and Mrs. Regis Philbin; and a few others. Reporter Robin, from Audrey's account, described in great detail their ensembles, the band, the décor, and even the table's floral arrangements—lilies (which my wife hates).

That part of the article was what my wife and I had envisioned: a fluff piece that wouldn't stir up the proverbial pot and would also be kind to our friend.

The more significant and disappointing feature was that Ms. Robin White had the full cooperation and input of Megan Kelly, who voluntarily made available personal photographs. Her insinuation that she possessed incriminating information and that the police were acting incompetently all made for a great story. Those facts led off the piece, the social info provided by Audrey filled the interior portion, and the fact that there was no prime suspect ended the story.

Later that morning but surprisingly before noon, we received a phone call from the one and only Megan Kelly. She must have read the latest edition of the *Palm Beach Daily News* and was in a critiquing mood. A call from Meg before noon was an oddity. "Well, they got everything right except for the jewelry," she began.

Before she could elaborate on the irrelevant discrepancy, I interrupted her. "Meg, I don't think it is wise for you to proclaim to whoever will listen that you know who the murderer is." I quickly added, "I think you should calm down, and let the police do their job."

"The police?" she screeched. "Excuse me, but that Gerity guy wants to lock me up and throw away the key." She callously added, "I might have been kept as a ready piece of ass for Vincent's pleasure, but I also heard a lot of shit. A lot of shit about Tri-State Tape."

I attempted to get Megan to elaborate on what she might have heard. But that was not going to happen during this conversation.

"I haven't been very smart about finances, so I have to make some moves before they throw my ass out onto the street."

I pressed her further. "Meg what have you heard? You must tell me."

"When the time is right, I'll have another little talk with Detective Gerity, and sooner or later he'll listen. He'll have to listen." She then hung up the phone.

I called Detective Gerity and asked him for an update on any new developments that might have occurred. I also thought he should know about my conversation with the quite insane Ms. Kelly. I told him that she insisted that she had heard something incriminating but wouldn't say what. "It was definitely about the company," I added. "She's pretty wired."

"And pretty dumb. Her comments to the press weren't such a great idea." Detective Gerity then brought me up to date on a few things. "The West Palm Beach police have been keeping an eye on her which has been a task. The woman doesn't live what you might consider a routine schedule." That at least made Megan's paranoid comments in regard to Chuck's intent to lock her up and throw away the key sound a little less absurd.

Detective Gerity relayed to me how, with Megan's meal ticket gone, she was scrambling to get some "do-re-mi," as she would say. She was trying to sell anything she could.

Her horse that Vincent had paid fifty thousand dollars for, not to mention the five to six thousand a month over the last year and a half for grooming, boarding, and training, now was for sale for fifteen thousand. Her two-month-old, five-thousand-dollar, handcrafted dressage saddle, custom designed for her height was worthless to anyone not six foot tall, but it was nevertheless listed for twenty-eight hundred. Her 1999 Jeep Cherokee with the dancing dressage-horse hood ornament had a sign in the window: "For

Sale $2,500. Will Negotiate." Lastly, to keep her in groceries, and most likely vodka, she had pawned all of her jewelry that had any value.

"I plan to bring her in again to address her allegations in the press. I'll keep you and Audrey out of that discussion. It would be useful if she continued to consider you both as her confidants." He then forcefully added, "But she has to realize that we are dealing with a murder, and there is still a very dangerous person or persons out there." Emphatically he gave a warning. "For her own safety, she has to keep her mouth shut."

Audrey came into the living room, and realizing that I was talking with Chuck Gerity, she interrupted, saying, "Ask him about Sammy and Christopher." I did.

He said, "We haven't located Christopher Hinkey yet, but Samuel Houten is scheduled to fly standby Tuesday, so it depends what flight has an open seat for him."

"That's just great." I wondered how Sam and Vince could have come from the same sperm pool. "Vincent's services are on Wednesday, and I can just picture his brother sitting in Albuquerque airport, still waiting for a plane while the minister is eulogizing his brother."

To calm my fears, Detective Gerity said, "We already checked seat availability, and it looks fairly certain he will get on one of the early flights. New Mexico state police agreed to ask the airline to prioritize his status. Other than buy him a ticket, there isn't anything else we can do."

Sheepishly, I remarked in an apologetic tone, "I'm sure you are doing your best."

Detective Gerity nodded. "There still isn't any sign of Christopher, but KCPD has been making inquiries, and I don't think it is going to be too difficult to track him down. It has been less than two weeks since he was last seen, so his trail isn't that cold. I'll let you know when something develops."

I was starting to feel better about the sharing issue we had with Chuck Gerity.

Just before hanging up, I was startled by a thought. "Oh Chuck, I almost forgot. We received a phone message from Peter Kunz Thursday night, and I did not think much about it until you voiced your concern for Megan Kelly's safety."

It wasn't really necessary to inform our friend, Detective Gerity, that Peter thought of him as a "clueless dick," so attempting to be politically correct, I merely stated, "Peter is obviously upset over his friend's murder and feels he is unjustly being considered a suspect. He said he was going to get to the bottom of this."

Chuck got the message right off. "Here we go with another loose cannon. Peter and Megan have no appreciation of the severity of the situation. All I can think to do is to ask the Kansas City PD to keep an eye on him."

I informed Detective Gerity that I tried to phone Peter just before I called him, but he did not answer. I told the detective that it was obvious that he, Peter Kunz, was still angry that we told him as much as we did about his finances. I then ended by promising to report back to Chuck as soon as I could make contact with Peter Kunz.

Frustrated, I ranted to my wife, "Between Peter going off on his own investigation, Megan going off on her own PR campaign, Sammy not even able to get to his brother's funeral in time, and Christopher disappearing, I feel like we are babysitters for the most childish group of adults that could possibly be assembled."

In response, Audrey said, "Only this is not child's play."

CHAPTER FOURTEEN

I spent a minute or two contemplating my wife's last remark. She was quite right. This was serious and definitely not child's play. I soberly considered the cast of characters who were now adding more fuel to the fire of complications.

"Audrey, I feel as though the walls of this apartment are closing in on me. I'm getting claustrophobic. Please let's get out of here. Can we drive down to Delray Beach where we won't run into anyone we know and get some lunch? We didn't have any breakfast, and I'm very hungry."

She agreed, so we drove to Delray, parked in the public lot, and began our walk along Atlantic Avenue, which over the past ten years or so has been transformed into restaurant row, with a number of boutique shops mixed in. We were not regulars to Delray, so we weren't sure which restaurant to choose. We walked three or four blocks east on the south side of Atlantic, then turned and walked back west on the north side of the street.

We were still having difficulty deciding because we passed so many quaint pubs and bistros. As we passed a corner shop named the Love Shack, a voice called out, "Aunt Audrey and Uncle Nate."

It was my wife's twenty-four-year-old niece, Rachel. She came running out of the shop where she was working and gave us both a family-style hug and kiss.

"I've been reading about your friend's murder in the papers. How awful. I know you were good friends. I'm so sorry."

"Oh, Rach, your father told me you were now living here, and with all that has been going on. I completely forgot. I'm so sorry. I've been meaning to call."

Sympathetically, Rachel replied, "You both must be going through a lot. The paper said you were the last to see Mr. Houten alive. Did the police question you?"

"Only daily." Almost pleading, Audrey explained, "It has been like a bad dream, but please don't ask us to recount it now. We came down to Delray to try to forget about it all for an hour or two and get ourselves some lunch."

I chimed in. "Which is well past due. My stomach is growling. Rachel, can you recommend a nice, quiet restaurant?"

"Oh, sure. Viamonte. It's just on the next corner. I'm dating the day manager. Just ask for Nick."

We said our good-byes with promises to meet up after things settled down and proceeded to her recommended Italian restaurant.

"I'm good with the restaurant, but please don't ask for Nick. I don't care for any idle conversation with your niece's latest boyfriend."

We took a sidewalk table. It seemed a good idea at the time. A sidewalk table gave us the ability to do some people watching, which would help take our minds off the latest developments, while enjoying an Italian dish hopefully with no interruption.

A bottle of wine, a basket of bread delivered to our table, and menus in hand, another familiar voice rose from the street, interrupting our planned solitude. "Audrey, Audrey we have to talk."

The sidewalk table that we anticipated would provide us with a temporary escape from our pressure cooker, with the added advantage of some delightful sunshine, was a bust.

The familiar voice was that of Salvatore Liguria, who was Megan Kelly's colorist, and who also colored my wife's hair on occasion. As Audrey had previously speculated, he was most likely having a sexual relationship with Miss Kelly.

Salvatore hurriedly proceeded toward the entrance of the restaurant, past the manager's stand and back to the outdoor sidewalk sitting area where we unfortunately were located. I took those few minutes to ask my wife to be polite but to get rid of him. It was not to be.

Salvatore kissed Audrey on both cheeks but barely acknowledged my existence. Without as much as a "do you mind," he called to a waiter, "We need another wine glass for this table." I thought, *What's with the "we" shit?* But I kept my mouth shut.

"Audrey, I was just talking to Megan about this morning's news story. She really thinks she has some very incriminating evidence on Joanie. We had quite a conversation." He purposely was being evasive to heighten the drama of what he was about to reveal. I found the last few minutes to be very annoying.

"Well, you sure had more success than I had," I offered, hoping to let the colorist know that we also were in the loop. "She called at about eleven, but she wouldn't talk to me about her comments in the *Shiny Sheet* regarding her suspicions. Quite frankly, Audrey and I are very concerned for her safety."

Smugly and with an air of superiority, he addressed his comments directly to me. "She wouldn't tell you anything because you obviously are not her confidant." He added in an insulting tone, "She probably thinks you are snitching to the police." Then redirecting his gaze to my wife, this presumptive twit stated, "I see you haven't ordered yet. Great! I'll join you so we can talk over lunch."

With that, he reached over and picked up my menu, which I hadn't even opened yet, and began reading it.

What a prima donna! He clearly believed that he had earned some imaginary, elite status based solely on the fact that an alcohol- and drug-abusing model (who was currently living hand-to-mouth, financed solely by the discounted sale of gifts received over the last three years from a man thirty years her senior and who could possibly be considered the prime suspect in his sensational murder) had made the misguided and thoughtless decision to confide in her pompous, freeloading, asshole colorist.

I didn't want to ask our intruder to leave. That would have been far too civil. I was developing a plan—a plan that I imagined would, at the appropriate time, encourage Salvatore to rise from his seat for some contrived reason. At that opportune moment, I would grab him by the throat and throw him over the box planter separating the café from the sidewalk with enough force to land him on Atlantic Avenue, hopefully in the path of oncoming traffic.

Audrey could see that Mount Vesuvius was about to erupt, so she put her hand on the prima donna's forearm and forcefully said, "Salvatore, we can order later. What can you tell us about your conversation with Megan?"

He began by speculating. "I'm not sure she would want me to tell you anything." This was another transparent gesture to prop up his imagined importance. "But she did hear some conversations over Christmastime that are quite revealing."

Impatiently, Audrey asked, "Such as?"

After a brief pause, he began revealing the information Megan had shared with him earlier in the day. "First of all, you should know that Vincent had become very agitated and was increasingly concerned about his company." After another pause for effect, he added, "Vincent received a Fed Ex package from the company two weeks before Christmas. Megan is pretty sure it was from his accountant and contained, among other things, his eleven-month year-to-date P and L report. It apparently wasn't good.

"She started to realize that he was suspicious of some kind of scam or theft because he started making calls to some of his long-time employees. He made those calls at about 7:00 p.m. That means after business hours in Kansas City. Most likely he was calling their homes, and some of the conversations lasted over an hour." There was another pause as he sipped some of my wine. We were going to have to tolerate this jerk and drag out of him what he knew piece by piece.

"OK," I began. "Vince gets a Fed Ex package. He gets one at least once a month. Megan thinks his P and L looks bad and he starts calling some trusted employees. Interesting but not very revealing. There must be more."

Salvatore relayed some of the comments Megan had overheard, and in my estimation, these comments taken individually were not very conclusive, but as a complete set, I admitted they appeared damning. In one instance, Vincent became impatient with his employee, and Megan heard him say, "I know all that. I need more. You got to get me more." Megan surmised this was Vincent attempting to recruit whoever was on the receiving end of the phone call as a spy. Maybe, but then again, maybe not. He might have been asking for sales information or a more detailed inventory update.

Salvatore kept the most interesting piece of hearsay for last. "One night, the week before Christmas, Vincent called Joanie. They had a very long conversation so Megan went upstairs to dress for dinner. When she started to descend the stairs, she paused to hear what Vincent was saying. She clearly heard him in a very threatening voice say to Joanie, 'If this is true, you are finished. I will throw you out of the company.' Megan said the next day he made plans to return to Kansas City immediately after New Year's, on January second."

Realizing that we had gotten all the news that's fit to print, I leaned toward our source of information and said, "Thank you, Salvatore. You can leave now."

In indignant protest, the colorist responded, "What about lunch? I'm famished."

I didn't hold back. "Audrey and I have been planning lunch for the last two hours. But sitting next to you only ruins my appetite. Go find some other sucker to buy you lunch."

He looked to Audrey for some sympathetic help, but she just looked away. He abruptly rose and thankfully left without another word. I opened my menu and motioned for the waiter. "Audrey, please make a choice quickly before I drop dead from hunger."

Our niece had made a great recommendation because the entrées included some real traditional Italian dishes. I ordered an appetizer of tripe over polenta and an entrée of bacallà in a caper-and-white-wine dressing over tricolore salad. My wife ordered a hamburger. Opposites attract. As soon as the waiter took our order and left our table, I opened my cell phone.

"Nate, who are you calling now?" my wife asked, apparently annoyed at the prospect of another distraction.

"I'm calling our friend, Detective Chuck. I'm sure that Salvatore will be a lot less pompous while waiting in the interrogation room for half an hour and then answering questions under a very bright florescent light."

With food on the way and the Delray police on the lookout for a egotistical colorist, I was starting to feel that things were finally moving in the right direction.

CHAPTER FIFTEEN

As soon as we returned from our Del Ray trip, my wife and I poured cocktails and rehashed all the information we had received that day. We deemed the travel schedule of Samuel Houten to be of little importance. The dissapearance of Christpher Hinkey was of more interest, and the revelations received from Salvatore Liguria were either very significant or just fantasy. Time would tell. They all however had to be considered.

We first addressed Vincent's nephew, Christopher. "Audrey, aren't you surprised to hear about Christopher?" Audrey and I hadn't talked to Vincent for some time, with the exception of a Merry Christmas call on Christmas Day. We had returned to New Jersey to celebrate the holidays with our family, so that all added up to about four weeks since our last contact with Vincent. Therefore, the revelation that Christopher was now among the missing was news to us.

"Yes, I'm very, very surprised. The last time we talked to Vincent, I remember was the first week in December, and he expressed that he was happy with the fact that Christopher had seemed to finally take to his latest position in the packaging and shipping department." She recalled Vincent telling us that his general manager, Bert Kelty, had even given him a raise and planned a Christmas bonus.

"Maybe the latest rehab stint did some good, after how many tries, dear?" I could hope but didn't have much conviction.

"I don't remember how many, but I think the first was shortly after high school. That's twenty years ago." She continued, "Nate, Vince talked more about Christopher than any of his other nephews and nieces. Even though he often screwed up, I think he was definitely Vincent's favorite nephew. He gave him so many chances."

I hoped there was some reasonable explanation for his latest disappearance, but it looked like the loser had fallen off the wagon again. My wife from Venus added compassionately, "When he finds out, Christopher is going to take Vincent's death very hard. If he doesn't already know."

Feeling that I had been just trumped by the how-Christian-are-you card, I asked, "Would you object to me changing the subject? I think I have procrastinated long enough. It's time I called Peter Kunz again and face the music."

"I'm going to change. I assume we're staying in tonight." Having lived through years of my lack of memory and attention to detail, she added, "Nate, don't forget a thing. I want a complete recount of the conversation."

Peter and I had each other's numbers in our cell phones, so he was certain to know it was me calling. Would he even take the call? I was relieved when he answered on the second ring. It was a good sign.

"Just calling to see how you are doing, buddy." I hoped the "buddy" angle would have the intended effect and then held my breath.

I didn't need to apologize because Peter, as if he had forgotten the voice mail he left on our answering machine some thirty-six hours prior, immediately responded. "There's something fishy going on at Tri-State Tape, and I'm just the guy who can find out exactly what it is."

Surprised at both his lack of anger toward Audrey and me after hearing the explicit voice mail just two days before, and by the intensity of this voice, I asked, "Peter, what the hell are you talking about?"

He didn't directly respond to my question but continued talking. "I don't want to say until I know more, but I talked to people at the company, and I heard that Vincent was ready to make some major moves."

"Peter, are you working with the police?" I was becoming alarmed at the tone of his voice and the direction of the conversation. He remained silent, and I became more frustrated. I repeated the question. "Are you in contact with the proper authorities?"

Again not answering, he said, "I'm meeting with George Cavallas on Monday to compare notes."

As I began giving him advice, reminding him to be careful to whom he talked, he interrupted me, signing off with "I'll be talking to you."

Audrey returned to find me deep in thought. "How did it go with Peter?"

"Terribly. I'm very concerned."

"Is he really that angry with us?" she asked, thinking that that was my concern.

"No, no, it's not about Peter's voice mail. It's just that Peter is going off on his own and asking a lot of questions." I added, "He seems to feel that Vincent was ready to shake things up at Tri-State Tape and that may have something to do with his murder."

I was relieved to hear that Peter was going to meet with Vince's long-time confidant and friend George Cavallas. Given my respect for George's competence, and his loyalty to Vincent, and despite how upset Peter appeared, I felt that he was at least taking reasonable action in meeting with George. If Vincent were planning a major change in his company, then George would certainly have knowledge of it.

"Nate, you know when we arrive in Kansas City, Joanie will be there, Peter will be there, the six heirs will be there, and now that Peter and Megan have implicated someone in the company as having a possible motive, all of Vincent's fifty or more employees will likely be there, nicely completing Detective Chuck's suspect list." She concluded, "We most likely will be in town for four days, in very close contact with the murderer."

"Or murderers," I said, correcting my wife. Then I added, "Not to mention Detective Gerity, the Kansas City PD, and the Missouri state police's special investigative division, collectively doing their best to stir things up so as to flush out the perpetrator."

Detective Edward Gerity, in my opinion, might have made a few false steps in the earlier stages of the investigation, but he realized the unique opportunity he was about to face. He knew that the murderer would be in KC, and he wanted this case solved. Without regard for sharing responsibility (and therefore credit), he summoned all the forces and expertise the city of Kansas and the state of Missouri could provide.

All things considered, it certainly appeared that the prevailing conditions were building up to a perfect storm, and we were scheduled to fly smack into the middle of it.

CHAPTER SIXTEEN

We were awakened Sunday morning by another Detective Gerity phone call. This time it was unusually early, slightly after six. I jumped out of bed and cleared my throat, grabbed the phone, and tried to sound as if I'd been awake for hours. Why did people feel the need to do that?

"Sorry to wake you, but I thought you would want to know."

He paused, and as my head was clearing, my anxiety was building. "What's up?"

"Megan Kelly was in an automobile accident at two this morning." He quickly added, "She'll be fine, but it was a serious accident. She is in the Wellington Medical Center. She suffered a broken bone in her foot and various bruises. I believe that they will keep her until tomorrow."

"Was she drunk?"

"I don't have anything more than that at this time. I should be getting a report from West Palm Beach later this morning. Her car left the road, hit a palm tree with a great deal of force, then spun around a hundred and eighty degrees before rolling over into a drainage ditch." Chuck sounded very tired. He must have been up since shortly after 2:00 a.m. He ended with "We'll talk."

Audrey didn't need me to explain. Her first words were "Is she all right?"

I relayed what Chuck had informed me about Megan's condition and that she had been in a serious accident, though her injuries were not life threatening. She now apparently was recuperating in the Wellington Medical Center.

"Nate, we have to visit her today before we leave for Kansas City."

I agreed but suggested, "Not before noon." I didn't want to sit in Megan's room watching her sleep.

We would have to make some adjustments to our planned flight arrangements, but first I made a pot of coffee before going online to check flight availability. The only nonstop flights to KC are out of Fort Lauderdale. The Fort Lauderdale airport is almost an hour further away than the West Palm Beach airport.

Audrey and I wanted to visit Megan but we also wanted to make our planned diner with Joanie Olsen in Kansas City. With that in mind but with the advantage of a one hour time difference between Florida and Missouri, I was able to get seats on the 3:00 p.m. flight arriving at 5:30 p.m. Kansas City time. Assuming no major delay, we could visit Megan at noon, make the 3:00 p.m. flight out of Fort Lauderdale and land in KC in time to check into the InterContinental and meet Joanie Olsen for dinner at 7:00 p.m.

Audrey was anxious to call Joan and Peter, but it was 5:30 a.m. in Kansas City and 4:30 a.m. in Aspen, so we had to kill some time. We had a cup of coffee and did some last-minute packing, and I whipped up two cheese-and-onion omelets with a side of bacon. I spoil my wife rotten.

Just before we left to visit Megan, and while I was taking the luggage to our car, Audrey made her phone calls. The first call was to Peter, the second to Joanie.

Having loaded our bags in the trunk of our old 1996 Jaguar XKS (a nice car, though not in Vince's collectible class, just classically old), I waited for Audrey at the front entrance of the lobby. I don't know what I expected but was surprised that in very short order, my wife appeared having already completed her phone calls.

We got into the car and started for Wellington, but before I even reached the street, I impatiently asked, "What did they say?"

"Peter was a little distant, almost distracted, but he seemed genuinely concerned about Megan's condition. He asked about the extent of her injuries." She paused as if trying to understand something she had just heard. Then she described Joanie's reaction. "Joanie asked me, 'Is she dead?' I know there isn't any love lost between the two, but it did strike me as a bit harsh."

We arrived at Megan's room in the Wellington Medical Center just before noon. We entered the room to find her with her cell phone in hand. "I was just dialing you."

Audrey was taken aback by her appearance and passionately said, "Meg, you look a mess."

"Thanks for the compliment. I didn't think I could feel any worse."

"I'm so sorry, but you look like you were beaten up. Are you in pain?"

Megan had superficial scrapes on the bridge of her nose that continued upward across her forehead, which were treated with a very unattractive yellow antiseptic. A large, half-inch-thick, white gauze pad covered what must have been a substantial bruise or gash on the left side of her forehead near her hairline. Meg's left eye was blackened and bloodshot, and her right foot was in a cast.

"My foot and face just throb. The pain meds are working, but my right tit and ribs are killing me. I get a spasm if I move." Looking on the brighter side, she added, "Since I don't feel like moving, at least I'm not temped to look in a mirror." Then she pleaded, "Could we please change the subject?"

"Meg," I asked, "you weren't wearing your seatbelt, were you?"

Megan snapped back, "Get off your soapbox and stop preaching. I was only going two miles."

I persisted. "But the airbag deployed, didn't it?"

Getting a bit agitated, Megan responded gruffly. "Yes, the airbag deployed. The fucking thing smacked me in the face."

I guessed from the facial scrapes and the broken foot that the steering wheel was not properly adjusted. With the wheel tilted too far upward, the airbag was aimed toward Megan's face, not her chest, thus causing the damage to her face. Additionally, it allowed her to forcefully slide under the bag, jamming her foot, which was most likely hard pressed against the brake pedal, resulting in the broken bone.

The injuries to her chest and the severe bruise to her forehead were most likely inflicted after the crash and after the airbag deflated while the Jeep was rolling over a few times before landing in the drainage ditch. Without the protection of her seatbelt, Megan must have been tossed about like a rag doll. The steering wheel, the console shift, the windshield, the roof, the driver's side window—all were potentially lethal objects.

I felt a little shudder go through me as I had a flashback of some of the many vehicular deaths I had dealt with through my career. "Megan, you are lucky to be alive."

At that moment, Detective Edward Gerity entered and was greeted less than cordially by Megan. "Great, now the gang's all here. Nice of you to visit, Eddy, but why aren't you out there finding the asshole who ran me off the road?"

My wife and I had the same stunned reaction. We looked to each other, then to the detective. Audrey asked, "Is that true?"

Insulted, Megan answered the question for Detective Gerity. "Of course, it's true. Some fucking asshole ran me off the road and into that tree."

Detective Gerity addressed Megan's inflamatory question about what they were doing to find the perpetrator. "Miss Kelly, we are investigating your accusation. We are not taking it lightly and have added security for your protection until the situation becomes clearer."

Chuck then turned toward Audrey and me and continued. "The vehicle was removed from the ditch and taken to the state police forensic garage for analysis. Although it was severely damaged, preliminary inspection did show the left front fender dented, and there is a trace of green paint."

The detective turned back to address Megan. "Now that I have your undivided attention, there are a few things I would like to review with you. You should know I had a long conversation with Salvatore Liguria yesterday afternoon."

Megan sighed. "Oh God."

"Detective Gerity," I interrupted. "We have a flight to catch. Do you mind if we leave now?"

"Not at all. This may take a while."

My wife gave Megan a gentle hug, and Megan gave her a classic response. "Do me a favor and send in a nurse. I want to know who I have to blow to get out of here."

On that note, and while unsuccessfully holding back our laughter, we headed out of the hospital and onto Fort Lauderdale Airport. *Kansas City, here we come.*

PART TWO

CHAPTER SEVENTEEN

By Sunday, the Vincent Houten murder was getting national attention. The New York and Chicago newspapers, with much of their readership personally familiar with Southern Florida, were covering the story. In the midwest where Tri-State Tape conducted most of its business, newspapers from Cleveland, St Louis, Omaha, and certainly Vincent's hometown of Kansas City were in regular contact with the *Palm Beach Post*, which was the far more credible South Florida news source than the high-society *Shiny Sheet*.

They all had assigned their top veteran reporters to the story. All the Florida dailies were sharing information and Detective Gerity was quick to employ their assistance.

"My name is Joe Winston. I'm calling about that picture in yesterday's Jacksonville Enquirer. The one of that missing person."

"Please go on. What can you give me?"

The voice on the receiving end of the call belonged to Al Morris, a member of the task force set up by Chuck Gerity in a makeshift situation room in the Palm Beach police station where the designated 1-800 phone call had been received and was instantly being traced.

"I think he's here. Well, he was here. I just checked him out."

"Just checked him out?"

"Yeah, I work at the Holiday Inn Express just off I-95 on Route 40 in Jacksonville. He checked out at 10:47 a.m. this morning."

"Mr. Winston, it's now 11:35 a.m. He didn't just check out. He checked out almost an hour ago." The officer's response was deliberately curt. "What took you so long to call?"

"Well, I wasn't sure it was him. I don't think I would have even noticed except he was real wired, very nervous, maybe even strung out. He looked like he hadn't slept much, and he paid with cash. We see lots of kinds come and go, but when someone acts strange and pays cash, red flags pop up."

Detective Morris encouraged Joe. "Please go on."

"It took a few minutes, then I remembered the photo. I remembered thinking yesterday that it seemed strange to have a photo of a thirty-seven-year-old missing person from Missouri on the front page of the local section of the *Jacksonville Inquirer.* I thought that guy must be important, and I guess I recalled his picture. After the strange guy checked out, I got a copy of yesterday's paper, and sure enough, it looked like him. Maybe he looks a little older than the photograph, but I'm pretty sure it's him."

The published photograph had been acquired along with a number of photos of Christopher Mosley from an extensive collection of photos in Vincent Houten's Palm Beach house. The collection included family and friends, some current, some recent, and some from the ancient past. Those displayed in frames on his piano were primarily reserved for Ms. Right Now, while the others arranged on tables and shelves were a form of decor. It was another example of the obsession of a collector.

The photo collection not only provided the photograph Detective Gerity had distributed to the Florida newspapers through the

Florida state police but proved additionally helpful in the investigation. The collection contained pictures of Joanie Olsen, Megan Kelly, Peter Kunz, Audrey, and me, but more importantly, it also included all the heirs and some key employees.

The task-force detective intentionally allowed Joe Winston to ramble on to give his informant some additional time and allow his techs the necessary time to trace the call. The detective didn't need any convincing. This was the first lead of any kind to the whereabouts of Christopher Mosley since the murder of Vincent Xavier Houten.

It had been five days since the murder of our friend Vincent but a little more than forty-eight hours since Megan Kelly was intentionally run off Southern Boulevard in West Palm Beach. Christopher was the son of Florence Mosley, sister of Vincent Xavier Houten, and the lone heir not to have been located since his uncle Vince's death. Christopher was a person of interest, to say the least.

The technical assistant to the task force had successfully identified the address of the Holiday Inn Express and immediately dispatched the Jacksonville and Florida state police to the scene. By the time Joe Winston could answer the next question, his hotel would be visited by no less than a half dozen police vehicles.

"Mr. Winston, I have a few more questions for you, but first will you please notify housekeeping not to clean or even access Mr. Mosley's room?"

"I'm in the back office by myself. I have to put you on hold. Is that OK?"

Morris responded, "It's very important. Do whatever you need to. I'll hold."

After several minutes, someone came on the line. "Hello, this is Sergeant Benson, Florida state police."

Detective Morris responded, "Hey, sarge. This is Detective Al Morris, Palm Beach police. What's the status there?"

Sargent Benson answered, "I have taken command of the scene until forensics and homicide detectives arrive. We're just getting organized."

Morris asked, "Anything you think I should know?"

Sargent Benson replied, "I instructed Joe Winston to keep housekeeping and anyone else out of that room."

"Can you confirm that has been done?"

"Already done. I have Jacksonville PD taping off the entire area, and they are now gathering guests with rooms in the vicinity of the suspects into one of the hotel conference rooms for questioning. We're treating this as a crime scene, no shortcuts."

"Great, Sarge. When you get a description of the vehicle, direction last seen, eyewitness accounts, anything, please keep me informed."

"Will do."

CHAPTER EIGHTEEN

"OK, OK. Let's review."

Detective Gerity, addressing the four-man task force, attempted to focus everyone's attention on the big picture. The purpose for scheduling the meeting had been to assure that all of the member's efforts would be coordinated while Chuck Gerity was in Kansas City. He was scheduled to leave 6:15 a.m. the next morning for what could be several days. Now there was a lot more to coordinate.

Gerity began. "A person resembling Christopher Mosley registered at the Holiday Inn in Jacksonville 7:12 a.m. Sunday under the name of Philip True."

"Excuse me, boss."

"Yes, Morris, go ahead. What do you have to add?"

"I think it's important to note that although hotel policy is to verify each guest's identification with a picture ID, the manager cannot confirm that the procedure was followed."

Gerity shot back, "Why not?"

"Who knows? Maybe she was tired at the end of her shift. Maybe he slipped her a few bucks. Maybe she just fucked up. The JPD is tracking her down for questioning but haven't located her yet."

Clearly frustrated, Gerity leaned his face toward Morris's and slowly asked, "Again, Detective. Why not? I'm not a mind reader."

"Sorry, Chuck. Nothing seems to be easy in this case. She has two regularly scheduled days off. She's not at her apartment so they are locating friends and coworkers to find out if she has a boyfriend, nearby or if she vacations in a particular area." Morris added, "You know the regular drill."

That statement riled the detective, and he jumped on it. "The regular drill doesn't cut it in this case. Get your ass up to Jacksonville tonight."

Detective Gerity was setting a tone, a tone of intensity and urgency. The detective continued. "So assuming our suspect is Christopher Mosley, we don't know if he has false identification of one Philip True, or if he just got lucky that he was not questioned. If he has a Philip True ID, he probably will use the same alias again." Gerity added, "We can only hope he does."

In an effort to redeem himself, Morris spoke up. "We do have confirmation that he was driving a green Toyota Corolla with damage to the right rear fender. He listed the license plate number as ZXN 537 on the registration form."

Realizing he had spoken too soon, the detective weakly added that the suspect failed to indicate a state on the hotel's registration form.

Detective Gerity addressed the four. "I don't have to remind everyone that green paint was evident on the Jeep Cherokee driven by Megan Kelly. As for now, we have to assume Christopher Mosley is our man."

Turning to Officer Jose Solemn, who was the technician responsible for performing the telephone wire trace, Gerity asked,

"Now that we have fifty states to consider, how do you plan to search with just the vehicle description and a plate number?"

Having just witnessed Detective Gerity's raw disposition, Solemn rattled off a detailed report. "Searches are already in progress. No vehicle with a similar description and plates comes up in Florida, Missouri, or Kansas motor vehicle registration. We have just started widening the search to nearby states."

Solemn continued. "It is more than possible that he registered a fictitious plate number on the hotel form. As of thirty minutes ago, no rental company has reported an overdue rental of that description. I also began a search with the cooperation of all major auto rental companies for a rental agreement in the name of Philip True, but that will take some time."

Impatiently, Gerity asked, "What kind of time are we talking?"

Officer Solemn responded. "Assuming that Mosley rented the Toyota before the Houten murder, we have to go back a week, maybe two. The search we did under the name Christopher Mosley that was done immediately after the murder took some time, maybe seventy-two hours, and that search was just a few days after we believe he rented the car, and it still came up blank."

"Good work, Jose. Just keep me informed." Then Gerity asked Morris, "Did Jacksonville homicide get anything from interviewing the other guests?"

"Other than confirmation of the damaged car, nothing. He checked in at 7:12 a.m. Monday morning. No one recalls seeing him. He didn't make any calls from the room phone or call for any room service. Twenty-six hours later he checked out, destination unknown. Oh yeah, I'm sure you'll love this. Forensics couldn't come up with any prints. Looks like he wiped the place down."

Under his breath, Detective Gerity murmured, "Audrey and Nate Stevens think Christopher Mosley is stupid."

It was almost six hours since Christopher Mosley had checked out of the Holiday Express. Even at the speed limit, he could be in anyone of six states. Every hour the search area got bigger. Gerity knew that the only hope for the task force nabbing him was for him to make a mistake.

"Boss," Morris chimed in, "if we're finished, I'm on my way to Jacksonville."

CHAPTER NINETEEN

Our Delta flight from Fort Lauderdale to Kansas City was fine. Because of the change from our earlier flight first class out of West Palm Beach, we had to settle for coach. But we were able to avoid a stop in Atlanta, and that wasn't a bad trade-off. We arrived on time, and the InterContinental arranged for a car service to meet us.

We were rushed a bit, getting from our visit with Megan at the Wellington Hospital to Fort Lauderdale airport. I was not familiar with the drop-off and long-term parking arrangements, so I was a little distracted, and conversation between Audrey and me was brief. Once settled in our seats though, we spent the first hour or so discussing Megan, both the seriousness of her condition and the hilarity of her humor. Then we eventually turned our thoughts to what we could expect when we met with Joanie Olsen for dinner.

We arrived at our hotel and had planned on walking to the Plaza III Steak House, not more than four blocks from the hotel, but the weather was quite cold. Once we were dressed and ready for dinner, we had few more minutes to spare since we would be cabbing it. We opened the minibar and mixed a couple of predinner cocktails.

I thought we should review tonight's strategy, which Audrey and I had discussed during our flight. "Honey, I know we have been over this before, but I just want to be sure we are not drawn into a discussion with Joanie on what we know about Detective Gerity's investigation." We knew we had inside information, information that Joanie and any other suspects would like to have.

My wife agreed. "We keep the subject to how much we miss Vincent and talk about the funeral arrangements. After all, Nate, Chuck will be in town first thing tomorrow morning, and I'm sure Joanie will be high on his list of interviews."

"That's why I want to be extra cautious. We made the mistake of telling Chuck more than we should have about our friend Peter's finances." I thought about how we could now jeopardize Chuck by telling Joanie more than we should about what we knew of his investigation.

We finished our cocktails, grabbed a cab, and arrived at the restaurant slightly after the agreed-upon seven o'clock reservation. I was not surprised that Joanie hadn't arrived yet. She was chronically late, and I was not annoyed this time because I was still a bit anxious as to what we were about to encounter. I welcomed another cocktail to dull the anxiety.

Joanie arrived just past quarter to eight, gave us both a cheek kiss and slight hug, took her seat, and without so much as a "so sorry I'm late," launched into her latest dilemma. "American Express somehow discovered Vincent has died, and they closed his corporate account."

Audrey innocently asked, "Doesn't he have other cards, Visa or MasterCard?"

Joanie responded indignantly. "Audrey, Vincent had American Express issue a corporate card to me in my name, and that is now cancelled. It's the only card I use."

Still not getting the picture, my wife continued. "What's the big deal? Just use your personal credit card, and the estate will reimburse you."

Joanie shifted a bit in her chair and seemed a little flushed in the face. "Audrey, I have had no reason to obtain any other card."

Well, well. It was no surprise to me, nor most likely to my wife, that Joan Olsen was a major benefactor of Vincent Houten's generosity. In addition, the fact that the success she had been claiming in her Aspen business endeavor was most likely highly overstated. Those factors could explain why she would be reluctant to use her own credit card. But for Joanie to not have any other credit, that was a bit of a surprise.

How broke was Mrs. Olsen? An interesting question no doubt, but how did American Express find out Vincent was dead? As the expression goes, "Somebody dropped a dime." In my mind, *who* had done the dropping was the bigger question.

Joanie then explained how this development further complicated present issues. "Nate, do you think the funeral home will require payment before the funeral service? Will the Newcomer Funeral Home extend me some credit? This could be so embarrassing."

My first thought was that, knowing what I now knew, I certainly wouldn't extend credit in my funeral home. Instead of fueling another fire, I simply replied, "I will go to the funeral home with you tomorrow. I'm sure they will extend a professional courtesy to us."

We ordered cocktails, Joanie's first, but our third. It was time to review the unfinished tasks at hand. Audrey and I had already completed most of the funeral arrangements over the past few days.

I had told my wife earlier, "Joanie is going to be of little help. She's far too busy following the money." And that was proving to be very accurate.

When Vincent was murdered, Joanie was in Aspen, and there was no need for her to come to Palm Beach. We could handle the logistics of arranging for Vincent's remains to be transported to Kansas City. It was pretty routine.

I contracted the Quattellbaum Funeral Home in West Palm Beach to remove our good friend from the medical examiner's facility once the autopsy was completed and prepare him for transfer to Kansas City. Newcomer Funeral Home was to remove Vincent from the KC airport and wait for Joanie's arrival to select an appropriate casket, provide clothing, and instruct them as to the visitation and service she thought would be fitting.

Audrey's attempts to assist Joanie by reserving a church for Vincent's service and a facility for his repast encountered some difficulties. But after a day or two of waiting hours for Joanie to return voice mails, sometimes well into the evening, she decided to take some liberties. She called Vincent's attorney George Cavallas.

George informed my wife early on, "Audrey, you know Vincent was such an optimist, he must have thought he would die in the middle of spring with the sun shining, and the flowers blooming."

The Houten last will and testament specified a graveside service followed by a house-and-garden reception at Vincent's residence. Well, it was January, and Mother Nature had just dropped seven inches of white stuff. The service had to be moved into a church, and we had to find a place for a reception for the hundreds we expected to come to enjoy Vince's hospitality one last time.

George Cavallas suggested, "Audrey, why don't you call the Country Club Church? It's just one block from Vincent's house, and I'll call the Carriage Club for the reception. They are both on Ward Parkway. I think that would be perfect."

Now over dinner, and in keeping with our strategy to avoid discussions of the murder investigation with Joanie, we moved the conversation to the progress that we had made regarding the funeral arrangements. So I took the lead.

"Joanie, I received a voice message as we landed this afternoon. The Country Club Methodist Church has agreed to allow a service for Vincent Thursday morning."

Audrey added, "I'm so relieved."

I was a bit pissed off when Joanie said, "You say that as if there was ever a question." Her statement and the tone of her voice were dismissive of Audrey's efforts.

"Hey Joanie, Vince was not only not a parishioner, but he hasn't set foot in any church since prep school."

That was being kind. I wanted to (but did not) remind Joanie that Vincent had a reputation in KC, and many Country Club Methodist Church parishioners had had firsthand encounters of some of his crazy parties a mere block away. Loud music, late night skinny-dipping, lawn sex, and once, at a party we attended, a woman took off her blouse and put her breasts in a birthday cake in Vincent's honor. Not to speak badly of the dead.

I added, "Joanie, it took some soul searching before the good pastor was convinced that the outsiders that would be drawn to the Houten service would show appropriate deference to his historic place of worship."

In true Joanie fashion, she said, "I still find it incredible that he would consider not memorializing a prominent citizen and next-door neighbor in his church."

I then told Joanie, "Nevertheless, he has agreed, and like it or not, we need to meet with him to help him personalize Vincent's eulogy."

Audrey jumped in with the assessment of the repast arrangements. "Joanie, we thought that since the church and Vincent's house are on Ward Parkway, the Carriage House would be a good venue for his repast."

Surprisingly, Joanie was positive and said, "I agree. That would be perfect."

My wife continued. "We are just awaiting confirmation that the Carriage Club is available Thursday afternoon."

"Is that a problem as well?" Joanie now was speaking to Audrey as if my wife were the hired help.

Keeping her cool, Audrey explained, "Well, yes and no. It's against club policy to entirely close the club to members for any occasion, and Vincent's send-off will require the entire club." My wife added, "George is working on it."

Quickly Joanie asked, "Why did you have to involve George?"

Now even my wife was getting testy. "Joanie, they turned me down. I'm from New Jersey. I don't know any members, and you were too busy to return a phone call. George said he could help."

I didn't like Joanie questioning Audrey's efforts. What the hell was her objection to Vincent's long-time attorney, George Cavallas?

Curtly, Joanie said, "I just wish you hadn't involved George." Before we could ask why, her phone rang. "I have to take this." Joanie left the table for privacy.

When Joanie was out of earshot, I turned to my wife. "OK, what's this about?"

"Beats me. Vincent always had confidence in George. They go all the way back to when Vincent bought Tri-State Tape. Now George can't be trusted to help arrange a simple luncheon?" She further speculated, "Maybe it's some kind of a battle for control."

If that were the case, the battle for control had to have started before Vincent's death because he was murdered only seven days ago, and Joanie got into Kansas City on Thursday. How much could have erupted in three days?

"Audrey, I'm just recalling something. Didn't Megan say she heard a phone conversation where Vincent told someone that if this were true, that person was finished? Do you think that was about Vince making changes at the company?"

"I don't know about what Megan recalls hearing, but if Vincent was going to shake things up, Joanie and George were going to be involved. And only one was going to be the winner." She was right. There was no question Vincent would have to pick sides.

A lot of things were not adding up, but the questions were— adding up, that is. I was getting the feeling that was a good development. In my mind, there were now a few different directions the investigation could take. Hopefully, one would be in the right direction.

I requested that my wife try to make some small talk, "Audrey, let's just get through dinner. We have to keep our cool with Joanie and meet with Chuck tomorrow."

I was not pleased with the mood of the conversation, but in hindsight I thought we all were feeling a mixture of grief and anxiety. That happened when someone didn't feel that his or her feelings were being acknowledged.

CHAPTER TWENTY

B etween a restless night's sleep, a three-hour plane ride and now a forty-minute drive from the Kansas City Airport to police headquarters, Detective Gerity had plenty of time to formulate his game plan.

He landed on schedule at 8:10 and was met by Detective Edmond Peterson. Detective Peterson had been serving as the liaison between the KCPD and PBPD.

Gerity greeted Peterson formally. "Nice to finally meet you, Detective Peterson. I have really appreciated your cooperation the past few days."

Peterson responded, "Glad to be able to assist, but can we cut the formalities? This is Missouri. We don't go for titles out here, and I hate Edmond, so if it's OK with you, please call me Ed."

"Fine with me. It's not Edward or even Ed for me, it's Chuck, and please don't ask why."

Detective Gerity's first order of business was to do an extensive review of the background checks of all Tri-State Tape employees with Detective Peterson, giving special consideration to Mrs. Joan Olsen and Mr. Bert Kelety.

"Ed, I'm anxious to review the background reports, then begin prioritizing interviews based on what we find, but everything has to be scheduled around Florence Mosley's arrival. She is priority number one."

Vincent Houten's sister, the mother of Christopher Mosley, would not be arriving until early afternoon. But Detective Gerity had decided that she should be met by KC police and transported to headquarters as soon as her feet hit the ground.

"I would like to make sure that your people are…let's say not too polite to Mrs. Mosley. She has been playing coy with me, and I think a very stern but professional approach as she lands might help her realize the severity of the situation."

Florence Mosley had been covering up for her son Christopher for so long it had become second nature to her. But this was not a bust for a simple drug sale. Christopher was now the prime suspect for the murder of Vincent Houten.

For emphasis, Chuck looked at Detective Peterson and said, "I want to have her undivided attention."

"That's no problem. We'll show her first-class midwestern hospitality. Additionally, Chuck's reports on all the employees have been prepared and are waiting for us at headquarters."

"Great." At that moment, Detective Gerity's cell phone rang. "Gerity here."

The voice on the other end was that of Officer Jose Solemn, the technical expert who had set up the computer capabilities of the Palm Beach Special Investigation Unit. He had been assigned to Detective Gerity's task force for a number of reasons, but most importantly to lead the tech effort to track down Christopher Mosley and his rented green Toyota Corolla with a dented right rear fender.

"What do you have for me, Jose?" Gerity asked.

"Not as much as I know you would like, Chuck, but Morris is in Jacksonville holed up with Jacksonville homicide. As we speak, he is interviewing the desk clerk that called in the lead on Mosley yesterday."

That was routine procedure, to interview the same witness the following day to see if he or she might have recalled some additional fact, or to trip them up if they had withheld some information. Chuck was impatient. "Come on, Solemn. Don't waste my time if that's all you got."

Solemn nervously added, "I have two other quick items. Morris says they have a lead on the night clerk who checked Mosley into the Holiday Inn Sunday morning. Jacksonville PD expects to have her in to interview in a few hours. And Nate Stevens called. He and his wife had dinner with Joan Olsen last night. They think you may want to talk to them before you meet with her."

"Have Morris contact me as soon as he finishes with the night clerk. I'll call the Stevenses when I get a chance."

At this point in the investigation Detective Gerity was not expecting anything from the Palm Beach County forensic report on Megan's Jeep, other than that the green paint on her fender was used by a half dozen auto manufacturers.

Additionally, he didn't think the day clerk would provide any more pertinent information, considering the clerk only saw Christopher Mosley for a few minutes. But a conversation with the night clerk who checked him in early Sunday morning at the end of her shift and an aggressive interrogation of Mrs. Florence Mosley, whom Detective Gerity was convinced had to have had recent communication with her son, could be fruitful.

CHAPTER TWENTY-ONE

While Detective Peterson was transporting Detective Gerity from the KC airport to KC police headquarters, Peter Kunz was pacing in George Cavallas's office waiting lounge. George was Tri-State Tape's corporate counsel and Vincent Xavier Houten's personal confidant. Peter was scheduled to meet George at 10:00 a.m., but he was far too anxious to simply be on time. He had thought of nothing else since Friday when he convinced George to rearrange his schedule and squeeze in thirty minutes for him to discuss his friend's murder and Peter's concerns.

George Cavallas arrived slightly after their appointed time. He walked quickly through the waiting room, past Peter Kunz, up to his receptionist, collected some messages, and before continuing to his office, finally turned and acknowledged Peter, saying, "I'll be with you in a few minutes."

"Bullshit!" said Peter and followed George into his office, brushing forcefully past the firm's receptionist who was attempting to detain him.

Peter Kunz had known George for as many years as Vincent had. He felt slighted by George's action. Peter simply felt that they were friends, and they could trust each other.

George closed the door behind them as they entered his office. He took his seat behind his desk then, apologetically, attempted to explain how busy he was with the affairs of Tri-State Tape since Vincent's death.

"Peter, I've been in meetings with Vincent's accountant and financial advisor since 8:00 a.m. You know them—Fred Fredricks and Randy Newman." Peter gave no reaction.

"I have a number of issues that need to be followed up. Reestablishing check-writing privileges with the company's bank, assuring vendors that the company is still a viable concern, and reviewing employment contracts to determine who may have a legally binding right to their position."

Peter's response was unsympathetic. "Well, George, since I'm a murder suspect in all this shit, I want to get to the bottom of Vincent's murder. I'm not interested in the new corporate structure of Tri-State Tape, so excuse me if I'm a little impatient. I want to know what you know and what you suspect."

George tried to defuse the conversation. "Peter, I'm the company's attorney, not a police investigator. You read the papers. There's a six-state all-points bulletin out for Christopher Mosley. He's the prime suspect, not you."

Peter leaned toward George. "Even if you think Christopher Mosley shot Vincent, you can't believe he did it on his own."

Peter continued, still leaning forward and attempting to gain George's cooperation. He tried to convince him with some common-sense reasoning. "You personally know Christopher. Now be honest, do you think he could have pulled this off alone?" Peter hammered home the final nail. "Anyone, and I mean anyone with a financial interest in Tri-State Tape or the Vincent Xavier Houten estate is a possible accomplice." After a silent pause, Peter offered, "That means you as well, George."

Reluctantly, George consented. "OK, Peter. What do you want from me?"

Peter was relieved. Without George's cooperation, he would be isolated. Peter needed a few of his own intuitions validated. He felt he had a lot to contribute to the investigation, but who would listen? With George's cooperation, he felt he would have a voice.

Peter now was the cross-examining attorney. "George, is it true Vincent had finally become serious about selling his company?"

George cooperated. "Yes, as we all know, he often talked about selling. However this time, yes, I believe he was serious. He was preparing the company for sale and structuring his estate."

Peter brought up his next point. "I know Vincent was upset with something at his company. Some people I talked to told me he was going to make some big changes. He was really pissed at something. If he was going to shake things up, you must have been in the know. George, what had him so upset?"

George hesitated then summarized. "In a nutshell, profits. Profits were disappointing. They were not only affecting the company value but changed Vincent's time frame for selling. He thought he had everything in order, then suddenly he realized he had a lot of work ahead of him."

Peter asked, "Was this a surprise to Vince? Did he not have a clue about his company's profitability?"

George shook his head and explained, "What he was obsessing about was how the company sales figures exceeded the best sale years ever, but expenses seemed to be out of control. It was a total shock to him."

Peter Kunz explained to George Cavallas how through the years, Vincent and he often talked about business and Tri-State Tape in particular. He told George what George already knew, that Vincent Houten always managed costs. Costs of goods sold, cost of labor, and cost of occupancy—all were in his domain.

Vincent Houten was a frugal businessman, and his management style reflected that. Sales were the responsibility of his sales manager, and Vince pushed him hard, but controlling costs was Vincent's baby. Now Tri-State Tape was only marginally profitable. Vincent obviously didn't buy the excuse that the escalated expenses were necessary to build market share.

Peter asked, "So Vince didn't think the increased expenses were directly related to an aggressive, expensive effort to increase market share?" After a pause for effect, Peter asked, "Did he think the expenses were a result of creative accounting?"

That was a rhetorical question. Peter Kunz knew that his murdered friend had a strong suspicion that someone in his company was either fabricating sale expenses, or manipulating inventory to exaggerate the cost of manufacturing. But for Tri-State Tape to be only marginally profitable would take a lot of fabrication and/or a lot of manipulation.

Vincent hadn't convinced Peter in the past when he voiced his concerns over the lack of loyalty in his company. After a few martinis, he often would wildly speculate about who was stealing from him. Peter had disregarded those rants in the past. But since the Vincent Houten murder, he was now convinced beyond a shadow of a doubt that his friend was right. Without letting George respond to the rhetorical question he had just posed, Peter continued. "Whom do you think Vincent most suspected, and whom did he most trust?"

George paused to contemplate the question, then answered. "The answers to both of your questions are the same. To those he gave his trust, he then suspected." George then added, "Peter, you probably know that Vincent was suspicious of everyone and was a bit insecure. It most likely was a result of his mother's financial roller-coaster ride that he experienced with her during his youth.

They would be living high one day and sleeping in the car the next."

"We know all that, George, but that's ancient history." Pressing the point, Peter again asked, "Who did Vincent most suspect, and who did he most trust?"

"I guess I would have to say Joan Olsen, whom we all know, his accountant, Fred Fredrick, who was the bearer of the recent bad news about the profits, and his general manager, Bert Kelty." After a slight pause, he said, "And me."

Peter knew that George had to include himself in that circle of trust. He was relieved that he did so; otherwise it would be obvious that he was attempting to shield himself from suspicion.

Peter needed George and wanted him to feel they were on the same team. "George, to begin, I wouldn't be here if I had any concerns about your loyalty. You have been with Vince for thirty years. So I would like to concentrate on the other three."

Peter Kunz remained silent for an awkward moment, hoping for George to voluntarily begin a review of the three players, but that was not happening.

Wily attorney that George was, he let Peter have the lead. He wanted to show no indication of who he might have suspected as a potential conspirator. In a well-played role reversal, George's silence was saying, "Peter, who do you most trust and who do you most suspect? You go first."

Finally, Peter began. "At the risk of stating the obvious, if someone in Tri-State Tape was involved in Vincent's murder, the motive had to be very strong." To further explain why he had begun with such a simple premise, he added, "I mean, covering up some kind of embezzlement or purchasing scam by it self doesn't seem to rise to the level of desperation necessary to commit murder."

Peter continued. "So I would like to discuss the possible motives of Vincent's closest confidants. Maybe we can find some underlying motive that may have driven someone to such an extreme measure."

With a tinge of sarcasm, George responded, "Peter, you're right. Motives could be obvious, and underlying issues could be complicated. That's why we should let the police do their job and let them conduct this investigation, not us."

"Bear with me a minute. I want to discuss three people, just three." Peter began with Vincent's accountant. "Let's talk about Fred Fredrick. As Tri-State's accountant, could he have cooked the books?" Peter answered his own question and then carried on. "Yes. Could he have overcharged the company for accountant services? Yes. Could he have manipulated inventories? Yes. If someone in the company was embezzling, was he the most qualified person to cover up for him? Yes."

Peter summarized. "So Fred Fredrick was in a position of trust that he could have used to illegally defraud Vincent and been a part of the systematic theft of funds from Tri-State Tape." Then, in an attempt to engage George in the speculation, Peter asked, "What do you think, Counselor?"

George impatiently responded, "Possibly, probably, maybe, but what's your point? There's no indication that he did any of the things you are suggesting."

Peter Kunz pursued his line of questioning. "That's exactly my point. Even if the wildest speculations were correct, they still don't add up to a motive for murder."

George, a little frustrated and annoyed that he had fallen into Peter's trap, responded, "Agreed. Let's move on."

Peter started the review of the next Vincent Houten insider. He began. "Joanie Olsen is far more complicated. She was a confidant to Vincent, a past live-in lover, one of the heirs of his estate, and now the executrix of his estate. She obviously had a financial interest in his death."

Peter turned to George Cavallas and asked, "Have any insights, George?"

"Yeah! I certainly do." Forcefully, George began. "First of all, Joan Olsen was more than a past lover. She was a valued confidant to Vincent for years, and to suggest otherwise would be grossly unfair."

Peter interrupted. "No one is suggesting anything, George. However, your point does not go to motive. The fact that she was a confidant, valued or not, is irrelevant."

George said, "OK, then more importantly, Vincent took very good care of her financially. She may be the largest recipient of his will, but considering how he had taken care of her financially over the past few years, why would she kill the goose that lays the golden egg?"

Peter thought George's analogy was weak, but he also considered that it seemed superficial and maybe a bit protective. Rather than risk getting into a testy exchange, he decided it would be better to move onto the next issue. "Thank you, George. I know your time is valuable. If you don't object, I would like your thoughts on Bert Kelty."

"I don't know what you expect to hear and I hate to disappoint you Peter, but as the corporate attorney I can tell you that Mr. Kelty would have been in for a nice bonus when Tri-State Tape was sold." For added effect he forcefully stated, "I wrote the contract. Anyone would be hard pressed to imagine he had a financial motive for murder."

Vincent Houten had given Bert a financially incentivized employment contract. George maintained that due to his successful management resulting in increased sales, Tri-State Tape's value had greatly increased. George insisted that based on the anticipated sale price Bert was entitled to a six-figure bonus upon the close of the sale of Tri-State Tape.

However since the death of Vincent Houten, the company's value most likely has been diminished. Since that occurred prior to any sale, George explained, it is unlikely that the contract granting Bert Kelty a performance bonus could be enforced against the estate. This fact gave further evidence that Kelty had no incentive to murder his employer.

Peter was puzzled. "Correct me if I'm wrong, but didn't Vincent's own last evaluation of his company show that sales were up but increased costs of goods caused the company to be only marginally profitable? Didn't that result in a reduction of its potential evaluation and sale price? And wasn't he additionally upset that those conditions were leaving Vincent with lots of work to be done?" Then Peter directly asked, "George, just what did Bert do to be entitled to a performance bonus?"

George felt Peter was challenging him and angrily replied, "The company is far more valuable today than before Bert was hired. That's what the employment contract is based on." He added, "Peter, you can't look at only the latest reports." After a pause, George concluded, "Bert may have, and I stress, *may* have, been financially motivated to exaggerate sales reports to elevate the value of Tri-State Tape, but Vincent's death did not help him. It may have cost him a few hundred thousand dollars."

"George, I never intended to upset you. Much of this information is new to me. I can't sit back and do nothing. I wanted to find out whatever I can to help find my friend's killer."

George Cavallas responded, "I hope you're satisfied with what I shared. Now Peter, as I mentioned earlier, I have an awful lot of work in front of me."

Peter pressed on. He wanted to pursue one last thing, "Where did Bert Kelty come from? What is his background?"

Frustrated, George responded, "I don't know, Peter. The company has his résumé. Please, please, let the police do their job and me, mine."

Accepting that he was not going to make any further progress, Peter ended the meeting. "Sure George, I understand. Thank you for your time."

Peter Kunz left George Cavallas's office, walked to the elevator, and descended the three floors to the parking area. As he did, he became more and more angry. He had expected cooperation and a sharing of information. After all, they were all friends—George, Vincent, and Peter—but he felt nothing but frustration. *Damn! What is George hiding?*

This morning, George was being evasive, acting like he was shielding or protecting something or someone. Their meeting left Peter with more questions than before he started. He was angry but every bit as determined as before.

When Peter opened the large glass door that separated the building lobby from the parking area, he was immediately met by two Kansas City police officers. Their actions were an obvious attempt to intimidate Peter.

Officer number one stepped in front of Peter and got chest to chest with him while officer number two was menacingly positioned just behind. The detective, his face only inches from Peter's, said, "Mr. Kunz, I am Detective Al Carlton, and this is Detective J. C. Wood. We would like you to come with us to police headquarters to aid in the investigation of the murder of Mr. Vincent Houten."

Peter was shocked out of his angry mood, and after no more than a second, he addressed the detectives. "I would be more than happy to assist in any way I can, but how the hell did you know I'd be here and at this time?"

Carlton answered, "Detective Peterson asked us to keep an eye on you."

J C Wood added, "As for this exact time, Detective Gerity thought that you may have more to talk about after your meeting with Mr. Cavallas." Then he sternly said, "Let's go."

CHAPTER TWENTY-TWO

We had contacted the West Palm Beach task force early Monday morning to ask that Detective Gerity call us. We thought Detective Gerity should know about our diner conversation with Joanie Olsen the previous evening. We requested that he call through the hotel operator so we could take the call in our suite and put it on conference mode.

We had a room service breakfast and anxiously awaited his call. We knew he was to land at approximately 9:00 a.m. But when and if he would call was unknown. His call came at 9:40 while he was en route from the Kansas City airport to the Kansas City police headquarters. The detective was attempting to squeeze a lot into his first day in KC.

Without hesitation, Detective Gerity spoke as soon as my wife answered the phone. He dryly said, "I understand that you had an interesting dinner with Mrs. Olsen last night."

Audrey responded with equally quick banter. "More puzzling than interesting, I would say."

I got right to the point. "Chuck, something has Joan Olsen and George Cavallas on different sides of the fence. There is no doubt that she either doesn't trust him or feels challenged by him."

Detective Gerity simply asked, "What the hell happened?"

My wife elaborated on the Carriage Club conversation. She described how Joanie seemed pleased with the planned locale for the funeral luncheon but disturbed that George had been asked to help in securing the venue. Audrey challenged the detective to consider how this conflict could have occurred in a short few days. Joanie had only arrived from Colorado three days ago.

She also mentioned Joanie's financial situation, regarding her lack of any credit. We both placed little importance on it because it was not a surprise to us. It just confirmed our suspicions that her claims of her business success were greatly exaggerated.

Detective Gerity seemed to be a bit more interested in Joanie's financial condition. He wanted to be sure that we were correct in our assumption that Joanie had no credit and that she was broke without the financial support of Vincent Houten. Audrey and I could not give him anything concrete, but we were pretty confident that our instincts were on point.

Audrey raised the question. "How did AMEX find out Vincent was dead? Either American Express has an advanced database connection to the pearly gates, or someone 'dropped a dime,' as we say in New Jersey."

Detective Gerity thanked us for the information and gave us a thumbnail sketch of his immediate strategy for the investigation. First on his agenda was to review the background profiles of all the Tri-State Tape employees with Detective Peterson—with an emphasis placed on the histories of Mrs. Joan Olsen and Mr. Bert Kelty.

Revealing some police strategy, Gerity added, "After that review, I'm confident that we will have an idea of what has the executrix and the corporate attorney at odds. Then we will decide who will be the first interviewed and who will follow. Usually the second is the more interesting."

Audrey and I thought it was important that we forewarn Detective Gerity of the apparent conflict between Joanie and George. We hoped to keep Chuck from walking into an interview cold and unaware of a very important dynamic. Of equal importance to us was what happened with the Megan Kelly interview in Wellington Hospital yesterday afternoon and what came from the Salvatore Liguria interview.

Additionally, during our phone conversation, I asked Gerity directly, "Chuck, I know your time is short, but give us an update on your interviews with Megan and Salvatore. Did anything come out of them?"

"Yes! Both interviews were significant. There is too much to discuss right now. I should be free later this afternoon. I'll be in touch then."

Not letting Detective Gerity end the conversation, and leaving the time frame open-ended, I said, "Chuck, can I suggest dinner at our hotel tonight? You're alone in KC, and you have to eat."

"Thank you. That sounds like it could work, but don't hold me to it. I'll call when I have a break." And Chuck hung up.

"Audrey, I hate police talk. What the hell does 'both interviews were significant' mean to you?"

"I don't know. We'll just have to wait. Let's go meet Joanie and arrange a funeral."

"Sure, but give me a minute. I better bring my checkbook."

CHAPTER TWENTY-THREE

Audrey and I picked up Joanie at Vincent's house on Ward Parkway a little after 10:00 a.m. She moved into Vincent's house as soon as she arrived from Colorado. Her two children joined her, along with their spouses upon their arrival for the funeral. Joanie was staking her claim, and the Houten family would have to fend for themselves.

Together, we drove one block to the Country Club Methodist Church to meet with Pastor Gunther as he had requested. We parked in the rear of the church and entered under the sign that read "Rectory Office." We introduced ourselves to the secretary stationed just inside the entrance. She was expecting us and immediately escorted us to the pastor's private office.

Pastor Gunther cordially greeted us at the doorway and offered us a seat at a small conference table in the front section of his office. The office was sparsely appointed, and there was little or no evident effort toward decorating the space. The conference table and chairs were comfortable and more than adequate to accommodate our meeting of four.

The pastor set the agenda. "I would like to know about Mr. Houten's professional life, his connection to Kansas City, and his family, but more importantly, I need to know what you can tell me about his personality so I may personalize the eulogy."

Pastor Gunther was quite thorough. We spent the better part of an hour answering his questions about Vincent's life experiences, his business development, and his convoluted family. We did our best to give him a feeling for the man he would eulogize. We relayed insights into his humor, his eccentricities, and most of all his zest for the fun in life.

When we left the church rectory, I for one had a good feeling that the reverend would do a good job eulogizing our friend. He assured us he would go light on the "resurrection" and the "eternal life" parts of the service and speak more heavily on who Vincent X. Houten was and what he meant to so many people.

When we got back into our car, I said, "Joanie, I really like Gunther. I'm sure he will deliver a very meaningful service for Vince."

From left field, Joanie said, "Yes, Nate, but you will have to handle the seating arrangements."

"The seating arrangements? What are you talking about?"

"I'm talking about his siblings, their families, three ex-wives, four or five lady friends, and maybe Megan Kelly for good measure. Who gets the front pew? Etcetera, etcetera. I can't imagine anyone more qualified than you to handle that assignment." Having no option but to accept my assignment, I drove us to the Newcomer Funeral Home, pouting all the way.

The branch manager, Joseph Day, greeted us. He was professional, maybe a little stiff, but very accommodating. Joanie selected an expensive but elegant casket insisting that Vincent deserved the best, an opinion with which Audrey and I agreed.

I waited for an opportunity to get Mr. Day alone. So when Audrey and Joanie began selecting memorial cards and reviewing service programs, I took the initiative. I asked Mr. Day if I could see the visiting room.

Joseph Day excused himself and directed me toward that section of the building. As soon as we reached the visiting room, I raised the issue of payment. "Listen, Joe. I want to let you know, Mrs. Olsen is in no position to pay for this funeral, and the estate could take months."

I was well aware the estate of my friend Vincent Houten was in the area of several million dollars (as in tens of). The issue was whether there were any readily available assets to pay the Newcomer Funeral Home. I wanted Joanie to have to figure that out herself. But if necessary, I felt I would do whatever was required.

Joseph Day was not the owner of the funeral home; he was a branch manager of a corporately owned establishment. I knew that he was required to follow company policy and had little or no authority to extend credit. I wanted him to know that I would not put him on the spot and ask for a professional courtesy of another funeral director.

"So Joe, let me be clear. I assure you that I will pay Newcomer's bill if all of Mr. Houten's funds are tied up in the estate. The estate could take several months. I just don't want Mrs. Olsen to know that I'm willing to pay for Mr. Houten's final expenses just yet."

Manager Day seemed to catch on. "I think I understand, and that is very generous of you."

I don't know why, but at hearing that comment, a wave of emotion came over me, and I had to choke back tears before I could respond. "He was a very special friend."

I collected myself and wanted to make sure Joseph Day understood my position, so I very directly added, "If I make it too easy for Mrs. Olsen, she will see no need to do anything, and I will be the one waiting for months to be reimbursed instead of Newcomer."

We took a few minutes to discuss a strategy and then returned to complete the arrangements with Joanie and Audrey.

As we approached the conference room, my cell phone rang. It was Peter Kuntz.

I excused myself and let Joseph Day return to complete the financial portion of the funeral arrangements. I took Peter's call. "Nate, I just got out of police headquarters. I would like to talk to you and Audrey. Are you free?'

I wasn't surprised that Peter had had a conversation with the police. After all, everyone I knew in Kansas City I had met through Vincent, and most likely, they all would be paying a visit to KCPD over the next few days, but I feigned concern. "Police headquarters? Is everything OK?"

"Everything is as fine as can be expected." Then Peter asked, "What's your schedule?"

"We're almost finished at Newcomer. We're taking Joanie to lunch. Let's meet at the InterContinental lobby bar, say two thirty. Can you tell me anything now?"

"Not now. Two thirty sounds good. See you then."

Apparently, by the time I entered the conference room, Joseph Day had reviewed the expenses and just informed Joanie of the company payment policy.

Incredulously, Joanie asked, "You are telling me that you want half paid by the day of the funeral Thursday, and the balance paid in ten days?" Joanie looked to me for support, but Joseph Day, as planned, played dumb and simply asked, "Is that a problem?"

"Mr. Day, the Vincent Houten estate is quite substantial. You can certainly be assured that your bill will be paid."

Politely, Joseph Day responded, "I hope I didn't suggest that was my concern. Our concern goes to timing. Estates can take months and sometimes years." He continued, "Mrs. Olsen, in situations like this, we would like to speak to the estate's attorney to determine what the funeral home can expect."

That set a fuse under Joanie. She leaned forward and, in a high-pitched voice that I don't ever remember hearing before, stated, "The estate's attorney? I'm the executrix."

This was another George issue, I suspected, one that was a little more pronounced than "Why did you have to ask him for help with the Carriage Club?" but still on the same theme.

Calmly, Mr. Day explained that the policy was a company policy not his policy, but that he did have some flexibility. The attorney, he explained, was in the best position to predict the schedule and timing of the liquidity of the estate. For him, as the branch manager, he had to have a reason to use his authority to extend some credit flexibility.

Joanie looked physically frustrated and agitated. "Well," she said. Then after a prolonged pause, she gathered her composure and finally consented. "Very well then."

"Thank you, Mrs. Olsen. If the estate attorney could call me tomorrow, I would appreciate it."

All things completed, we left the funeral home and headed to the KC Plaza for lunch. While driving, I was not able to speak to Audrey alone, so she didn't know that we had a meeting with Peter Kunz scheduled for two thirty. I had to let her know about the meeting and that Peter had just been interrogated by KCPD.

Meeting Peter was far more important than soothing Joanie's feelings. We needed to keep the lunch brief.

CHAPTER TWENTY-FOUR

Audrey, Joanie, and I, having completed the funeral arrangements at the Newcomer Funeral Home, agreed to lunch at the Classic Cup. The Cup, as the locals referred to it, was a quaint restaurant in the KC Plaza that we had had the pleasure of experiencing on a few previous occasions. During the fifteen-minute ride from the funeral home to the Plaza, Joanie said nothing. I thought I was getting the silent treatment. Her silence was saying "some help you were" loud and clear.

After we were seated, Audrey and Joanie were chatting about something or other that I had no clue. I tried to move things along at the restaurant without being too obvious. My wife had to be informed that we had a schedule. I was anxiously wondering when one of the ladies would go take a piss so I could finally tell Audrey of our schedule.

Finally, Joanie saw some business acquaintance being seated on the other side of the dining area. She excused herself and crossed the restaurant to greet him. I was then able to tell Audrey of our meeting with Peter and briefly explain that he had been interrogated earlier that morning by KCPD. From that point on, I was relaxed.

Audrey and I were on the same page, and the timing of things was now going along fine. We finished lunch. I paid the check, and then we drove Joanie to Vincent's house on Ward Parkway. Joanie was anxious to be reunited with her children.

After dropping Joanie and exchanging some obligatory pleasantries with her children, Audrey and I were able to return to our hotel by two fifteen. Peter Kunz was already at the lobby bar, thirty minutes early, and with a half-finished bourbon and soda in front of him.

My wife hurried to the bar and gave Peter a strong, lingering hug. Although we had spoken a few times since our friend's murder, this was the first time we were together face-to-face. I waited my turn.

As Audrey released Peter from her embrace I could see that she was softly crying, which didn't help me at all. I grabbed Peter's hand, pulled him close, and threw my left arm around his shoulder. I spoke into his ear. "This is a nightmare, Peter." It was all I could do not to break down.

"Bartender, please transfer Mr. Kunz's check to our table." I turned back to Audrey and Peter and pointed to a high-top table near the floor-to-ceiling windows overlooking the hotel's snow-covered pool. "Let's sit there. It looks quiet."

We took our seats and gave a waitress our cocktail order with instructions to back up Peter's bourbon and soda. My wife started the conversation:

"Peter, it's so good to see you. How are you holding up?"

I for one was a bit surprised by Peter's mood. During our phone conversations over the past week, he had expressed some emotion, mostly anger at being considered a suspect in his best friend's murder. He now was calm, and he even seemed reflective or somewhat distant.

In response to Audrey's question, Peter answered dismissively, "I'm fine, just fine."

Audrey insisted, "Peter Kunz, 'fine' is not enough. Let's start with the fact that you were at the police headquarters this morning. What the hell happened?"

Before our drinks arrived, Peter began recounting the police experience he had earlier in the day. "After a lot of time spent on interrogation and pursuing timelines, I think that they finally believe I had no idea that I was named in Vincent's will. The KC detectives spent a lot of their time on that issue." Peter continued without pause, "I also think they believe, or at least Detective Gerity believes, that a car and a few hundred thousand dollars is not a strong enough motive to kill a friend of over thirty years."

Audrey reached over the table and squeezed Peter's hand. "That must be a big relief."

Peter agreed, "I have to admit, it is a very big relief."

Peter then retreated back to his reflective mood and after a second or two said in a low voice, "I'm convinced that I personally know who my friend's killer is, but I don't know who he is. I just can't let it go till it's done."

I was still concerned for Peter safety. "Peter, I'm glad that you are now working with the police and not going at it on your own."

Peter snapped out of his black mood and stared into my eyes, forcefully stating, "The police take too long." Then he took a large swallow of his bourbon and soda.

"Peter, they're just doing their jobs." Then I added, "What is your issue?"

"Well, for starters, I met with George this morning for about forty-five minutes. He couldn't wait to get me out of his office. He wasn't interested in sharing anything."

We could feel Peter's frustration growing. Peter continued, "I've known George for over thirty years. Ever since Vincent bought Tri-State Tape. I expected some give and take this morning. You know, two friends of Vincent trying to get to the truth. Instead I got a lawyer who seemed lawyered up."

Audrey, applying female logic, suggested a different possibility. "Peter, this is a murder investigation. Don't you think an attorney would go to his professional training and instincts and be naturally evasive? Especially an attorney who was the victim's confidant, and who may be a suspect himself?"

Peter thought for a minute. "OK, that could make sense, but when I asked George what Bert Kelty's background was and where he came from, he lied."

"Lied?" I was surprised that Peter could accuse George of any wrongdoing. I stayed calm and asked, "What did he say?"

Peter was going the long way round answering my question. "He wanted to end the meeting. I guess it went past the thirty minutes he had set aside. So when he said it, I thought he just wanted me out of his office, not that he was trying to mislead me. After all, I still considered George a friend of Vincent and me."

Almost shouting with frustration, I asked again, "What did he say that was a lie?" After all, Audrey and I had been in regular contact with George regarding Vincent's wishes for his funeral, and we had thought George was beyond reproach and a true friend of Vincent Houten.

After a minute or two, Peter Kunz answered, "He said he didn't know Bert's background. He said the company must have his résumé."

A little confused, I wondered aloud, "And that was a lie?"

Peter's voice was insistent. "Absolutely. One of the detectives who questioned me today told me that George had introduced Bert to Vincent. George recommended Bert Kelty for the general manager's position at Tri-State."

I looked to my wife. We were both shocked, and she turned to Peter. "Maybe there's a simple explanation, but I agree with you, Peter. It does seem very suspicious."

I said, "Peter, the detective just came right out and said George recommended Bert to Vince?"

"Well, no. Gerity asked me what I knew of Bert, and did I know his background." Peter was now trying to be accurate and was guarding his words. "I told him I didn't think Bert was well known in town. Not many people I know knew him. That's when Detective Carlson let loose and said, 'Well, Mr. Cavallas knew him well enough to recommend him for the general manager's job.' Maybe the officer slipped up, but that's what he said, plain and simple."

Peter still trying to recall the conversation in detail. "The fact that George recommended Bert to Vince surprised me, but then Detective Carlson let something else slip. Bert is an attorney but hasn't practiced in several years. When I asked why, Detective Gerity cut the conversation off."

Peter Kunz then speculated that there might have been a connection between the two lawyers. "Maybe that's why George said he didn't know Bert's background. That I can easily find out." Peter then stated quite forcefully, "I'm going to find out."

It was obvious that Peter was going to continue his own investigation. In a futile effort to discourage him, I asked, "Peter, what do you think you can do that the police can't?"

Audrey added, "The police have all the background information. I'm sure they are investigating any connection between George and Bert."

"I'm KC born and raised," Peter stated defiantly. "If I don't know somebody in this town, then I know somebody that does. I have been a trader in this town for forty-five years. I have contacts all over Kansas City and most of the state of Kansas and Missouri. I can and will find out Bert Kelty's background, where he worked, with whom, and probably most of his client list." He leaned back in his seat and with a smile added, "All the dirt that's fit to print."

We ordered another round of cocktails and tried to lighten the conversation. We discussed details of Vincent's funeral arrangements, and without pressing, we encouraged Peter to work with the police.

We talked about some of the good times we had shared in Palm Beach. Then Peter suddenly became quiet and reflective again. After a second or two, Audrey, obviously concerned, put her hand on his forearm and asked, "Peter, are you all right?"

Slowly snapping out of his funk, Peter answered, "Oh yeah, I'm fine." Then after a short pause, he said, "I have to go." He seemed to be still in another place and didn't get up immediately but then suddenly popped up out of his chair and without as much as a thanks for the drinks said, "I'll be in touch." With that, Peter Kunz headed for the lobby exit, leaving us bewildered.

I asked my wife, "What do you think?"

She said, "I think he just figured out who his first contact will be." Then she added, "I hope he doesn't get in over his head."

"Well, if that's true, and he has just decided who his first contact will be, then he already is in over his head." I said it, but I was hoping I was wrong.

My wife and I slowly finished our cocktails. We now just wanted to kill some time. It was going to be a long and anxious hour or two before we would hear from Detective Gerity. Would he accept our invitation for dinner, or would he leave us terribly disappointed? There was so much to discuss. If he accepted, my wife and I were in agreement—the wait would be well worth it.

CHAPTER TWENTY-FIVE

Audrey and I had spent the last few hours since Peter left us at the hotel lobby bar, killing time. We went to our room, called our kids, took another shower, did whatever we could think of while anxiously waiting to hear whether Chuck Gerity would accept our dinner invitation or blow us off. When he accepted and then arrived forty-five minutes late, I had little or no patience left.

"So what's so significant?" Those were my first words to the good detective when I finally faced him in our hotel lobby.

Chuck gave me a puzzled response, "Significant? I don't know what you're referring to."

"Significant. Significant. Chuck, that's what you said about the Megan Kelly and Salvatore Liguria's interrogations. So Audrey and I have been sitting on the edge of our seats, waiting to know what happened. What's so significant?"

"Oh, I forgot that I referred to the interviews that way." Chuck leaned back in the comfortable club chair we had selected in the bar lounge. We sat on an overstuffed love seat facing him. Audrey put her hand on my forearm as if to tell me to be patient and quiet.

Detective Gerity remained silent for a minute or two, apparently organizing his thoughts.

A cocktail waitress asking us for a beverage order broke his silence. He ordered a Pinot Grigio. Audrey and I ordered vodka rocks. After the waitress left, he turned to us and began his review of the day's events. Audrey's hand was still on my forearm.

"There have been a number of developments over the last twenty-four hours that I would consider significant." Then there was another pause, which I considered annoying, but not so significant since my wife was now squeezing my arm. I waited for the next bit of information.

Finally, he said something. "This morning, Detective Morris located the Holiday Inn Express night receptionist who checked Christopher Mosley into the hotel the morning after Megan Kelly was forced off Southern Boulevard in Wellington."

I thought: *How hard was that? It's only been two days.* It wasn't as if the receptionist was in hiding. I didn't think that was great detective work, but I was glad I didn't say so because Detective Gerity explained that she, the night receptionist, had left immediately after her Monday-night shift to party with some friends on the Carolina Outer Banks, north and east of Myrtle Beach.

The receptionist was four hours from Jacksonville and not in the habit of keeping her parents informed of her whereabouts. It suddenly became apparent to me that some things just take time, especially in an investigation of other peoples lives, lives that have their own schedules and priorities. I needed to get a grip.

More importantly, Chuck informed Audrey and me that the night receptionist did in fact follow procedures and remembered a Kansas state driver's license issued to Philip True.

That was a real breakthrough. If the investigation could not verify that Christopher Mosley was assuming the name of Philip True, the chances of finding him would be greatly reduced. Now a computer program could check thousands of transactions every minute to flag Philip True, as opposed to the local police attempting to identify the suspect by memorizing emailed photographs of the suspect that might or might not be current.

The receptionist also positively identified photographs of Christopher Mosley that Detective Morris presented to her as Philip True, whom she had checked into the Holiday Inn Express three days ago.

I asked a rhetorical question. "Chuck, doesn't that mean that he will most likely use that ID again? And the more he uses it, the better the chance of locating him?"

"Exactly," Chuck agreed and added, "Mrs. Mosley has finally been convinced that the best way to help her son is to cooperate."

She was further advised that, due to her financial interest in her brother's estate, she could be detained as an accomplice to his murder. That, Detective Gerity speculated, might have had some bearing on her change of heart.

"So Christopher has talked to his mother?" Audrey asked.

Chuck responded in his trained police vernacular, "There has been no direct conversation between the parties. We have however been able to obtain two voice messages left by Christopher for his mother Florence Mosley."

I was again feeling Detective Gerity's elusive attitude. In an effort to get to the heart of the matter, I forcefully asked the good detective the pertinent question. "Damn Chuck, what were the messages?"

Chuck began explaining, "You have to understand that in any investigation there is a limit to the information that can be shared." He continued in his strange tone, "Technically, it is only appropriate and procedurally acceptable to share information if in the sharing of that information may result in the obtaining of additional information significant to the resolution of the case."

Detective Gerity had been sharing information ever since we developed a relationship during the early stages of the investigation—all the way back to Palm Beach, which now seemed like a century ago. I turned to my wife with a quizzical expression as if to say, "Where is this coming from?"

Audrey spoke first. "Chuck, based on your criteria, everything you know should be shared with us. What have you told us that didn't result in obtaining additional information?"

Maybe I was getting some investigative insight after two weeks of concentrating on Vincent's murder, but I had a strong suspicion something new to the case had just altered Detective Gerity's position. It had to be about Audrey and me. Something that Detective Gerity didn't want us to know, most likely something about our safety.

The detective began explaining that the voice messages were not important and did not provide any relevant information to the investigation. Audrey remained silent and continued to look into Chuck's eyes. Without saying a word, she delivered her message, "When is this bullshit going to stop?"

Chuck got the message and reluctantly agreed with Audrey's logic. He then relayed what he was unwilling to share. "The first message Florence Mosley received was Thursday afternoon. 'I should never have listened to them. Peter Kunz and the Stevenses better watch out,' her son said. The second was early Sunday morning: 'There's only one person who can help me. I'm going there.'"

Chuck vocalized the obvious question that he had been struggling with. "Who are 'them'? And who is the 'person' he is going to?"

Audrey wasted no time interjecting her opinion. "I don't know for sure who 'them' are, but I'm fairly certain he is going to his uncle Samuel."

Detective Gerity nodded. "Mrs. Stevens, I agree with your assumption, but why do you think so?"

My wife began. "First of all, Vincent told us that Christopher regularly disappeared for a week or two, and he believed that his nephew often went to New Mexico and spent the time in the out-doors with his uncle Samuel—most likely getting stoned together."

Detective Gerity found that interesting since Christopher's mother didn't know or maybe hadn't mentioned that her brother was an enabler and more importantly, that the two were that close.

"Secondly, Chuck, Christopher is obviously scared. Sammy, as you probably know, is a New Mexico nature photographer and supplements his income serving as a nature guide in the Santa Fe area. Christopher's last chance is his uncle Sam, and probably the reason that Sam is running late to his brother's funeral is because he is trying to help Christopher."

Nodding in agreement, Chuck said, "I learned of Samuel's profession just this morning. The Kansas City police department's background profile of Samuel Houten was quite detailed."

Samuel Houten had spent years in the Santa Fe National Forest and the Pecos Wilderness. He mostly made his living as a contract freelance photographer. He would go to the most remote locations in his passion to bring the beauty of the southwest back for all to enjoy through his still and video photography. Additionally, to supplement his income, he served as a guide, working out of the town of Torero.

Torero, New Mexico, was a mining town at the end of the nine-teenth century and early twentieth. It was now a stopover for hiking enthusiasts and for those on multi-day nature excursions into the Santa Fe National Forest or the Pecos Wilderness. The Wilderness is the site of Pueblo Indian ruins currently being protected in their natural state. The area provides miles and miles of undisturbed terrain, ideal for two men to disappear into.

"So where does that leave us?" I asked.

Detective Gerity summarized. "We now at least have a destina-tion. We can assume that Christopher will continue to drive to New Mexico. That will take a few days. We have calculated the most likely routes from Jacksonville to Santa Fe and put out an all-points bulletin along those corridors. That's a very extensive area. However, the closer he gets to Santa Fe, the fewer the route options, and the tighter the noose."

After a pause, the detective concluded. "The reality is that our best chance will be if he makes a mistake. If he gets to Samuel, it could take a long time to find them. A very long time."

Audrey interjected, "Samuel has to get to Vincent's funeral. If he doesn't, it could expose him not only as aiding and abetting Christopher but as a possible suspect in his own brother's murder, and one with a strong financial motive as well." We all concluded that either Christopher would take a detour for a few days while his uncle, Samuel Houten, attended his brother's funeral, or Sammy had set up a temporary safe house where Christopher could lay low until Sammy got back from the funeral.

Everyone was in agreement about just who was the only person Christopher Mosley felt he could trust. But he additionally told his mother that he should not have listened to "them." Who the "Them" were was still a mystery and the heart of the investigation.

I speculated aloud. "Without Christopher Mosley, it will be hard to determine to whom he was referring to in the voice message he left for his mother."

Chuck responded, "A cooperative Christopher Mosley would make it easier, but you must know that we take his warning about the safety of you and Peter Kunz seriously. The investigation will continue vigorously, with or without Christopher Mosley." That was a sentiment that I certainly appreciated.

Before our discussion went any further, Detective Gerity asked that we consider moving to a table and ordering dinner. It had been a long day, and he had been nourished by coffee, donuts, and a hot dog. Not exactly Palm Beach cuisine. We apologized for being poor hosts and asked our waitress to move our cocktails to a table in the dining room.

CHAPTER TWENTY-SIX

Peter Kunz wasted little time before pursuing his independent investigation. He left my wife and me after we shared a few cocktails at the InterContinental lobby bar, drove the few blocks to the Kansas City Plaza, and directly to the Capital Grill.

Kansas City trading desks opened and closed with the New York Stock Exchange. The hour time difference between New York and KC meant that the trader's day was approximately 7:00 a.m. to 3:00 p.m. The Capital Grill's bar served as their regular afternoon cocktail rendezvous.

Peter Kunz had been retired for the last few years but still made frequent afternoon visits to the Capital Grill to meet up with past friends and colleagues. Old habits are hard to break. They die hard. He was hoping on this day that his former partner and fellow retiree Jefferson Coulson would be doing the same.

Jefferson Coulson was now past eighty and had been retired for over ten years. Even at his age, he was still a big, imposing man. Six foot four, and north of two hundred and fifty pounds, he possessed a deep, husky, contagious laugh. In his prime, he had been the consummate, stereotypical, slap-you-on-the-back salesperson.

Jefferson mentored Peter in the early years of Peter's career. They worked side by side for the next thirty years. He was a father figure to Peter. Jefferson was well respected by the latest crop of young traders, who enjoyed his endless stories of the good old days.

When Peter entered the Grill, he found Jefferson at a high top near the bar, having a jovial conversation with three younger traders. Jefferson Coulson greeted Peter warmly. Pete, not wanting to be rude and interrupt Jeff's story, proceeded toward the bar and ordered his usual bourbon and Coke, then casually returned to the high-top where Jefferson was still holding court.

Peter was becoming impatient but waited for his opportunity to get Jefferson's attention. Peter did not want the whole of Kansas City to be aware of the investigation with which he was now obsessed.

While Jefferson was loudly reminiscencing for all to hear, Peter took a different tack and casually raised a leading question about the good old days. "Jeff, didn't we trade for the Coffer, Gallo, and Angali law firm back in the seventies?"

Addressing not only Peter but the young traders, he waved his right arm for effect and answered with a deep laugh. "Oh yeah, back then they could really load up those pension contributions for the partners and not much else for the underlings. We had a lot of capital to play with." Then Jeff looked at Peter. "What made you think of that?"

Peter coolly responded, "I had a conversation with George Cavallas this morning, and I kind of remember that he began at Coffer, Gallo, and Angali before starting his own practice. I don't know why, but it just came to mind."

Jefferson confirmed what Peter had suspected, and that gave Peter the confidence that Jeff had a good recollection of that law firm. Peter was new to trading back then and had little contact with the principals of Coffer, Gallo, and Angali. Now he anxiously waited to get Jefferson alone so he could press his friend for more important information, questions meant for Jefferson's ears only.

Peter and Jefferson continued their regular routine of bantering with their colleagues, although Pete's heart was not in it. He was waiting to get Jeff alone. They both were now finishing another drink, Pete's fourth and Jeff's, well who knew. Nothing out of the ordinary for either of them. They weren't kids any more, but they could still keep up with the best of them.

Jefferson took the back of Peter's neck in his bear-like hand and pulled him close. "Kunz, how about we have one more, and I'll call Gloria to pick us up?"

Without a second's delay to consider the suggestion, Peter responded, "Coulson, that sounds good to me. This round is on me, but I'm fine to drive. No need to bother Gloria. I'll drop you off on my way home. I have something quite important I would like to talk to you about. I think you can be a big help to me."

Jefferson felt the seriousness in Peter's voice and said, "Get us the drinks, and let's sit over there where we can talk." He pointing to a high-top at the far end of the bar area and instructed Peter to get the refills while he secured the table.

As soon as Peter reached the table, Jefferson asked him, "How can I help?"

"Well, it's about the Houten murder. You may not know this, but at first, I was a suspect because Vincent put me in his will." Peter explained how insulted he had been that the police considered him to have a motive due to the bequest of car and a few thousand dollars. "That really pissed me off." Peter Kunz truly felt the idea that he would kill his best friend for a car and a few thousand dollars was absurd and insulting.

Peter Kunz was getting a bit excited. "Jeff, at first I wanted to prove to those red-neck morons in Florida that I know more than they do, and I can solve this. But now, Jeff, I really think I'm onto something, and I can't let go."

Peter had his friend's undivided attention, and Jefferson responded, "All right, Peter, take your time, and bring me to up speed."

Peter began. "I had a meeting with George this morning that let's just say didn't go very well. Then I spent two hours with Kansas City's finest getting the first degree. After thinking about it and putting the two events together, I think I have a connection. I hope you can help me tie it together."

Jefferson didn't completely understand Peter, but he did understand that Peter was seriously and deeply involved in the murder investigation. "What connection?"

Peter leaned closer to Jefferson, lowered his voice and said, "George Cavallas and Bert Kelty."

Quietly Peter explained the reasons for his suspicion. "George Cavallas, as Vincent Houten's attorney and confidant, introduced Bert Kelty to Vincent, suggesting he serve as Tri-State Tape's general manager. George does not want it known that he has known Bert for years, nor does he want it known that he even recommended him for the position. Bert, on the other hand, doesn't want it known that in the past he was a practicing attorney and most likely had a past relationship with George." He lowered his voice still further. "I think it goes back to Coffer, Gallo, and Angali. I have a hunch that Bert worked there and something happened, good or bad, to cement his relationship with George. I need to confirm that Bert in fact worked at the firm, and then I want to know why he hasn't he practiced law since." Peter then asked Jefferson, "Do you have any sources?"

After a minute's pause to search his memory, Jefferson responded, "I can tell you that I don't have any recollection of Bert Kelty working at the firm, and until just now, I didn't even know he was a lawyer. It was a very big firm and still is. The firm still continues to use the original name, but Coffer and Gallo are long gone. Angali is the only surviving original partner, but I don't know how active he is."

Peter almost desperately asked, "Do you think you can find out about Bert?"

In his raspy voice, he gave a soft laugh and assured Peter that he would deliver the goods. "I still see Tony Angali around town from time to time. I can give him a ring. I'm sure he will take my call."

"That would be great, Jeff. It's very important."

Without hesitation, Jefferson committed to assisting his friend. After all, at eighty-plus-years-old, where did you find excitement like this? To be involved in a case of murder, a murder of someone he knew and for good measure for one of the suspects to be your longtime partner and very close friend, there was nothing to consider. "OK, old buddy, are you sure you can drive me home? I have some work to do."

CHAPTER TWENTY-SEVEN

When Peter Kunz pulled up to Jefferson Coulson's home to drop off his old friend, Jefferson stepped out of Peter's sedan, leaned back into the car, and in an effort to reassure his retired partner, he said, "Pete, you'll hear from me sooner than later."

Jefferson Coulson then walked in the front door of his house and immediately called to his wife, "Gloria, do we have Tony Angali's cell number?" He was not about to waste any time.

Gloria was a bit taken aback by Jefferson's directive. "I'm sure I have it. Why do you need it now?"

"I'll explain later. Just please get me the number." Jefferson was single-minded in his mission.

In a forceful tone, Gloria informed her husband that he had had enough to drink, and whatever this was about, it could wait till the morning.

"No, honey, it can't wait. Kunz needs my help. I'll explain after I talk to Tony."

Anthony Anagli took Jefferson's call. "Hi, Tony. Hope I didn't get you at a bad time. I was hoping I could rattle your brain for some info from the good old days."

Angali responded good-naturedly. "Jefferson, it's always a pleasure to talk to you, my friend. I'm just about to go out to dinner, but I have a few minutes."

"I won't take more than a minute of your time." The salesman would say anything to get the information he was looking for. Jefferson got right to the point. "I was hoping that you might remember a young attorney who worked for your firm back in the seventies. Bert Kelty."

"The seventies. That was a long time ago and a lot of lawyers since. I don't recall a Bert. What was his real name?"

"Good question. I don't know."

Angali said, "What's this about?"

Jefferson responded, "Well I've been asked to do a little research. Bert Kelty has been working at Tri-State Tape for the last two years, and since the death of Vincent Houten, he is under consideration for chief executive officer."

Jefferson Coulson might have been retired for the last decade, but he still had the skills to ruse someone for information. "Those involved in his will and estate are looking for some help in judging his background, his ability, and his trustworthiness."

In a tone that Jefferson interpreted as somewhat unconvinced, Tony asked, "How did they get you involved?"

Anthony Angali was not someone to take lightly, even though he was in his late seventies. Tony considered Jefferson Coulson's request for information, even though it appeared to be irrelevant ancient history, as something that Jefferson had to earn. Nothing came without a price.

"Well, there are a few factors involved with the estate and the continuation of the operation of Vincent Houten's company. And

I have been asked by someone involved to see what I could find out as an impartial observer."

"Call me tomorrow, and see if you can get his real name." That felt like a brush-off to Jefferson.

The night was still young, so Jefferson called Peter Kunz to brainstorm. Jefferson informed Peter of his unproductive conversation. "Tony Angali wants me to call him tomorrow with Bert's real name, but I don't think it's going to get us anywhere. He seemed a little cautious. We might have to take another approach."

"Jeff, we must know a retired attorney from Coffer, Gallo, and Angali, or one who had contact with the firm back in the seventies. I can't think of anyone, can you?" Peter's disappointment came through in the tone of his voice.

Excitedly, Jefferson said, "Kunz, it just came to me. Tommy Brennan. He's at least ten years older that me but still sharp as a tack. He knows every lawyer in the state."

Peter asked, "You mean Judge Thomas Francis Brennan?" He continued after a brief pause. "Jeff, the last time I saw Judge Brennan was when I was in front of him on a DUI charge. The reason I got off was because I had just dropped his daughter off at her house after a short stay at the Hilton. Her husband was away on business in Atlanta. You say he's sharp as a tack, but let's hope he's not all that sharp."

Jefferson was not dissuaded. "I'll leave you out of it. If I can reach him tonight, I'll call you back."

Before he hung up, Peter could hear Gloria in the background. "Not another call. You're so drunk, you don't even know it."

Maybe Gloria was right, but Jefferson was determined. Jeff poured himself a fresh cocktail while Gloria reluctantly gave him the phone number of the Honorable Thomas F. Brennan.

Jefferson took a more subtle and tactical approach than he hD with Anthony Anagli. "Judge, I'm happy you could take my call."

In anticipation of Coulson's motivation for the phone call, the judge asked, "Jefferson, what's the charity of the month that you would like me to endorse?"

"Tommy, I've been off that circuit for years. But I would like your assistance in some information gathering. Would you rather I call you in the morning?"

"No, it's fine. What's up?" The judge at his age had a very limited social calendar. He was at home with only television for company.

Employing a different approach than the one Jefferson used with Tony Angali, he sheepishly addressed the judge. "Well, Tommy, I would like to ask you about some ancient history, if you don't mind. Specifically, I hope you may have a recollection of an attorney who worked in the Coffer, Gallo, and Angali firm back in the seventies."

"I don't know if I can help, but let's find out. I had a lot of dealings with the firm from their start in the late sixties to my retirement in 2005. Good and bad."

Jeff Coulson poised the question. "Do you recall Bert Kelty?"

"Of course I know Bert Kelty. And I know Bert has been working at Tri-State Tape. I'm just a little surprised he is still working there. He usually moves from company to company pretty regularly."

"Do you know his real name?"

"Albert Keltenski. He shortened it after he was disbarred. I think that was in the early eighties, eighty-one or eighty-two."

After a short pause to recover from the shock of the last casual comments Jefferson asked, "Tommy, what was he disbarred for? This could be important."

"I can only tell you what I heard. I was not a judge until eighty-eight, and if I were, I couldn't tell you anything that I learned from the bench."

Jefferson almost desperately addressed Judge Brennan. "Judge, it's important."

There was silence for a minute or two while the judge collected his thought and called up his memory. He was unsure that he should partake in pure gossip. What good could come of it? Before discussing anything further he asked Jefferson, "How important? What's this about?"

Rather than try to ruse Judge Brennan like he had tried with Anthony Angali, Jefferson took the direct and honest approach, "Tommy we have a suspicion that Bert Kelty is indirectly involved in the Vincent Houten murder. We also believe that there is a connection to George Cavallas, a connection that started back in the seventies while they were both employed at CG&A. But we have not been able to confirm that Bert Kelty, or whatever his name was, actually did work there. Until now."

Coulson let that information sit with Judge Brennan and remained silent until the judge asked, "You say 'we' have a suspicion. Who are the 'we'?"

Sheepishly Jeff answered, "Peter Kunz, me, and the Stevenses." Sarcastically and using a financial industry reference, Judge Brennan responded sarcastically, "Peter Kunz? How reliable. Tell me how he passed the series ten for criminal investigation at the Capital Grill? And who on earth are the Stevenses?"

Forcefully, Jefferson answered, "Tommy, we may not have the credentials you would like, but Kunz has been a friend of Vincent Houten for over thirty years, and I've known him just as long. The Stevenses have become Vincent Houten's best friends. Over the last fifteen years they partied, traveled, you name it, together. And by the way, they were the last to see him alive."

Jefferson took a sip of his cocktail, caught his breath, and continued, "I think it's apparent that we are looking for answers. The Houten murderer is probably here in KC as we speak. We're trying to find the murderer. We are not chasing the pot of gold. There are enough people doing that."

The honorable Thomas Francis Brennan was convinced. He began relaying whatever he could recall.

Albert Keltenski, a young and ambitious attorney, was assigned a minor case for a large client. A case objecting to a variance granted to a competitor of the CG&A client. He apparently missed the forty-five-day deadline to contest the variance, and his client could no longer object. The variance stood, and the Coffer, Gallo, and Angali client was not happy.

Jeff interrupted. "So he was disbarred for that?"

"No, the client was very important to the firm, and young Albert felt the pressure. He backdated documents, forged signatures, and lied to the judge."

Encouraging the judge to further search his memory, Jeff asked, "Can you remember who the client was?"

"I think the company was called FBC Contractors, but I don't know what it is called today."

Jefferson knew FBC. Back in the day, the Sacco crime family ran FBC. He knew the firm because he traded the union pension fund. Jeff informed Judge Brennan that FBC now operated as KCMO. He then asked, "Tommy, do you know if the Sacco family still control the company, and whether there is a connection to George Cavallas?"

"I'm not sure, but somehow Bert Kelty keeps getting management positions or consulting contracts in midsized companies. They usually last a year or two, then he moves on. This last one with Tri-State Tape has lasted a bit longer. That may lead back to George; Coffer, Gallo, and Angali; the Saccos, or all three. I don't know."

"Tommy, I can't thank you enough." Jefferson Coulson hung up his phone, poured himself another drink, sat in his favorite chair in his den then picked up the phone and called his friend Peter Kunz. "Peter I got some real good shit for you."

CHAPTER TWENTY-EIGHT

"Salvatore?" My wife shook her head incredulously.

We had just gotten settled into our dining room chairs at the InterContinental when Detective Gerity decided to inform us that Salvatore Liguria had been arrested. That was information out of left field.

Puzzled by the circumstances, Audrey asked, "Salvatore may not have shared all the information he had, but how does that get him arrested?"

On this, I had to disagree with my wife. I had the feeling that the detective had good cause to arrest Salvatore.

In the restaurant in Delray, I had wanted to throw Salvatore into oncoming traffic. He bragged about how much Megan trusted him and not us, and how much more inside information he had. Maybe I was too infuriated by his pompous attitude to be objective.

Holding back, or more accurately "withholding" evidence from the police was a criminal offence, and I now was anxious to hear Detective Chuck's account. Why exactly had the Palm Beach PD arrested Mr. Liguria? I had the feeling Salvatore had somehow painted himself into a corner.

"It really began with your account of your lunch in Delray," Detective Gerity told us.

I was taken aback. "Chuck, I didn't think we gave you very much. Tell me, what part of the conversation we had with Salvatore did you find important? What did we tell you that struck a nerve?"

"OK, be patient. Let's start from the beginning. Not your lunch encounter with Salvatore, but the night of the murder."

Detective Gerity began in a monotone. "Vincent Houten holds a pre–New Year's Eve cocktail party at his residence at about seven p.m., a party that you both attended. That was nothing out of the ordinary. He had many cocktail parties similar to this and there were no incidences reported at this event by you or the other guest we interviewed. The collective party of six proceeds to the Mar-A-Lago Club at approximately nine p.m. to attend the New Year's Eve formal ball. They use three separate cars for the short trip."

The detective continued, still sounding like Detective Friday from the seventies TV series *Dragnet*. "The short version is that sometime into the evening, there is a quarrel. Megan Kelly, Mr. Houten's date, leaves the premises, as do his guests from Kansas City, Mr. and Mrs. Robertson. This is nothing new or significant in itself since quarrels between Mr. Houten and Ms. Kelly have happened with some frequency before, but it plays a part in the overall investigation.

"Nate, you and Audrey remain and accompany Mr. Houten to the west end of the Mar-A-Lago estate near the Lake Worth bulkhead to watch the New Year's Eve fireworks. After the fireworks, you leisurely walk back toward the valet stand."

Detective Chuck paused for effect. He looked directly into my eyes, turned toward Audrey, and looked into her eyes a little while longer. "You both go toward the guest valet stand, and

Mr. Houten goes to the employees' secluded parking area. Vincent is now alone. He gets into his car, and before he can start the engine, someone puts a bullet behind his left ear."

Audrey and I were dabbing tears away. I pleaded with Detective Gerity, "Oh shit, Chuck. You don't know how much listening to your chronology upsets us. Please get to the point."

"I'm sorry to have upset you, but we have to break it down piece by piece." Detective Gerity then got to the point. "Someone was waiting at Vincent Houten's car. Waiting for him to come back to the car after the party. He or she didn't even wait for Mr. Houten to start his car. The murderer anticipated approximately when he would get to his car, and he or she patiently waited."

After another slight pause for effect, the detective asked, "How did the murderer know?"

Wow! That question hit me hard. But after a minute to reflect, I thought that any one of a hundred people could have known that Vincent Houten would be attending the Mar-A-Lago gala. As an active member of the club, he had attended the New Year's Eve ball for the past three years, and who would not assume that he would not leave until after the fireworks display? I could see the detective's point, but was the timing a real mystery?

My wife was one full step ahead of me. "Chuck, for someone to select New Year's Eve at Mar-A-Lago as the right time to murder Vincent and risk being seen by any one of over five hundred guests and employees, that person had to know he would have parked where he did."

Now my light bulb was starting to go on and bring me some clarity. How could I have been so ignorant? It was not *who* would know Vince's schedule New Year's Eve. It was who and how did the murderer know that there was an opportunity to commit the murder based solely on where Vincent parked.

Chuck's question of a few minutes ago was now much more meaningful. He had asked, "How did they know?"

Detective Gerity answered his own question in the same dry monotone. "Megan Kelly was the only one who could have had the particular information of where the 1956 Jaguar was parked and be able to approximate the time that Vincent Houten would be leaving the party. Passing that information onto the murderer allowed him to hide in the shadows near the secluded parking area. He most likely waited patiently and eventually watched Mr. Houten walk across the front of the Mar-A-Lago estate house and over the croquet lawn toward his car.

"With hundreds of guests scurrying for their cars at the valet station, some one hundred yards away, no one would have notice an unauthorized person lurking on the grounds. No one would hear the pop of a Saturday night special, especially not after the Grucci family fireworks, and no tired waiter or staffer would bother to question a classic car left on the grounds as they left work after a very long evening. They were focused on going home and going to bed." Ominously, Chuck concluded, "It was the perfect location and the perfect situation for the murder."

As soon as the detective took a breath from his reenactment, I broke in. "Chuck, you don't really think Megan could have given that information to the actual murderer?"

Chuck responded very emphatically, "No, I don't think Miss Kelly *could* have given that information to the murderer. I firmly believe that she *did* give that information to the murderer."

Silence. One second. Two seconds. Five seconds. I took a big swallow of my vodka, but waited. Finally, after Detective Gerity had let enough time lapse for his intended effect, he said, "Megan most likely did not have any knowledge of the plot."

Assuming Megan did not know, and that the investigation unit was correct about Ms. Kelly being the only possible source of the information, then who other than Salvatore Liguria could come to mind? He had to be the provider of the crucial information.

Chuck concluded, "Regardless of whether our assumptions about Salvatore Liguria are right or wrong, Megan Kelly knows the murderer, or at least his accomplice. She just doesn't know who he or she is."

The way Salvatore bragged to us during our lunch in Delray about how much Megan confided in him raised the detective's suspicions. And Megan Kelly had confirmed her relationship with Salvatore to Audrey and me and again to Detective Gerity in the Wellington Hospital. Someone was passing on information, and Salvatore Liguria had the information that was being passed along. But Detective Gerity had to have more than suspicion to arrest Salvatore.

The next step in the investigation after Detective Gerity's hospital interview with Megan was to determine Salvatore Liguria's schedule at the time of the crimes. That investigation revealed that Salvatore was at the Polo Club the night of the attempted murder of Megan Kelly, the night her car was forced off the road in Wellington. That was a very important breakthrough.

Detective Gerity shared that big break with us. Then explained how he played it out with Megan. "I had the evidence that Salvatore was at the Polo Club that night, so before I confronted him, I asked Ms. Kelly if she saw him there. Her answer was, 'Yes, we had a few drinks together.' Voila!"

The rest was child's play. "We talked to Salvatore, who denied everything. Then we went back to Ms. Kelly, who put two and two together. She drew her own conclusion. 'Salvatore tried to kill me!' Ms. Megan Kelly's Irish temper came through orange, white, and green. I guess you could call it a coming-to-Jesus moment, and she began cooperating." Detective Gerity casually stated, "We're still waiting for Salvatore to come around. He's resisting now, but we know he eventually will."

We ordered a fresh round of cocktails, and Detective Gerity excused himself to use the restroom.

Having been seated in the dining area at a table overlooking the snow-covered courtyard, we awaited Chuck's return. My wife and I took the opportunity to hash out a few possibilities. More importantly, we tried to agree on which part of the investigation we most wanted to pursue with the detective. We had his undivided attention, but for how long? We wanted to make the most of our time with him.

We both felt we had spent enough time on the Megan-Salvatore drama, and although that was interesting, there were other issues that we needed and or wanted more clarity. We knew we didn't want to waste time on the manhunt for Christopher Mosley. That would be a time-consuming review of police procedures and interstate operations. That issue we dismissed immediately.

Audrey and I agreed that what we needed to know most was what Detective Gerity might have discovered about the obviously and suddenly cold relationship between Joanie Olsen and George Cavallas. After all, the detective had told us earlier in the day that they were high on his list to be interviewed.

We also thought of the safety of our friend Peter Kunz, who we believed was intent on investigating on his own. As we considered his safety and what he shared with us about his day's experience and his suspicion of George's honesty, we came to the same conclusion: George was the real unknown.

Who really was George Cavallas? What had Chuck Gerity found out about him? We couldn't wait to talk to Detective Gerity when he returned to our table.

My wife and I were now anxious to continue our conversation with Detective Gerity as we watched him walk back toward our table. We were united in just what blanks we both would like to ask the detective to fill in, but when he reached our table, he didn't move toward his seat. He stood between Audrey and me and apologetically said, "I'm afraid I won't be able to stay for dinner. We have just located Christopher Mosley."

I began to say "Great!" but he had already turned and briskly walked out of the dinning room and toward the lobby exit. I could only think, *Now what?*

CHAPTER TWENTY-NINE

Detective Gerity received the news of the discovery of Christopher Mosley from Detective Jose Solomon, the technology expert on the Palm Beach PD task force. "He is in a Motel 6 on Route 136 just outside of Amarillo, Texas. The Amarillo PD called in the Texas Rangers, and they're on the scene, awaiting confirmation before they move in and apprehend him."

Chuck was apprehensive. "Are they sure it's him?"

Solomon answered with confidence. "I'm sure. Everything checks out: Mosley's description, the car, and its dented fender, and the same MO as in the Jacksonville Holiday Inn Express—registered under the name of Philip True, listed a false license plate on the registration form, and paid with cash."

Gerity impatiently asked, "So what are the Texas Rangers trying to confirm?"

"Boss, the suspect is assumed to be armed and dangerous. Texas is new to this case. It's only right that they take what time they need to do this right. They are calling it confirmation; I'm calling it CYA. We would do it the same way."

Quick to compliment, Chuck said, "You're right. Good work, Jose."

"I'd like to take credit, but we didn't locate him by way of the database search I set up. That didn't produce anything. It was a suspicious clerk who checked the registration form and noticed the false plate that he listed. She contacted the Amarillo PD, and the rest is history."

"Good work just the same." Chuck then informed Jose, "I'm leaving the InterContinental and heading to KCPD headquarters to meet Detective Peterson. I'll be there in twenty minutes. Stay in touch if anything develops."

Detective Gerity retrieved his car from the valet at the InterContinental and headed for the Kansas City police headquarters. This was what he had been hoping for, the big break.

Christopher Mosley was the odds-on favorite to be the shooter, even though everyone considered him a pawn in this case. Whose pawn was the question? Christopher's interrogation could put all the pieces together.

When Chuck arrived at the police headquarters, Detective Ed Peterson was waiting for him. Peterson reassured Gerity, "Chuck, I have been in contact with the Texas Rangers and the Amarillo local PD. They are taking every precaution and are now ready to move in."

Gerity and Peterson waited for the latest update from Amarillo, Texas. Detective Gerity suggested that he and Ed review Christopher Mosley's profile. The conclusion was that he was a scared, remorseful young man with no prior indication of violence.

Gerity speculated aloud. "Ed, this should go down pretty easily, don't you think?"

"Yes, I agree. Based on his profile, he should not pose any resistance or make an attempt to flee." After a pause, Peterson added to his analysis. "But based on his profile, there is also no indication that he would commit murder."

Detective Peterson finally said, "Profiles are not infallible. Police profiles can only give a reasonable indication of how an individual might react in a given situation. Based on Christopher Mosley's profile, the real question is, how did someone convince him to kill his uncle?"

Chuck Gerity let that question go unanswered while they contemplated the possibilities. Detective Gerity began telling Detective Peterson that they should begin scheduling a flight to Amarillo when a loud ring interrupted their moment of concentration. Detective Ed Peterson answered the call on the first ring. He was silent, just listening to the information that was being relayed to him. Gerity saw the look of disappointment on Ed's face. He knew the news was not good. Chuck simply asked, "What's up?"

"He's dead." Detective Peterson was blunt but not intentionally. He was just shocked by the latest development.

"Dead?" Gerity asked. "The Rangers killed him?"

"No, they didn't even move in." Peterson relayed what the caller, Jose Solomon, had just informed him, "As soon as Mosley saw the police activity around the Motel 6, he put a bullet in his head."

"Ah, shit." Detective Gerity felt the heavy weight of frustration. Nothing easy was going to come of this case. His empty stomach went into a spasm. Detective Gerity shook his head and turned to Detective Ed Peterson. "It's pretty hard to get information from a corpse."

CHAPTER THIRTY

With cocktail in hand, Jefferson Coulson's speech was beginning to slur a bit. He and Peter Kunz had had more than a few at the Capital Grill, and against his wife's advice, he did not stop even while making contact with Anthony Angali and Judge Thomas Brennan. However, now he was on the phone with his friend Peter Kunz, and with perfect clarity, he relayed to his friend Peter the conversation he had had with Judge Brennan.

Judge Thomas F. Brennan had confirmed that there was indeed a connection between Bert Kelty and George Cavallas and also affirmed a possible connection to the Sacco crime family who ran FBC Contractors.

Jefferson Coulson was pleased with himself. It didn't take thirty minutes for him to get the information he was able to share with his friend Peter Kunz. After relaying it to Peter, Jeff concluded, "The plot thickens my friend." His old friend then cautioned him. "Watch your back."

Peter Kunz expressed his gratitude to Jefferson and then spent a moment or two contemplating what it all meant. Jefferson

patiently waited through the silence until Peter finally commented, "Jeff, I have some thinking to do."

Peter asked himself the same question that he had posed to
George Cavallas two days earlier. *Who had a motive strong enough to
murder Vincent Houten?*

The question rolled around in his mind while he drank another bourbon and Coke, then another bourbon and Coke until
he fell asleep in his den in his lounge chair in front of his blank
TV screen. He woke a little after six with a fuzzy head. He poured
himself a cup of coffee and reviewed in his mind what information
he had found out about his friend's murder.

In his attempt to put the puzzle pieces together, Peter Kunz
considered Vincent's family and their potential financial windfall.
He thought about Joan Olsen's monetary benefit, and he reviewed
in his mind every word of his meeting with George Cavallas. He
also reconsidered his opinion of Detective Edward Gerity. He still
wasn't convinced of the detective's professional competence, but
Peter had come to appreciate his single-minded tenacity.

Peter wisely decided to contact Detective Gerity directly. He
decided it was time to cooperate with the police.

It was clear to Peter Kunz that if the investigation pursued the
connection among Bert Kelty, George Cavallas, and the Coffer,
Gallo, and Angali law firm, then the motive, whatever it might be,
should become clear. Peter's 8:00 a.m. call to the KCPD didn't connect him to Detective Chuck Gerity, but he left a message with
the police receptionist, and his call was promptly returned by
Detective Gerity at 8:10 a.m.

"Mr. Kunz, I'm at Tri-State right now conducting some interviews. Is nine thirty at headquarters convenient for you?" A meeting with Peter Kunz was far more important than canvasing the
opinions of the employees of Tri-State Tape.

Kunz responded, "That will be fine with me."

Detective Gerity closed his phone then called to Detective Peterson, who was conducting an interview in the company conference room. "Let's wrap it up. We have to go."

Detective Peterson ended the interview he was conducting without question and collected his notes. Detective Gerity informed Peterson that Peter Kunz had new information and now wanted to cooperate.

Detective Peterson nodded to Gerity, a gesture acknowledging the importance of the situation. He made two phone calls to inform headquarters of the change in their plans and then followed Detective Gerity to the exit.

The Kansas City police headquarters was less than twenty minutes from Peter Kunz's house. In order to be prompt for his nine thirty appointment, Peter got into his BMW at eight forty-five. As he backed out of his garage and into his driveway, he noticed a dark sedan proceeding very slowly past his house. Peter reached up to activate his automatic garage door closer, then looked into his rearview mirror to see if the sedan was still there. It was nowhere in sight.

Peter backed slowly and cautiously into the street, looking in the direction that the sedan was traveling, but it was gone. He thought, *I'm getting a little paranoid.*

Peter Kunz's thoughts now went back to the information that Jefferson Coulson was able to gather from Judge Brennan. He became engrossed in strategizing how he would relay that information to Detective Gerity. Peter decided, rather than try to speculate or lead Detective Gerity and Detective Peterson to his opinion, he would lay out the facts as he knew them and let the detectives take it from there.

Peter approached the police station and found a parking space on Twelfth Street, just a half block from the entrance. He was a bit early. He leisurely returned his coffee mug to the console cup holder, unbuckled his seat belt, and began to open his door. At that moment, the sound of a car horn blasted at him from behind.

Peter had partially opened his door. He turned to look over his left shoulder to see what the commotion was all about. A dark sedan, most likely the same sedan Peter had observed near his house, roared toward his car. With its horn still blowing, it side-swiped Kunz's BMW and tore the driver's side door off its hinges.

The blow caused the dark sedan to skid sideways and to the left, into the lane of oncoming traffic. The driver quickly regained control of the vehicle, swerved back into the correct lane, then sped away.

Peter was badly shaken. He had been a second or two from stepping out of his car and possibly losing a leg or his life. The force of the impact was enough to send the BMW's right front wheel over the curb and onto the sidewalk. The front left bumper went into the rear of the pickup truck that Peter had parked behind.

The noise of the car horn blowing followed by the sound of the crash had police and witnesses in the immediate area running to Peter Kunz's assistance. Fortunately, he had not been ejected from his car. Almost in unison they all pleaded, "Don't move. Don't move."

CHAPTER THIRTY-ONE

Detective Gerity's 9:30 a.m. meeting with Peter Kunz at KCPD headquarters was now a 2:00 p.m. meeting in Peter Kunz's recovery room in the Kansas University Medical Center. My wife and I got to the medical center before noon. Detective Gerity was kind enough to inform us of the incident immediately after it occurred. No one was calling it an accident.

We had spent most of our time in the medical center waiting for Peter to complete tests. He had two MRIs, multiple x-rays, and several physical exams that were conducted by physician after physician.

Peter had turned to look over his left shoulder when he heard the car horn blowing just before the crash. That left him now with severe pain in his neck, left shoulder, and his upper lumbar region. By midafternoon, the shock had worn off and the pain, discomfort, and realization of what just happened was setting in.

Peter Kunz's friend Jefferson Coulson was informed of the incident shortly after it occurred. The information came from a friend of his in the KCPD investigative unit. Kansas City was just not that big of a town. It didn't take Jeff long to put two and two together and realize that he and Peter had unearthed some very pertinent information, information that someone desperately wanted to keep quiet.

Jefferson asked his contact in the investigation unit to contact Detective Gerity for him. He wanted to discreetly relay the information he knew that Peter Kunz was about to discuss with Detective Gerity at their scheduled nine thirty meeting. Discretion was imperative considering how dangerous the atmosphere had become.

By the time Peter had completed the arsenal of medical tests and physical exams, the Vincent Houten murder investigation was proceeding with renewed energy and with new direction and new urgency.

Peter Kunz was now resting comfortably, having been given a mild sedative and some powerful painkillers. My wife and I were pacing the room. This was getting scary.

Unannounced, Detective Chuck Gerity entered Peter's hospital room with Detective Ed Peterson following just behind. He gave my wife and me a trite greeting. "Hi." Then he pulled a chair up to Peter's bed and sat looking directly into his face. "How are you doing?"

Chuck's tone was not what you would consider compassionate. It was more like *let's get the pleasantries over with and get down to business.*

Peter instinctively knew that the detective really didn't care about how he felt but answered the question just the same. "I guess I'm not doing too badly, considering that someone just tried to kill me."

"I'm glad you're feeling better." Chuck apparently felt he now had the green light to get back to the investigation. Pleasantries exchanged, he asked, "It may appear to you, Mr. Kunz, that someone tried to kill you, but in reality, if 'they' tried to kill you, you would

most certainly be dead—despite our best efforts to protect you."
He continued, "Mr. Kunz, what you received today was a warning."

Peter was not convinced. "I think that I was as close to being killed as a person could get."

With the air of a teacher talking to a student, Chuck said, "Mr. Kunz, you turned to see your attackers because they were blowing their car horn. Someone who is intent on killing does not warn his target before he strikes." Detective Gerity continued. "The fact that today's warning was so violent indicates that you have gotten close, made a connection, and got somebody concerned. Concerned enough to want to send a message."

Detective Peterson took up the story. "Your car was intentionally struck just one half block from police headquarters in broad daylight. Several police and civilians witnessed the collision. It was a warning to you, Mr. Kunz, but it was also a message, a message to everyone else involved in this case."

That was a sobering thought to me. I thought to myself, "Who are those guys?"

Detective Gerity then informed us that he had not yet interviewed George Cavallas because he had been in court since ten o'clock. More significant was the fact that Bert Kelty also had not been interviewed for the simple reason that Bert Kelty had disappeared. Chuck Gerity made light of those developments and reassured us, "There still has been some significant progress in the investigation today."

Detective Ed Peterson took over the discussion, "Mr. Kunz, following your lead, and with some help from your friend Mr. Coulson, we have been able to discover that Coffer, Gallo, and Angali represented the Sacco family from the sixties through the seventies—the same time frame during which Bert Kelty and George Cavallas were employed there together."

This information was new to Audrey and me, so I asked, "Who is the Sacco family?"

Chuck Gerity informed us that they were a Kansas City and Midwest-region crime family. He then motioned to Detective Peterson. "Ed heads up the KC organized-crime unit."

I was totally taken by surprise. "Are you saying that the Italian Mafia is here in KC? What do they do? Corner the market on long-horn cattle?"

Peter answered from his bed. "Nate, they go back to the turn of the century. They got big during Prohibition. Mayor Ward wouldn't enforce Prohibition, and KC rocked. That's where the song 'Going to Kansas City' came from. The whole Midwest, including Chicago, came to KC for jazz and bootleg."

Detective Peterson then continued. "The Sacco family members were the bootleg suppliers. They have since gotten more sophisticated and now do a little corporate embezzlement, among other things."

My wife and I looked at each other with equal concern.

Ed Peterson addressed Peter Kunz as directly as he could. "Mr. Kunz, the information you and Mr. Coulson were able to uncover was very crucial to our investigation, but now I must highly recommend you return to South Florida as soon as physically possible. We can not ensure your safety." Detective Peterson concluded. "This is not only about the embezzlement in Tri-State Tape. It's about exposing and possibly cracking the Sacco family's organized corporate embezzlement program."

Detective Gerity then added, "Mr. Kunz, please inform me of your travel plans as soon as you have finalized them."

With that, the detectives turned and exited the recovery room. My wife and I watched the detectives leave. Then we both turned toward our friend Peter and Audrey asked, "Peter, I think that's good advice. What do you think?"

Peter took a minute to respond, then said, "I helped connect George to Bert, Bert and George to the Coffer, Gallo, and Angali law firm, and made it easy for the detectives to connect the law firm to the Sacco family." He added, "I'm no hero. I have accomplished what I hoped to accomplish for my own satisfaction. The Saccos delivered a message to me, and I got it loud and clear. If the hospital releases me today, I'll be on the first flight to West Palm Beach tomorrow." Peter wiped away a tear. "My only regret is that I will not be at my friend's funeral service. But it's done, and I'm done."

When my wife and I finally left Peter's room, Audrey turned to me and said, "That's good news. Peter is finally acting sensibly and leaving."

I responded, "Yeah, but the bad news is that we now know who the 'them' are." They were the same "them" whom Christopher Mosley had referred to in the voice message he left for his mother before he blew his brains out.

CHAPTER THIRTY-TWO

As we left the hospital lobby, it was still light, but the light was fading. I didn't want my wife to see my concern; however, until this afternoon, I had thought the "them" that Christopher Mosley mentioned in his voice mail to his mother referred to two or three co-conspirators. Maybe Joanie, maybe Bert, maybe George, but I had never given a thought to the idea that they might be professionals.

I tried to make light of it when a black-and-white was waiting at the exit of the hospital parking area and followed us to our hotel. But it was definitely a big relief. We pulled up to the entrance of the InterContinental, where the valet took our car. I waved thanks to the patrolmen who had just escorted us in safety. He did not respond and nor did he leave.

We entered the hotel and without taking a vote went directly to the lobby bar. We ordered our cocktails: vodka rocks, vodka grapefruit.

My wife had been putting up a good front. She hadn't shown one sign of concern or fright. She was now about to reveal a kink in her armor. We sat in silence until our drinks were delivered, both trying to put things into perspective.

We sipped our first cocktail of the day, which had been delayed due to Peter's incident. Then Audrey leaned forward, placed her left hand on my right hand, gave it a gentle squeeze, and said, "Nate, we have to think this through. We have to decide what's best for us. I think we should book a flight back to Palm Beach as soon after the funeral service as we can."

I wholeheartedly agreed. Now that the Sacco family and organized crime were involved, we had to look at the big picture. My cell phone rang. I excitedly told my wife, "It's Chuck."

"Hey Chuck, we really did appreciate the escort today to our hotel."

Without acknowledging our expression of gratitude, Chuck went into his hard-ass policeman's role. "I have the same advice for you as we gave to Peter Kunz. Go back to South Florida or to New Jersey. But leave."

My wife and I were not oblivious to that fact that the danger level for all concerned in this case had just escalated. But we still had an obligation to our friend. "Chuck, we have a funeral to attend in less than forty-eight hours. And I'm the master of ceremonies. We promise that we will be careful, lay low, and then get out of KC."

Chuck Gerity responded, "If I can't convince you to leave then you must agree to two things."

"OK, what?"

"First, you must let me know what you are doing every day. You can call or text me, but every time you leave the hotel, I expect to hear from you."

"And?"

"And have your rental car company pick up your rental car at the hotel. Don't drive it back to the airport; don't drive any car in KC. Use taxis or a car service only after you inform me where you are going. Understood?"

I responded, "If you insist, but that is a bit of an inconvenience."

To get our attention, the detective said in a very serious tone, "Listen to me carefully." Then he spoke very deliberately, "I have just been informed that Curtis Thomas was found in his car shot dead, one bullet, small caliber, behind his left ear. Sound familiar?"

"Yes, but who is Curtis Thomas?" I asked.

Chuck informed us that Mr. Thomas was a forensic accountant hired by Vincent Houten before his murder. He was in contact with the investigative unit, and the unit was anxiously awaiting any information he could provide. Not surprisingly, all of Mr. Thomas's records and his computer hard drive were now missing.

Chuck then said, "It sure seems that someone is showing a fondness for cars. Don't you think?"

Vincent was murdered in his '56 Jag, Megan was forced off the road in her Jeep in Wellington, Peter Kunz's car was sideswiped in front of police headquarters, and now the forensic accountant was found shot in his car.

The detective had a point. "Say no more. My next call is to Avis."

PART THREE

CHAPTER THIRTY-THREE

Audrey and I spent most of Wednesday in our hotel. We were not just lying low to avoid potential danger, nor were we hibernating just to pass the time. We were on a mission—a mission to complete Vincent Houten's funeral arrangements. We spent the day constantly on the phone, fulfilling one request after another.

To begin with, in response to Joanie Olson's instructions, we arranged for four of Vincent's prized autos to be stationed in front of the Country Club Church on Ward Parkway, to be on display prior to the arrival of those attending Vincent's service. "Make sure they are prominently displayed but not in the way of the hearse or the limousines." She informed us where they were garaged, but it was up to us to have them cleaned and to find drivers to transport them. "Just ask your concierge" was her curt advice.

Shortly after our first assignment, and before Audrey and I had a chance to even complete it, we were asked, or more accurately instructed, to have four additional autos on the front lawn of the Carriage Club. That involved one more complicating detail for us to arrange. The recent seven inches of snow cover would have to be plowed to make room for the display Joanie envisioned.

Transportation was next on Joanie's agenda—a limo to collect Joanie and her family from Vincent's house one hour before his service; another limo to pick up his third (and most recent) ex-wife along with her two daughters from their residence, and lastly, a courtesy limo for the mayor and city council members of Kansas City to be picked up at city hall. "Have them billed to Newcomer Funeral Home. Tell them to put it on the funeral bill."

Throughout the day, Audrey answered phone calls and took detailed notes of Joanie's wishes. That was the easy part. Keeping me from blowing my top was the real challenge. "Nate, we're doing this for Vince not Joanie."

The public funeral service was scheduled for 11:00 a.m. in the Country Club Church followed by a private, family only committal service at his family cemetery plot. On the morning of the funeral, Audrey and I planned on leaving the InterContinental separately. I needed to be at the church early to make sure everything was as we had planned and put out any fires that might erupt. My wife would meet up with me later at the church for the official service.

Thursday morning at nine, I gave Audrey a kiss, and I told her, "I'll see you at the church. Just stay in the rear vestibule until I have everyone seated, and then we can sit together for Vincent's service."

I left our room and proceeded to the hotel lobby, then exited our hotel and asked the doorman to hail a cab for me. There were several cabs available, and I noticed that one cab pulled in front of two others to pick me up. However, there was no commotion or disagreement among the drivers. I thought nothing of it.

I seated myself in the cab. "Country Club Church, Ward Parkway." My driver made a left out of the hotel entrance, and when he reached Ward Parkway, he turned right and east, not left toward the church. I quickly confronted him, "Hey! Don't you know where you are going?"

In a very calm but firm voice, my driver replied, "Mr. Stevens, I know where I'm going, but my people want to know where you're going."

Audrey and I had already been briefed that the Sacco family were most likely involved in the murder of our friend Vincent, as well as the disappearance of Bert Kelty, the murder of Curtis Thompson, and the warning delivered to Peter Kunz. It didn't take a genius to recognize that the *family* was now paying me a visit.

Following Detective Gerity's advice, my wife and I had agreed on our immediate travel plans. We would attend our friend's church service and get out of town ASAP. I had instructed our travel agent of our wishes but had not gotten confirmation. It was very possible and acceptable to both of us that we would miss the committal service as well as the repast at the Carriage Club that Audrey had spent so much time arranging.

Audrey and I realized the seriousness of the situation. We wanted to be on the first available flight out of KC. We would have preferred to wait until after our friend's funeral service and luncheon, but if that meant delaying our departure, Joanie would have to get through the luncheon without us.

Without hesitation, I nervously addressed my driver/kidnapper. "Sir, I get your message, and I receive it loud and clear. My message to you and your superiors is this: my wife and I feel obligated to attend our friend's funeral this morning. Immediately after the service, we are in the process of arranging our return to South Florida, never to be heard of again."

There was silence. He was still driving east; Royal Stadium was now in view. We were now five or six miles away from the Country Club Church and approaching Royal Stadium. I was now getting very concerned—not about arriving late to Vincent's funeral service, but for my own longevity.

I sheepishly offered, "Sir, if that's not the message you want to hear I can change it. I'm flexible."

"I like your flexibility, Mr. Stevens. That's real good. But to be clear, your message is not the message we want to hear. The message we want to hear is that you will help clean up all of this shit. The family doesn't like shit coming down on them, especially where they're not involved."

I surprised myself that I had the nerve to ask, "The Saccos aren't involved? Are you telling me that your people didn't warn Peter Kunz by sideswiping his car?"

Impatiently, my newest friend responded, "Anybody who knows the Saccos knows that they don't do high-profile shit like that. If the police don't know that by now, they're fucking morons."

The good news was that my driver had now turned around and was driving west, back toward my original destination. I was relieved that my life did not seem to be in danger, but I was still concerned what role the Saccos expected me to play. I felt it was better to wait to hear what he was going to tell me rather than to ask for my marching orders. What did he want me to do to "clean up all this shit," as he said.

We drove in silence throughout the remainder of our twenty-minute drive. We approached my destination and my cab driver stopped a full three long Kansas City blocks from the Church. I did not open the door or ask if I could leave because I knew he had not completed his message. You know, I was just "showing respect." It's a Jersey thing.

Without a preface or "if you please," the messenger stated, "Mr. Stevens, we expect you to stay in town for as long as it takes to clean this up. You and your wife are the only ones who have no financial connection to this fucking mess. No motive. Not suspects. So we have decided to appoint you as our unofficial liaison."

"Sir, until this morning, I thought it was all cleaned up. I thought it was a simple case of an employee embezzling from his employer but with the assistance of organized crime. The only question was who all were involved? I can't see how I can help clean this up. I'm lost."

My chauffer stated, "I already told you the Sacco family is not involved. Tri-State Tape is small potatoes. You should start by checking out Grizzly Adams."

"Grizzly Adams?"

Sarcastically, my driver explained. "Yeah, you know. Brother Sammy from the New Mexico survivalists' colony. All things lead to him."

"You obviously know more than me." He remained silent for effect. I finally asked, "If I'm your liaison, I guess you want me to update you on developments. How do I reach you?"

"Don't be stupid. We will reach you."

I opened my door, thinking the session was over, and my driver quickly turned to peer at me over his right shoulder. It then dawned on me that this was the first time I had seen his face. It was very fair, and he had a full head of reddish-blond hair. He was probably in his late forties. *Not very Italian looking,* I thought.

His voice was now quite forceful. "Understand this: We're counting on you to straighten this out, but if this is not cleaned up quickly, the family will then get involved and clean it up." For emphasis, he added, "Completely clean it up. Capiche?"

That was pretty intense, but being from New Jersey, I certainly did "capiche." I exited the car, started my three-block walk toward the church, and quickly came to the realization that if the Sacco family was truly not involved in Vincent's murder, then we had the same motivation to solve the murder, albeit for different purposes. The walk was doing me a little good.

I slowed my pace to think through the new scenario. The false idea that this was a case of employee embezzlement with the assistance of organized crime had made sense. It tied all the ends together. The only question remaining was whether Bert was doing it alone or if George or Joanie were involved.

I made the assumption that the Saccos didn't go to the trouble of recruiting me just to throw the investigation off of them and onto Samuel (Grizzly Adams) Houten. So I began thinking of all that we knew in the connection of the series of crimes we were facing, but now without the involvement of organized crime. I tried imagining how Sam Houten could have played a roll in all of this from New Mexico.

I thought that Bert Kelty's disappearance left only Joan Olsen and George Cavallas as suspects until the Sacco representative said, "All things lead to Sam." How does Sam Houten fit in? Joanie and Sam hated each other, and that was a fact. Did George and Sam have a relationship? I didn't think so. The thought that we were no closer to solving Vincent's murder now than when we got to Kansas City was making me dizzy.

I reached the Country Club Church, came out of my contemplative mood, and paused at the foot of the church's front steps. Before ascending, my last thought was *What the fuck?*

CHAPTER THIRTY-FOUR

My circuitous cab ride and three-block walk got me to the church closer to 10:45 rather than my planned 9:30. Several people had already arrived, and there was now a steady flow of attendees ascending the church steps. Many guests had already taken their seats. My task as head usher was now far more hectic.

There were a number of KCPD patrol cars and officers gathered as an unofficial honor guard in tribute to a very prominent Kansas City citizen. But they also were on official deployment to observe and provide a show of force at the funeral service of a murdered prominent Kansas City citizen, a murder that was still under investigation.

The police also were there in anticipation of some dignitaries, all of whom I was to properly and prominently seat along with some of the family, three ex-wives, four stepchildren and a number of past and present lady friends. It was a little awkward and a bit nerve-racking, but I had to keep reminding myself that it was an honor to do it for my good friend.

We were expecting the mayor and a couple of councilmen but were surprised by the lieutenant governor, and the US congressman from the district. Both were accompanied by a handful of aides. Now who got the front row?

There were over seven hundred in attendance. Due to the obvious involvement of Christopher Houten as the suspected murderer of his uncle Vincent, Samuel Houten was the only family member in attendance. I sat him with Joanie Olsen and her children. I thought I should keep the heirs together.

George decided to sit along side Bert Kelty in the section I had reserved for the Tri-State employees. There were at least fifty of them, which I thought said a lot about our friend.

Vincent's sister and her husband had returned to Pennsylvania immediately after receiving the news of their son Christopher's suicide. Their children also cancelled their travel plans to attend the funeral. Who could blame them for not wanting to attend the funeral of the uncle who their brother had murdered?

I had been keeping my eye out for Chuck and Ed, but if they had arrived, I missed them. Audrey arrived shortly before the start of Vince's service. I had reserved seating for us that gave Audrey a chance to closely observe the service yet gave me the freedom to leave and return as the need might arise.

Before I was able to seat Audrey, she informed me in a relieved tone, "Nate, Patty called. She got us on a three thirty flight to Fort Lauderdale; it arrives at seven forty. I told her to book it." She must have felt my silence. "Isn't that OK? It's what we agreed upon last night."

I didn't want to worry her, so I casually responded, "That will most likely work. We'll have to see. Something has come up, so we may have to put it off till tomorrow." To avoid further discussion at this time I said, "I'll tell you about it after the service. It's about to begin." I then escorted her to the seats I had selected for us.

The service began close to schedule. The Reverend Gunther began the service with a "Welcome to all" message. Then the organist played "Going to Kansas City" as Vincent had requested in his last will and testament. The reverend then spoke of what he had learned of Vincent's life, the good and the not so good. Gunther addressed the fact that success was not the only goal in life for Vincent or for any of us. The number of friends and associates who were here were a testament to Vincent's personality and his good soul. He expounded on Vincent's philanthropy and personal service to the Kansas City community.

I thought, *Bravo, good job!*

He then, with what could be described as brutal honesty, told of Vincent's childhood years—years that had left him with emotional scars, scars created by an unstable mother, experiencing poverty one month and riches the next. The church was silent. Gunther ended this segment of the service with the song "Somewhere Over The Rainbow." This was a song that he said was Vincent's favorite, and having just heard the minister's description of Vincent's early years, it was so moving.

Sammy and Joanie declined to give a eulogy but George Cavallas did address the congregation. His comments were brief. "If you were lucky enough to know Vincent Houten, then you have an experience to cherish. I ask the hundreds here in attendance, why are you here?" Answering his own rhetorical question, he said, "You have to honestly answer that Vincent Xavier Houten added to your lives."

George's comments, though brief, were very touching. If I were convinced George was not involved in Vincent's murder, I might have even been moved.

There were a few testaments, mostly political proclamations that meant nothing.

After the proclamations were read, the reverend concluded the service with an insight into the gospel passage where Jesus tells his disciples that His Father's mansion has many rooms. Gunther then interpreted that reading to mean that there was a room for all sinners in heaven, and he gently pointed out that there was not one here today who was not a sinner. I concluded that meant there was therefore a room for Vincent Xavier Houten.

The service now ending, I approached the casket, motioning to the pallbearers to join me. I instructed them to turn the casket toward the church's gothic doors and wait until I had assembled the family and close friends. Sam, Joanie, and her family exited their pew and stood directly behind the casket. I turned toward the other side of the main aisle and mentioned to George that he should join the procession, which he did.

With the procession assembled, we slowly proceeded down the aisle, and the organ began playing "The Saints Go Marching In." The whole church sang along. They started joining in slowly, but by the time we reached the rear of the church, the place was rocking. It had the feeling of an authentic Kansas City jazz funeral.

Vincent's casket was carried to the hearse. I had set Joanie, Sammy, and George shoulder to shoulder in a receiving line to personally thank all who had attended the service as they exited. Who they wanted to invite to the luncheon at the Carriage Club was up to them. The plan was to have Sam, Joanie, and George follow the hearse in their limousine to the cemetery for a brief committal. Then they would join the guests at the Carriage Club.

It took more than thirty minutes for the receiving line to thank all of the guests. The hearse and the limousine had been waiting at curbside in front of the Country Club Church as planned. Joanie, Sam, and George started down the church steps toward the limousine, and then George stopped, turned back toward us, and said, "Aren't you joining us?"

The last thing I wanted was to spend one minute in a limousine with three of the most likely murderers of my good friend. It was hard enough to be civil to them for the funeral service. I did not know what to say. Thankfully, my wife was in agreement and quickly said to George, "This is a special time for all of you. We'll see you later at the Carriage Club."

As the hearse and limo departed, I turned to my wife and asked, "Where the fuck are Chuck and Ed?" I guess my concern shocked her.

Audrey looked to me with a puzzled expression. "I don't know why that is important." Then with a woman's instinct, she asked the probing question, "What changed our travel plans?"

I hesitated, then began to explain to my wife but then hesitated again. How do you explain to your wife that you have been chosen to be the liaison to the Sacco crime family? How could she understand that being a liaison is only a temporary position and an unofficial position at that.

I finally brought myself to tell Audrey an abridged version of my morning encounter. "Honey there is no reason to elaborate, but I did have a visit from a member of the Sacco family when I left the hotel this morning."

I quickly added more information so as to try to limit the conversation, "Audrey he seriously and completely convinced me that the Saccos are not involved in this murder. That's good news that the Mafia is not involved in the Houten murder, don't you think?"

Not to be snowed (an expression we use in Jersey), my wife asked, "Nate, you were met by a member of the Sacco crime family and all he wanted was to tell you was that his family was not involved in Tri-State Tape or Vincent's murder?"

"Well, it was a little more than that. But that was the major theme of the conversation."

"Well, since I don't believe for a moment that you are being the slightest bit honest with me, I feel the need to ask what the minor theme of the conversation was. The not-so-major theme."

"It's no big deal. Honestly! They just asked that we say in town for a while longer to help straighten out the situation. And also to keep them informed of our progress." I sheepishly added, "Almost like a liaison."

Audrey was not buying it. "We are now the Sacco family liaison? And you say it's no big deal?"

I said, "I think when this is over we will have nothing more to do with the Sacco family. I don't know if I should even tell Chuck."

I was trying to shelter my wife from the fact that we were now involved in a crime that involved organized crime. In desperation, I suggested, "Let's change the subject, honey. I have a car service waiting to take us to the Carriage Club. Let's go to Vincent's luncheon, try to enjoy some of his friends, and then contact Chuck."

Learning of my encounter with a member of the Sacco crime family quickly changed Audrey's demeanor. My wife angrily said, "I can't believe Chuck wasn't at the service today. He told us they would be there. I'm not letting you change the subject. Call Chuck right now."

CHAPTER THIRTY-FIVE

As directed by my wife, as soon as we got into the car-service sedan, I called Chuck Gerity's cell phone. I was not convinced that I should tell him about my morning encounter with the Sacco family's representative. Not just yet. To my surprise he answered my call on the second ring as if expecting my call.

"I thought you would be at the service today. Was I wrong to assume that?" I was having a difficult time controlling my frustration. I felt my wife and I deserved a little handholding from Chuck and Ed.

The detective explained, "There are a number of breaking developments that consumed our time. And as I'm sure you are aware, there were a number of police officers at the church. We felt that your safety was never compromised." Then with an air of sarcasm he said, "I'm sure the attendees at Mr. Houten's funeral service didn't miss us."

I don't know about all of the attendees, but I know after my cordial meeting with the Sacco representative, I would have welcomed their presence. I waited for the right time to bring up the Sacco encounter.

Detective Gerity elaborated. "Ed and I are trying to tie up loose ends. Salvatore Liguria is starting to cooperate. Florence Mosley has been giving us some more insight into the Christopher and Samuel relationship, and we are making every effort to investigate the relationship between George Cavallas, Bert Kelty, and the Sacco family." Chuck once again sarcastically concluded, "I felt that was more important than listening to eulogies."

I bit my tongue and simply asked, "Are you planning to be at the Carriage Club for the luncheon? There's a thing or two that I think we need to discuss."

"Yes. Ed and I plan on being there no later than two. We hope to have enough put together to bring the three into custody and bring this to a close." That was good news, to say the least. It made it easier to go to Vincent's luncheon and put up a good front.

I decided to put in a dinger and let both detectives know of my visit from the Sacco family. "I'm glad to hear that you can make it to the repast since you were too busy to attend the funeral service, and I guess things were a little bit too busy this morning when I left the hotel to go to the church."

Detective Gerity then directly asked, "How was your discussion with Pauli Ferguson today?"

I didn't get it. "OK, Chuck. Let's stop with the games. Who is Pauli Ferguson?"

Detective Peterson had briefed Gerity about the Kansas City crime family and the identity of my driver. He answered my question. "He is the son of Angelica Sacco Ferguson. Angelica is Vito Sacco's sister. Vito is the head of the family. This case has to be very important to the family to have his nephew Pauli come to visit you."

I asked, "How do you know it was Pauli?"

Peterson answered. "We had a plainclothes detective posing as a cabbie in one of the taxis in front of the hotel. He was supposed to pick you up and serve as your ride. He was fortunate enough to ID Ferguson in one of the other cabs. Wisely he backed off and radioed in for assistance. We set up a tail. The tail was on you all the way around KC and then to the church."

"That's reassuring, but tell me more about Pauli. How much more scared should I be than I am right now?"

Detective Ed answered. "There's not much to tell. Pauli is family and moving up in the ranks. What did he want from you?"

I told the detectives the basics of our conversation. I could see my wife stiffening with concern as I detailed Pauli's denial of the Sacco family involvement and his appointment of me as his information gatherer. I relayed that the Saccos knew a lot about the case because he said that Audrey and I were the only ones who didn't have any financial connection or motive.

I ended by telling them the last thing Pauli said to me, his warning: "If you don't clear this up soon, the Sacco family will get involved and clean it up—completely."

CHAPTER THIRTY-SIX

Audrey and I arrived at the Carriage Club. It was crowded with Vincent's saddened friends and some of those best described as moochers, who were mourning the loss of Vincent's many parties rather then the loss of Vincent.

Audrey and I decided that we should serve as the unofficial host and hostess until Joanie, Sam, and George arrived from the cemetery. So we moved through the crowd saying hello and exchanging brief memories with those we knew and introducing ourselves to those we had not previously met.

I took a minute to text our travel agent Patty to instruct her to cancel our flight reservations. There was no way to get out of this puzzle and make a three thirty flight.

The party of three arrived from the brief committal service within the hour, as was expected. Joanie entered the Carriage Club with the air of a socialite at her coming-out party. George remained his lawyerly, subdued self. Sam, on the other hand, went directly to the service bar and ordered bourbon rocks.

Surprisingly, it was a pleasant event. Sharing stories of Vincent's pool parties and the countless impromptu cocktail parties was like reliving them. Each person who offered his experience added a new layer to the memory picture that we, and I assume the others, wanted to hold onto.

Shocking to me and to my wife was that a few women, some single and some not, were willing and surprisingly anxious to confess to their sexual dalliance with our deceased buddy. A quickie here, an afternoon there, and the occasional business trip to Vince's Goodtime Villa. He was quite the guy, but we knew that already. Audrey commented to me, "Nate, I think I'm one of the only women under seventy here that hasn't slept with Vincent." That honestly had never crossed my mind, but I was a bit relieved just the same.

Two o'clock came and went. My wife and I were not clock watching, but when it got close to three, we realized that the good detectives were past their designated schedule. We had had a few vodkas, and we were quite tired from the emotional strain of the day. Audrey and I didn't think waiting for the police to bring a conclusion to the case would change anything, so we opted to leave.

We said our obligatory good-byes to Joanie and then to George, but when we found Sammy, he was sitting at the service bar and appeared quite drunk. I started the conversation mundanely, "Sam, I'm glad we were able to be a part of your brother's service. I hope that we will have a reason to meet up with you in the future."

Sam slurred a "thank you for your help," then said, "Let me walk you to your car."

"Sammy, that's not necessary. We called a car service. It should be outside, waiting for us." Samuel Houten would not take no for an answer. We walked together out the front entrance and started toward our right and the waiting hired sedan, which was no more than twenty-five feet away.

A now very sober Samuel Houten said, "Not that way. This way." He showed us a pistol that he was now pointing at us. He held it close to his side and below his waist. It was partially covered by his blazer so as not to be visible to someone passing by. "I thought you two would never leave."

I tried to do a cool you-don't-scare-me act. "Sammy, you play a very convincing drunk. What is it that you're playing now?"

"I'm not playing anything now, but if you don't do as I say, then you are playing with your lives. My car is the gray Jeep near the end of the driveway. Let's go." Sam made his point. His voice was a little high pitched. He sounded anxious, maybe even a bit scared. Audrey and I did as we were ordered.

We got into the back seat of his Jeep and were instructed to put on the seat belts. "If I hear a buckle open, I won't ask who. I'll just shoot you both. Understood?"

I wanted to say "Capiche," but I knew this was no time to try humor to lighten the tension. I replied, "We understand."

Sam got in the driver's seat and, still holding the pistol in his right hand, buckled his seat belt using only his left. He turned to check us out and make sure we were buckled in as he had instructed. He then backed out of the parking space and drove toward the exit and onto Ward Parkway, all while still holding his pistol.

Audrey calmly but with a stern voice asked, "Sammy, why are you doing this? Where are you taking us?"

Sammy seemed irritated by the question. "I know Gerity and Peterson are getting close. It's time for me to cut my ties. I'm going to New Mexico, and you're going as far as I need you to help get me there. You two keep getting in my way. Now you're going to help me for a change."

Audrey waited a moment and then said, "I don't understand, Sam. How are we always getting in your way? We hardly know you."

"You two enjoyed more of my brother's money than his whole family. We got nothing. All I tried to do was get some help through some tough times, but Vince was too busy partying with you two in Palm Beach." Samuel Houten was obviously bitter, more bitter than we would have anticipated, and he was directing his bitterness toward us.

My wife switched to a softer, more soothing voice to try to reason with Vincent's brother. "Sam, you're not suggesting that Nate and I allowed your brother to pay for our entertainment. We never needed your brother's money to enjoy Palm Beach. We just needed your brother's company."

Sammy snapped, "I don't believe that for a fucking moment."

My wife continued in the same soft voice, trying to calm him down. "OK, Sam, even if you're right, it's Vincent's money after all. He should have been able to spend it as he pleased."

Shouting at Audrey, Sam Houten said, "No, it's not. It's not his money. He got the oil wells, the only ones that paid off. He tricked our mother just as he tricked Janet Harding into marrying him and then took over her family's business. Florence and I got the worthless stock. He used mother's money to buy Tri-State Tape."

My wife and I didn't have to say anything, or in any way attempt to communicate with each other. We knew that we were in the back seat of a car driven by a psycho. I knew there was no need for Audrey to continue to try to soothe the beast. We had to escape. I was waiting for an opportunity.

I kept looking out the window, hoping for inspiration. With my right hand, I held my wife's left. As we passed street after street, I knew our chances of escape grew slimmer. Once we left Kansas City and entered the highway, we were going to be in for a long ride.

CHAPTER THIRTY-SEVEN

Detectives Chuck Gerity and Ed Peterson had just left KC police headquarters and were headed to the Carriage Club for Vincent's luncheon when they learned of our predicament from the KC cops who were suppose to be protecting us. They immediately notified the hostage management team of the Missouri state police. Arresting Joanie, George, and Sam would now have to wait.

The detectives were in their police cruiser on speakerphone and receiving advice from Captain O'Neil, head of the state police special unit. Detective Peterson informed the captain that Samuel Houten was driving through KC business district in a late-model Jeep and appeared to be heading for Route 35.

O'Neil spoke in an unemotional, routine voice. "The initial strategy is always to defuse the tension. I suggest that we allow him to leave Kansas City, then set up the first confrontation a few hours later, maybe at the Oklahoma border. That will give him five or six hours to calm down."

Detective Peterson took the lead. "Captain O'Neil, please arrange for that, but we are going to try to catch up with the Houten vehicle. We have two patrol cars following it as we speak, and we are hoping that there may be an opportunity to intercept Samuel Houten before he reaches Route 35."

Captain O'Neil advised, "Proceed very cautiously."

I didn't know that two police cars were following us, but if I did, I didn't think it would have changed my decision to try our escape. In hindsight, I was glad to be oblivious to the hostage management team's plan for us to spend countless hours driving with a nut until we reached the Oklahoma border. Knowing that plan would have probably made me more desperate to escape and most likely act more recklessly.

We approached a traffic circle that had a considerable amount of congestion. As we approached, we could see that the congestion was caused by a broken-down service delivery van in the left lane. I thought it was now or never.

I squeezed my wife's hand, not to reassure her but to alert her that she was about to be ejected. I slowly reached for the rear car door handle and we both took hold of our seat belt buckle. Due to the traffic, our car slowed to about ten miles per hour. I leaned slightly over my wife and reached for the door handle that would free my wife, and as I did, the windshield popped.

Our abductor Samuel Houten slumped down into his seat. Audrey and I were startled enough to freeze in confusion. For the first second or two, I didn't know what had happened. But as Sam slowly settled lower in his seat, I could see the bullet hole in the windshield.

Our car drifted across two lanes of traffic and settled on a landscaped berm. We were fortunate that we didn't crash into other cars. From the time of the gunshot until the car stopped, things moved in slow motion. It was quite surreal. We heard the pop sound from the windshield. Then the car seemed to float across the traffic lanes unto the grassy divide before settling on the raised landscaped berm. No crash, no trauma, just a feeling of floating, then stopping.

My wife was quite shaken to say the least and with little composure angrily rambled, "That was reckless. We could have been
killed. How could Chuck have put us in such danger."

Audrey assumed that the police had shot Sammy in their attempt to rescue us. I hadn't thought that far ahead. I was trying to
figure out what just happened. I began by questioning where the
shot could have come from. Was the shooter in a passing car, or
was he on a rooftop, or could he have been behind a fence on the
grassy knoll or in a book depository, JFK style?

I looked back toward the traffic circle were the Jeep had been
when the bullet struck the windshield. I tried to envision being the
shooter. Where would I choose to position myself to get the best
shot? As I contemplated the shooter's options, I suddenly noticed
that the disabled service van that had caused the congestion was
now gone.

Audrey, still anxious, asked, "Nate, what do you think we should
do now?"

I didn't want to spend any more time in the car with our dead
driver but the obvious question was, where were we safer to wait
in the car or out in the open? In answering my own question I
thought that Sammy wasn't very safe in the car, so I suggested,
"Let's get out and wait for the police, they wouldn't be long."

Within three minutes or so, two unmarked cruisers drove over
the landscaped area between the road and the berm, directly toward us. They stopped about thirty feet from us. I had a feeling of
relief. My anxiety and fear for my wife's safety were quickly subsid-
ing. That lasted until the two police officers exited their vehicles
with guns drawn. "On the ground, face down."

I looked to my wife and moaned, "What the fuck?" That was
becoming one of my more regularly used expressions.

"I said down. Now!"

We did as ordered. One officer stood over us while the other
inspected the car. He must have quickly determined that Sammy

was dead, and the officer had to observe that the bullet came from outside the car. I thought this should be over soon. Not as soon as I was hoping.

Audrey and I remained on our bellies on the wet, melting snow while the officers decided what to do with us. The officer who inspected the vehicle came back to where his partner was standing watch over us. He then leaned over us, and after giving us a thorough pat-down, he told his partner, "They're clean. Let them up."

By the time we got to our feet, the officer who patted us down was on his radio describing the scene to someone on the other end. His partner said nothing but still held his gun drawn. I wasn't face down in the snow, but I wasn't completely relieved, not yet and not with a police pistol pointed in our direction.

Audrey was beginning to shiver. Who dressed for the possibility of being frisked while lying face down in four inches of wet snow? In any case, she never did do well with the cold.

Next, just to make things more bizarre, two marked Missouri state-police vehicles came roaring toward the berm from opposite directions with their sirens howling and lights flashing. Their tires tore through the wet snow, causing grass and mud to fly up in their wake.

It now looked like the set of a B movie. One clueless officer had a gun pointed at the victims, another was talking on his radio, and two state police officers stood in the background looking like they were deciding whom to shoot first.

Finally, another unmarked cruiser approached to join the show. In contrast to the prior dramatic entrances, it approached slowly and quietly. After the car came to a stop in what was becoming a police parking lot, out stepped Detective Gerity and Detective Peterson.

Detective Peterson walked directly toward our guard. "You can stand down. Secure your weapon." Peterson was the ranking officer on the scene. The hostage rescue unit was part of the state police, and since we were no longer hostages, that unit no longer had a role in the situation.

Detective Peterson summoned the other police officer who had guarded us, and the three walked toward Sammy's car, away from Audrey and me. The hostage rescue unit decided, or I suppose they might have been ordered, to leave the scene. Both of their vehicles slipped and slid as they attempted to exit the grassy area. They seemed to have had no regard to the damage their tires were causing to the half-frozen grass.

Detective Gerity walked up to us and asked, "Are you both all right?" The hectic scene had played out in no more than ninety seconds.

I wasn't certain if I wanted to hug Chuck Gerity or punch him in the nose. I knew that he and Peterson would quickly relieve us from any suspicion as to Sam Houten's shooting. But where had they been when we needed them? I simply said to Detective Gerity and without emotion, "She's freezing."

CHAPTER THIRTY-EIGHT

We sat in the detectives' police car for about twenty minutes. The car heater made the time we spent there more pleasant than standing out in the cold, but not by much. A car heater does not dry wet clothes very quickly.

Both detectives Peterson and Gerity got into the car at the same time. Ed Peterson informed us that we were going to police headquarters to review the details of this afternoon's event and inform us of what he and Chuck had uncovered since our last in-depth conversation.

The last in-depth conversation in which my wife and I felt that we were receiving open and honest exchange of information was more than forty-eight hours ago. If the detectives were going to have another open and honest conversation, we could be looking at a very lengthy meeting. That type of exchange we probably could have endured, but I had my doubts about just how open and honest they would be.

I wasn't going to allow my wife and me to be subjected to a common jailhouse interview. I said forcefully, "No, we're not going to police headquarters. We're going straight to the InterContinental. Our clothes are wet, and my wife is freezing."

Detective Peterson informed us in an official tone that there were procedures to follow and then added, "I must insist."

"Fuck you and your procedures." Enough was enough. What more could they want from us? I wasn't finished. "Where were you two when we needed you? What procedures did you follow when you let me be hijacked by the Sacco family, when you didn't show up for the funeral service, when you assigned a couple of KC traffic cops to protect us?"

Audrey then joined in. "What procedures did you follow that couldn't even protect us from being kidnapped by Sammy Houten in broad daylight? And where in your procedure manual does it say that after the kidnapper is shot that you then assume the victims become the suspects and make them lay face down in the snow?"

Detective Peterson began to respond, but Chuck sheepishly intervened. "Ed, it can wait. Let's go to the hotel." He then looked back over the front seat and said, "How about we give you a few hours to clean up, and we'll meet you in your suite?" That suited my wife and me just fine.

When we got back to our suite, Audrey jumped into the bathroom first. I got out of my damp clothes, put on the hotel's terrycloth robe, and hit the minibar. I had just taken my first sip when the phone rang.

I let the phone ring a few times while I considered whether to answer it or not. I just wanted to chill out and have my drink. But so much had happened that day that I thought I had better pick it up.

The voice on the other end was a familiar one. "Hey, just wanted to apologize for the extra excitement today."

It was Pauli Ferguson, and although I hadn't anticipated a call from the Saccos, it wasn't a complete surprise. My response was nonconfrontational. "It was a little over the top."

Pauli began giving me some information without admitting anything. "Mr. Stevens, how much did you and your wife want to take a long ride with your host, Grizzly Adams?" It was a rhetorical question so I waited, saying nothing. Pauli continued after a minute or two. "Someone, I can't guess who, thought the PR was bad enough here in KC, but if there was an O. J. Simpson-type car chase, well, let's just say it's better that it came to an end."

I knew I was speaking to Pauli Ferguson, but I didn't want to use his name on the phone. I thought of it as an effort to win some trust from him and to maintain deniability for both of us if that issue ever became necessary. I asked, "Sir, my wife and I had two Kansas City police assigned to us for our security. How did you know we were being abducted right under their noses?"

"Oh please, I thought you were from Jersey. Whatever the police know, we know first. They were watching the crowd. We were watching Sammy Houten."

Pauli seemed to be dropping his guard a bit, so I pressed my luck. "Then your people arranged for the delivery van to break down to slow the traffic?"

Pauli seemed to catch himself. Maybe he was saying too much, and he suddenly became cautious. "I'm not saying yes, and I'm not saying no. I'm saying that whoever helped relieve you of your driver, well, that was child's play." He then delivered the message that he most likely was sent to deliver. "I'm being nice to you because we feel you both got caught up in something that you had nothing to do with. But now since this is cleaned up, it's time to go. The sooner you leave Kansas City, the sooner the publicity dies down."

I immediately responded that that was exactly our plans but asked one last question. "Can you help fill in some blanks?"

Pauli, right in character, said, "Maybe yes, maybe no."

I pressed on. "We thought George and Bert were working together and with you. Now that we know that you or your family were not involved, and Sam and Christopher Houten have been exposed. Can you tell me if I can trust George Cavallas?"

Pauli Ferguson let out a little laugh. "You're a smart man. You spent enough time this afternoon with Grizzly Adams to come to your own opinion. Christopher Houten, Bert Kelty, the accountant Curtis Thomas, and Sammy Houten—all dead. Who's left? Joan Olsen and George Cavallas. Enough said. Now you should make some travel plans."

I responded, "Capiche."

With that, Pauli Ferguson chuckled and hung up.

I heard movement in the bathroom. I had only a minute or two before Audrey would be joining me. I frantically tried to develop a plan and a plausible explanation that my wife would think was not completely crazy. The detectives wanted to talk to us and the Mafia wanted us out of town. My vote was to get out of town. I didn't want to have to explain all this to Audrey after the day we had just experienced.

CHAPTER THIRTY-NINE

While Audrey was monopolizing the bathroom, I ran a few possibilities through my mind of how to escape our Kansas City trap. We could lie to Detective Gerity by telling him that we would meet with him in the morning, then sneak out the service entrance, just bolt to the airport, and take any plane that was going to South Florida.

I also contemplated just blowing him off and not agreeing to cooperate. After all, what more did we owe him? That strategy would most likely entail bunkering down in our hotel suite for God only knew how long. Other than those two options, I was coming up blank.

The idea of refusing to cooperate was stupid because even if we were within our rights as witnesses to decide not to cooperate, Chuck and Ed could most likely restrict us from leaving KC for some time. That would mean engaging a lawyer and filing objections and on and on. Anyway, despite not having a plan, I called our travel agent Patty and asked her to get us on the earliest flight to Fort Lauderdale the next day. We would just have to deal with Detectives Gerity and Peterson and throw ourselves on their mercy.

Audrey came out of the bathroom in the matching terry-cloth robe. Her hair pulled back, she now appeared far more relaxed. I asked if she were ready for a cocktail, which she acknowledged would be very welcome, but before I got to the minibar, she said, "I heard the phone ringing while I was taking my bath. Who was it?"

Buying myself an additional minute or two, I said, "Let me make your drink. Then I'll tell you."

I iced a cocktail glass. Then I opened a nip of Gray Goose, located a can of grapefruit juice in the well-stocked minibar, and assembled my wife's favorite cocktail, vodka on the rocks with a splash of grapefruit. I wasn't really stalling per se, but I wasn't rushing. I was deliberating.

I decided to answer Audrey's question without delving into great detail. I simply told her that Pauli Ferguson called, and he suggested that we leave town so that the bad PR his family was receiving would die down. I thought that that was vague enough, but as it turned out, it was more than enough to cause her to become very anxious once again.

Audrey's eyes widened, and she spoke very quickly, almost tripping over her words, "Nate, I don't care if they are in Kansas City, Jersey City, or Brooklyn, New York—the Mafia is the Mafia. They are serious about their business and you are now on a first name basis with the Kansas City don's nephew. This is nuts!"

I wanted to calm my wife, but she was absolutely right. In New Jersey, there had been occasions where Audrey and I would be at an event where some of the guests were obviously "connected," as the northeast expression goes. But seeing members of the Mafia from across a dining room or saying hello over a cocktail was not the same as riding in a car against your will and receiving phone calls with specific instructions. This was definitely nuts.

There were still a lot of questions that we would like answered by our detective friends. Many things just didn't add up, and I (and I'm sure my wife) still wanted to be involved in solving the murder of our friend Vincent Houten. Right now, however, like our good buddy Peter Kunz, we were done. Emotionally drained.

Audrey and I were committed to leaving Kansas City sooner than later. The only things in our way were the Kansas City police, the Missouri state police, and the Palm Beach police. What complicated things even more was that although the Vincent Houten murder had occurred in Palm Beach and was technically under the jurisdiction of the PB detectives, the murders of Samuel Houten and Curtis Thomas, as well as the unsolved disappearance of Bert Kelty, all had taken place in Kansas City. Now the Palm Beach police, specifically, our friendly Detective Gerity, had less influence in this case with every new development.

I suggested that I could try to put the detectives off until tomorrow. Once we heard from Patty and knew when we could leave, we could then decide how to deal with Chuck and Ed. I told Audrey that I didn't think they would agree to wait till tomorrow, but I would try.

If the detectives insisted on meeting in our hotel suite, then I thought it best to give them our full cooperation. If they were satisfied by what we could contribute in our meeting, than hopefully leaving tomorrow wouldn't be a problem.

I began thinking that maybe I had just developed Plan B, but then realized that plan number Plan B was out of our hands. It most probably was not going to be our brainchild to implement. It was going to be up to the detectives.

My wife asked me, "Can they make us stay?"

I wanted to be positive, but I really didn't know. What little legal experience I had gained over the years did not involve murder. I speculated anyway. "We are witnesses to a crime, not suspects in that crime. We have cooperated with the police throughout this investigation, and that should hold some weight."

I went on. "What would be the benefit of detaining us in Kansas City when we would be just as cooperative in Palm Beach?" A thought suddenly came to me: maybe we could convince Chuck and Ed that we would be more cooperative in Palm Beach, since there we would feel a lot safer from the Sacco family.

I didn't wait for Detective Gerity to contact us. I initiated the first call, "Hey, Chuck. I got a call from Pauli Ferguson: not very important, nothing exciting. How about we talk about it tomorrow? Audrey and I could use a break." I really didn't think that approach would go over very well, but I gave it a shot anyway. I also knew as soon as I mentioned Pauli's name, it was a mistake that I would regret.

"Sorry, Nate, but it can't wait. We're on our way. Ed and I should be there in fifteen minutes."

Audrey was sitting across the cocktail table from me and heard my end of the brief phone conversation with Detective Gerity. She didn't need to guess what he said. She just asked, "How much time do I have to get dressed?"

"He said they're on their way."

My wife was not pleased. She looked emotionally exhausted. She pulled herself up from the club chair and slowly walked back into the bathroom to do her makeup and such, leaving me to wait my turn for the bathroom once again.

CHAPTER FORTY

Our travel agent called me in our hotel suite while Audrey and I were waiting to meet with Detectives Gerity and Peterson. She notified me that the earliest available flight the next day to Fort Lauderdale was at 11:45 a.m. I wouldn't say that yet another change in our plans was annoying her, but she sounded a bit frustrated, which was understandable. This was the third change in twenty-four hours.

"Do you know how much you have incurred in flight cancelation and rebooking fees?"

I didn't know, but I thought maybe we could charge them to the Kansas City police department or the Vincent Houten estate or for that matter, the Sacco family. Just dreaming.

I got out of the hotel robe I was wearing, threw on a pair of kakis and a golf shirt, and waited for the detectives with a cocktail in my hand. Soon, Chuck Gerity called from the hotel lobby to ask if it was OK to come to our suite. The suite was quite nice. It had a bedroom and a separate sitting room but just one bathroom, of which my wife had still not relinquished control. I told him it would be fine. "Come right up."

I knocked on the bathroom door to give my wife notice of the pending arrival, and as I did, the door opened. Audrey stepped into the sitting area looking stunning. She immediately noticed the cocktail in my hand and said, "That looks good."

"Vodka and grapefruit juice?"

"Why not?" she responded.

I handed my wife her cocktail and put a few extra ice cubes and an additional splash of vodka in mine. I thought a little extra fortification was in order. After all, this could be a lengthy meeting.

The two detectives entered our suite looking very serious. Audrey and I sat together on the love seat, Chuck Gerity took the club chair, and Ed Peterson sat in a desk chair I had brought over from the other side of the room. The first thing I wanted to know was where were the two detectives had been throughout the day, but it was their meeting, and they were not going to talk about anything until we first discussed my conversation with Pauli Ferguson.

Without even the briefest of pleasantries, Detective Gerity flipped open his note pad and leaning forward. "What time did he call?"

I paused before responding. I knew we had substantially assisted in the multiple investigations, but my wife and I were not Gerity's police partners nor his subordinates. We were in fact victims, victims of abduction and kidnapping, as well as emotional victims as witnesses to violent trauma. Our kidnapper/chauffer, Sammy Houten, had been shot and killed not more than two feet away from us. It would have been nice to have a little recognition of that.

I gave a curt response to Chuck's question. "What time did who call?" After a pause, I added, "And how has your day been?"

Detective Gerity ignored my wisecrack and then simply asked, "What did Pauli Ferguson say?"

I snapped back, "He said that whatever the police knows, he knows first." I took a sip of my vodka for effect then added, "Based on the events of today, I find it hard to dispute that. What do you think, Chuck?" I still wanted their reason, their strategy, and their excuse for not supporting us throughout the day, a day not like any other in our lives.

Detective Peterson intervened with a little more compassion. "OK, Nate. I understand you had an unusually difficult day, but we are dealing with the deaths of four individuals and the disappearance of another. These are not common, everyday events for any police department." The tension in the air could be cut with a knife. Detective Peterson let the tension settle for a moment or two before saying, "I understand that you feel that we let you down, but one of the important elements of this case is the Sacco family. We need to have an understanding of the Sacco family's involvement, and you are the only one to have any firsthand contact."

I took a deep breath and dropped the attitude. Busting the detective's chops any further wasn't going to accomplish anything. I tried to recall every word of the conversation with Pauli Ferguson.

I expressed my opinion that Pauli's claim made earlier that morning of his family's lack of involvement in the Houten murder or the embezzlement from Tri-State Tape were true. I relayed that his main concern now was to put this whole episode behind and let the publicity die down. I explained that his message to me was a simple one. "Now it's time to go."

I told the detectives that Pauli implied that he had arranged the shooting of Sammy Houten, but he was careful not to actually admit to it. Whether the detectives gave any credence to my insight was up to them.

Audrey looked toward me a bit confused and said, "You never told me that."

Now I was confused. "What did you think happened?"

She then sheepishly confessed, "I thought Chuck and Ed arranged the shooting."

Detective Gerity shook his head. "Audrey, no police department would take that type of action and place civilians in that much danger." He then continued to explain that whoever did shoot Samuel Houten was either a marksman or a very lucky shot because the bullet was a direct hit to the heart causing near instant death.

We returned to the details of my conversation with the don's nephew, reviewing word for word what I could recall. During that time, Audrey and I found out that a bullet to the torso was not as reliable a causer of immediate death as a bullet to the head. Peterson said, "The shooter was obviously taking your safety into account."

No additional information was necessary for me to appreciate that the torso shot was far safer for us passengers in the rear seat of the car and, just as important, far less messy. I thought, *How thoughtful of Pauli.*

Detectives Gerity and Peterson finally ran out of questions for me regarding my brief conversation with Pauli Ferguson. If the detectives had come to any conclusions about the Sacco family, they didn't share them with Audrey and me. Before I could ask Chuck and Ed what the fuck they had been doing all day, my wife far more diplomatically said, "Please tell us what was going on behind the screen today."

Detective Peterson answered defensively, "We had you covered throughout the day. The decision to allow Pauli Ferguson to pick Nate up at the hotel this morning was based on a few assumptions, and those assumptions ultimately proved correct." He then explained, "Pauli had to know that Kansas City police had been assigned to protect you. He most likely didn't even have a weapon in case we decided to confront him. If the intent of the Sacco family was to harm you, they would never expose someone as high up as the don's nephew to do it."

From that, I surmised that they—they being the joint police brain trust—decided to follow Pauli and me so as to let me be the gatherer of information and then unceremoniously become the liaison to Sacco Incorporated. Ed Peterson's point was that I was really never in danger…well, not grave danger. OK, really?

I took a little while to absorb Peterson's account of my trip with Pauli Ferguson. I concluded that considering all that happened throughout the day, my ride with Pauli was not the highlight of the day after all. I was not the target of a hit or anything. How silly of me to have been so upset.

I tried to convince myself to get over it. What the police brain trust did was take a calculated risk that had worked. I could accept the reasoning behind their decision. I was just glad that the abduction didn't include my wife.

Detective Peterson continued to recount the day's activities. "When you were in church for the funeral service, Chuck was in constant contact with Palm Beach while the interrogation of Salvatore Liguria was going on. Since Pauli Ferguson and the Sacco family just entered the picture, I was running down our contacts inside the Sacco organization." Peterson reflectively added, "It was a pretty hectic time."

Chuck, appealing for our understanding, said, "Nobody could have anticipated Samuel Houten kidnapping you both at the repast."

I thought, *Well, Pauli did,* but I thought better of saying it aloud. What I did say was that somehow Sam Houten knew or had enough information to anticipate that the police were getting close to arresting him, and he then obviously panicked.

The InterContinental was a first-class hotel, but it wasn't home. My wife and I had been through enough. We wanted to get back to familiar surroundings. We were fine with going to Palm Beach rather than New Jersey so as to be available for Detective Gerity, but we wanted out. We had a flight scheduled for 11:45 in the morning, and I was determined that we would be on it.

There was more to discuss: George, Joanie, Salvatore, and who knows what else might come up, but I wanted to wrap this session up. "Gentlemen, I think any more conversation will be either speculative or redundant. I suggest we call it a night. It's been a long day." Both Chuck and Ed seemed to agree with my suggestion, but when I then told them quite matter-of-factly that we would be leaving in the morning, they had a different reaction all together.

Detective Peterson was first to comment. "This investigation is far from over. There is no way we can allow you to leave." He continued very sternly, "You both are important participants, and we are sure to need your continued cooperation."

I then responded emphatically and without hesitation. "Detective Peterson, you will have our complete cooperation just like Detective Gerity had our complete cooperation in Palm Beach when this all started."

My statement surprised the detectives. They looked at each other, and although they didn't say anything, both appeared to be thinking of the consequences that might result from our leaving KC. They remained silent for more than a minute or two.

After waiting for the two detectives to come to a consensus on how they felt about Audrey and me leaving, I decided to let them know how strongly I felt about the issue. "Let me recap. First thing this morning, I get a tour of Kansas City with the famous Pauli Ferguson. He wants me to clean 'this' up. He says if 'this' situation doesn't get cleaned up soon, the family will clean it up—completely. Pauli must have gotten impatient because six hours later the situation was cleaned up. He then brags to me how easy it was to do and tells me that my wife and I should get out of town."

Detective Peterson continued to take the lead in this discussion and continued sternly saying, "All that is very true, but we need you both to stay for at least a day or two. We will give you twenty-four-hour protection."

I calmly responded, "No offense, Ed, but we had protection today and got mixed results. We are dealing with professionals."

I decided to ignore Detective Peterson and directed my comments to Detective Gerity. Looking only at him, I began by reminding him just how professionally Pauli Ferguson had acted today. I began in a calm but deliberate voice. "Despite knowing that I had police protection at the hotel this morning, Pauli boldly posed as a cab driver and gave me an unsolicited tour of Kansas City. Then while the KC police were 'protecting' us at the luncheon from whatever our protectors thought was important, Pauli was watching what he thought was more important—Samuel Houten."

I continued to make my case. "Twenty minutes after Sam kidnapped us, Pauli Ferguson somehow was able to arrange for a delivery van to break down in the middle of a traffic circle, and just to show off a little, he had a sharpshooter in place waiting to take out Sammy Houten. Wow!"

I waited a minute for the detectives to consider the events of the day and then commented, "Pretty impressive and quite professional, I would have to say. Unless you good detectives are prepared to place us under arrest, we are going to get on the eleven-forty-five flight back to Fort Lauderdale tomorrow morning, where our car has been gathering dust in long-term parking. I don't think that is being the least bit unreasonable."

CHAPTER FORTY-ONE

After Gerity and Peterson finally left, Audrey and I spent the rest of Thursday evening in our hotel suite. We survived on room service and cocktails. We were quite tired and emotionally spent, but as the time passed, our interest in our friend Vincent Houten's murder gradually returned.

Maybe the cocktails were an elixir for our renewed passion, but regardless, we began discussing the multitude of unresolved possibilities and suspects. After our discussion met one dead end after other, we decided to call it a night. The case would have to wait. We would be seeing Detective Gerity in the morning, and for now, sleep was the priority.

Reluctantly, Gerity and Peterson had agreed to allow us to return to Palm Beach on our scheduled—or I should say rescheduled—flight Friday morning. However, Detective Gerity insisted that he personally drive us to the airport and that until then, we were not to venture out of the hotel, not even for a local breakfast or to buy a New York newspaper. Those conditions were easy to agree to. We would have agreed to far more just to be able to leave Kansas City behind us.

Chuck Gerity instructed us that he would be picking us up at the InterContinental at 10:00 a.m. Considering that we had an approximately forty-five-minute ride to the airport, that should enable us to arrive comfortably one hour ahead of the flight time.

Audrey and I had room service for breakfast and packed our bags rather quickly. I guess we were a bit over anxious to leave town because we now had some time to kill. We called for the bellman, checked out of our suite, and by 9:15, we were sitting in the hotel lobby bar with two Bloody Marys in front of us.

Chuck texted me that he was on his way and that he shouldn't be more than ten minutes. I texted back that we were in the lobby ready to go. I thought of asking if he would like a Bloody Mary for the road but thought better of it.

Chuck entered the hotel lobby almost at the exact time he had suggested. My wife and I had selected seats with a direct view of the front entrance of the hotel, so we saw him as soon as he arrived. It only took a minute or two for our gazes to meet, and Detective Gerity walked toward us. As he approached us, I motioned to our waitress to bring our check. Chuck didn't seem to have any reaction to our early morning cocktail and merely said, "I think we should go."

I settled our bar tab, and then my wife and I met Chuck at his cruiser, on loan from the Kansas City police pound. His car was standing directly in front of the hotel's main entrance, and the bellman was already placing our bags in the trunk. Nice service when you can get it. I opened the front passenger side door for my wife, but she countered by opened the rear door herself and sliding into the car before there could be any debate. I took the seat next to Chuck.

Detective Gerity drove out of the hotel entrance, made a left turn toward Ward Parkway, then headed east toward Highway 40. That was the same route I had had the pleasure of taking with Pauli Ferguson one day earlier. We hadn't gone more than a mile when Audrey asked very directly, "How does Salvatore Liguria fit into this picture?"

Detective Gerity didn't bother to review the facts that brought him and his team to the conclusion that Salvatore was the one who had passed along Vincent Houten's movements the days and hours before his death. He had shared his complete analysis of that with us not forty-eight hours earlier. The relationship between Megan and Salvatore and the question of who could have known where Vincent would park did not have to be repeated.

Chuck Gerity began answering Audrey's question by explaining the investigative process that he and his team followed. "The three questions we needed answered about Salvatore Liguria were these. Who did he pass the information to, what was his motive for passing along the information, and did he know the information he provided was part of the plan to murder Vincent Houten?"

Audrey impatiently waited for Chuck's answers to those three questions and when the detective remained silent for the next minute or two my wife exploded. "Enough of this cat-and-mouse game. Please answer the damn question. How involved was Salvatore Liguria?"

Detective Gerity, unfazed by Audrey's frustration, continued unemotionally. "We started to get results to our interrogation when Mr. Liguria realized he was considered an accessory to murder, wittingly or not."

Chuck summarized Salvatore's assertions for us in a nutshell. "First, Salvatore never met Christopher Houten and only spoke to Samuel Houten. Secondly, he claims that he had no idea that Samuel was planning to murder his brother. Lastly, and you'll love this, Salvatore was in love with Megan Kelly. Salvatore was jealous of Vincent Houten but he also viewed Vincent as a selfish woman-izer who used Megan as a convenient sex partner and treated her very disrespectfully. Salvatore had witnessed more than one inci-dent of Vincent verbally abusing and humiliating Megan in public, usually after far too many glasses of wine. Those incidents infuri-ated him."

I was trying to absorb the new twist Chuck was introducing to us. My wife had been correct a week ago when she speculated to Detective Gerity that Megan and Salvatore were most likely having an affair, although I'm sure she never contemplated how serious Salvatore's feelings were for Megan. Now we needed to know what made Salvatore switch from lover to informant on his lover's move-ments. He'd handed out the information that nearly got her killed.

Before I could ask the question, Detective Gerity detailed Salvatore's first encounter with Vincent's brother Samuel Houten. They were both in Palm Beach. Sam was making his infrequent but obligatory visit to his brother on his drive through Palm Beach to the Florida Keys, and Salvatore was in town just doing a dozen touch-ups or so before the Heart Ball.

Chuck recounted what Salvatore had told him, "A group of seven met at Vincent's house for cocktails, then went to the Colony Hotel for a poolside dinner. The group included Vincent and Megan, Sam, Peter Kunz, Salvatore, and the two of you, of course."

Audrey probably remembered the night in every detail, but I was struggling to recall even meeting Sam Houten in Palm Beach. We both remained silent and let Chuck continue to paint the pic-ture. I had always found history fascinating.

According to Salvatore's testimony, after dinner the group of five returned to Vincent's house while Audrey and I returned to our apartment. Apparently all involved had more than enough to drink, and an argument broke out between Megan and Vincent. Vincent decided to leave and go to the Chesterfield Hotel's Leopard Lounge for another glass of wine or two.

The Leopard Lounge was a one-block walk from Vincent's house and a frequent after-hours stop for him to, as he always said, "check the traps." Peter Kunz decided to follow his friend. That left Megan, Salvatore, and Samuel to stew over Vincent's behavior. The three had several more drinks until Megan fell asleep or more likely passed out on the couch. That's when Samuel and Salvatore revealed to each other their hatred for Vincent.

Audrey and I had the answer to the question of Salvatore's motive. It was clear what had inspired him to become an informant. It also reinforced what we believed was Samuel Houten's passionate jealousy toward his brother. That jealousy was what drove him to extremes.

We were also interested to find out from Salvatore's claims that he only spoke to Sam Houten not to Christopher, the shooter. If that proved true, then the only question left was whether he had known that there was a plan to murder Vincent Houten.

We both thought that Salvatore Liguria could never have been willingly involved in the murder plot. It didn't add up. It made far more sense to categorize him as a romantic caught up in a B-type TV episode than an accomplice in an A-type series of murders. But the question that still remained was: Why did he relay where Megan was the night she was forced off the road in Wellington?

We were approaching the airport exit, and although I would have liked to conclude the discussion of Salvatore's involvement, I was anxious to talk about George Cavallas and Joan Olsen before our time with Detective Gerity was over. I asked, "Chuck, before you leave us, can we talk about Joanie and George's involvement?"

Detective Gerity's tone of voice suggested he was in possession of information that we would like to have, but that he was reluctant to share it with us. He had been acting strangely the entire trip to the airport.

He addressed the question of Joanie and George's involvement sheepishly, "I could give you a little information, but I think it would be better if, before we speculate on their involvement, we let a few more things play out. I will tell you that it was George who hired Albert Thomas to search Tri-State Tape's books. That's quite revealing." He then said nothing further.

I looked over my shoulder to the back seat and saw my wife shaking her head in frustration. Then she asked, "Is that all you can tell us? What type of things are you expecting to play out?"

Detective Gerity began speaking almost defensively, "For one thing, the forensic accountant we hired to continue the work of the murdered Albert Thomas is due to give us a preliminary report today." A pause. *One Mississippi, two Mississippi...* I was waiting for another eruption from the back seat. Restraining herself, Audrey asked through clenched teeth, "OK, Chuck. What would be 'a second thing'?"

We were pulling up to the United Airlines terminal, and I was getting as anxious as my wife. Chuck stopped the cruiser, put it in park, and then turned to reluctantly address both of us. "What I'm about to tell you must be kept in the strictest of confidence. This is information that we definitely don't want anyone to know yet, especially not anyone in the Sacco family."

I replied, "We capiche." Neither Chuck nor Audrey thought that was funny.

Detective Gerity's next words were not funny either. They shocked both of us. "Bert Kelty is coming in."

CHAPTER FORTY-TWO

The call had come into the Kansas City police department automated answering system. The caller waited through the very annoying prompts (press one for this, press two for that), and then finally he heard, "Hold for an operator." The caller held for a minute or two before a live voice came on the line. "How may I help you?"

Without any emotion in his voice, the caller just gave a name. "Peterson."

"Please hold." There was a pause before a new person came on the line.

"This is Officer Wood. What can I do for you?"

The caller repeated the name. "Peterson."

Officer Wood, who was just doing his job, asked, "Who's calling and what is this in reference to?"

The caller stated firmly, "You can tell Detective Peterson that I have information about the Vincent Houten murder. That is all you need to know."

Wood, trained to avoid confrontation, simply replied, "I'll see if he's free."

"Peterson here." Detective Peterson agreed to accept the call as soon as Office J. C. Wood relayed the caller's message. He was anxious to hear what information this yet-to-be-identified person had to offer about the Vincent Houten murder investigation.

"Detective Peterson, I represent Albert Keltenski. I believe you know him as Bert Kelty. Mr. Keltenski has some information that he believes you may be interested in." The caller then identified himself as Anthony Angali, the same Anthony Angali that both Albert (Bert) Keltenski and George Cavallas had worked for as junior attorneys years earlier.

Attorney Angali then stated, "At this time, I am only interested in discussing my client's safety, and the provisions you can provide to ensure that safety." He paused.

Then the counselor added, "After that is resolved, we can begin discussions of immunity for his cooperation."

Detective Patterson didn't hesitate. "Of course we are willing to provide whatever level of protection necessary to satisfy Mr. Keltenski's concerns for his safety. I would like to add that I'm pleased to hear that he is well. We were quite concerned for his life after his sudden disappearance."

"I'm sure you are more than happy that he is still alive. You haven't had much success keeping people of interest in this case breathing." Anthony Angali ended the conversation by saying, "Come up with a plan, and we'll see if it's acceptable. You can reach me through my office." He was purposely abrupt. He knew the entire conversation was being recorded.

Detectives Peterson and Gerity developed a plan for the safety of their newfound star informant. They assigned Detectives Al Carlton and J. C. Wood to find a safe house. Both were assigned to the organized-crime task force under Ed Peterson but had been assisting on the Houten investigation. Their work on this investigation began when they introduced themselves to Peter Kunz after Peter's meeting with George Cavallas on Monday. Now their instructions were simple: find a safe place, not a hotel, but a house, preferably in a field for optimum surveillance.

That task proved to be a relatively simple one for a couple of local boys, both of whom had been born and raised in the area. They were further instructed to equip the building with surveillance cameras and install trip cameras and motion detectors around the perimeter of the building.

Before Detectives Ed Peterson and Chuck Gerity were ready to brief Counselor Angali on the planned safe house, they worked on a draft of an immunity-from-prosecution agreement. Bert's attorney, Angali, was trying to take every advantage of his unique position and dictate all the terms of his client's safety provisions as well as his further condition to testify. There was only one small relevant fact that stood in his way, Bert Kelty might be the only living cooperating witness, but he also was a potential accomplice to murder.

Detective Gerity decided to set the terms for immunity. He huddled with the Kansas county prosecutor and worked on a draft that would help turn the tide in their favor.

Attorney Angali couldn't possibly object to the plan for his client's complete protection. The provisions were more extensive than those that Detective Peterson had arranged for some Mafia informants he had dealt with in the past. But before Bert Kelty could come in and receive police protection, he would have to first agree to the terms of the immunity-from-prosecution agreement.

Detective Gerity personally hand-delivered the document to Tony Angali. It was not lengthy but to the point: Full disclosure of all activities at Tri-State Tape, complete details of the involvement of all participants in the embezzlement scheme and his role in it, in return for freedom from prosecution for embezzlement, but not murder or conspiracy to murder.

Mr. Angali's initial response was noncommittal. "Thank you, Detective. I'll review this with my client." Detective Gerity was being dismissed and was unsure how to read Angali. He and the prosecutor laid out a strategy that they felt would work, and Chuck Gerity delivered it. Now it was time to wait for the Kelty side to make the next move.

Chuck Gerity participated in strategizing the Bert Kelty situation with the Kansas county prosecutor and personally delivered the final proposed immunity agreement to Anthony Angali. How that was received was now out of his hands. It was time for he, Ed Peterson, and the prosecutor to meet with the forensic accountant, Fred Ryder, to review the findings of Ryder's investigation.

CHAPTER FORTY-THREE

Audrey and I checked our bags at the airport terminal and found a cheesy grab-and-go sandwich shop and bar in the Kansas City airport. Nothing against KC, but there wasn't anything memorable about the culinary options in the airport terminals. We were able to find two open barstools and ordered a couple of bloody marys of the premixed, watered-down variety—one last reminder of how much we missed our friend Vincent and his over-the-top bloody marys.

Audrey suggested we call Peter Kunz and give him our travel itinerary. We agreed that we should catch up with him as soon as possible once we returned to South Florida. Peter answered my call and immediately asked, "Where are you? Are you back in Florida yet?"

Peter's voice was slightly high pitched, and his speech was fast. He was obviously anxious to hear from us first hand about what had developed since he left KC two days ago. He breathlessly commented, "Jefferson Coulson told me about some of the shit you went through since Wednesday."

"Peter, we're still in KC, but we are at the airport. Our flight leaves at eleven forty-five and is scheduled to arrive in Fort Lauderdale at three fifty-five." Our friend offered to pick us up at the airport. I reminded him that our car had been in long-term parking for more than a week. With that understood, Peter Kunz insisted on meeting us at our condo at five thirty or so. We would have a cocktail together, then an early dinner at a nearby restaurant. "We have to talk."

The flight was uneventful. We left on time and arrived ten minutes early. As soon as we landed, I activated my cell phone to find a text message from Detective Gerity. The cryptic message read, "The accountant strongly believes that Tri-State Tape was being robbed. Embezzlement, and most likely, for years. I'll have more to discuss tomorrow."

I showed the text message to my wife, and she responded with a sigh, "He's really starting to piss me off today."

Audrey didn't have to explain. Chuck was being very evasive, and we both felt we deserved better. "Let's just leave it alone till tomorrow."

We retrieved our luggage from baggage claim and made our way to the curbside pick-up area and took the courtesy bus to long-term parking. We got settled in our car, and as soon as we entered I-95 north for the forty-five minute drive to Palm Beach, Audrey called our friend. "Peter, we are on our way and should be at the apartment by five."

Kunz just said, "I'll be waiting."

The valet at our condo greeted us warmly as we pulled into the circular drive. "Welcome back, Mrs. Stevens." He then took our luggage from the trunk of our car, and we entered our condo lobby. The doorman smiled awkwardly and informed us that Mr. Kunz had already arrived and was waiting for us in our apartment.

I wasn't upset by the fact that Peter Kunz had let himself into our apartment, and I don't think Audrey was either. We had given him a key, and we even kept his favorite bourbon in stock. Peter was welcome anytime. Getting to our apartment before us was just another indicator of how anxious he was.

As we entered the apartment, we could see Peter on our balcony with a cigarette in one hand and a bourbon and coke in the other. Audrey was thrilled to see him and called out, "Peter, come here right now."

He gave my wife a lingering hug, then enthusiastically shook my hand and said, "You both look like you need a drink." Peter Kunz played host while my wife and I unpacked our bags and freshened up. He made us a cocktail and even prepared a plate of cheese and crackers.

Kansas City had initially been cold and snowy, and then the weather had turned less cold but wet. It was nice to be back in South Florida were it was now sunny, warm, and breezy. Without debate, we took hold of our cocktails and snacks and retreated to the balcony. There was still an hour or more of light. The ocean was a bit choppy but still aqua green; I just never got tired of that view. We enjoyed the tranquility and remained silent for a while, but we knew that it was only temporary. We all needed to talk.

Audrey spoke first. "Peter, do you have any injuries from your accident?"

"It's only been a couple of days, but my neck and shoulder suck. The doctor says it will be fine. Nothing major." Then Peter Kunz asked, "What happened to you two with Sammy? I heard it was crazy. Even the Sacco family got involved."

I didn't want to get into a blow-by-blow account of the last two days, so I simply told Peter that Sammy was scared. He was in over his head and when the police were about to arrest him, he panicked. I made no mention of the Sacco family or Pauli Ferguson.

Peter Kunz sipped his bourbon and Coke and became reflective. He obviously was deep in thought, so Audrey and I remained silent, trying not to interrupt his mental process. He finally said, "There are a few things that don't add up."

I completely agreed but responded, "Like what?"

Peter said, "First, I heard that George Cavallas hired the forensic accountant Albert Thomas. So I can't figure out why George would hire the accountant to discover who was stealing if he was the one stealing. And then kill him after he started to uncover what George had to know he would uncover."

I understood Peter's reasoning but asked, "Peter, where did you hear that George hired the accountant? We just heard that from Detective Gerity this morning."

"I got it from Jefferson Coulson. He and Judge Brenan can't get enough of this case. They are hitting up all their old sources." Peter added, "I think they even talked directly to George."

Peter was thinking rationally but seemed to be trying to convince himself of George Cavallas's innocence. "Jeff told me that George lied about not knowing Bert Kelty to protect me. He was trying to get me off the case for my own good. I don't know how he or the judge could have learned that except from George. If it's true, it could make sense."

It appeared that Peter Kunz didn't want to accept the possibility that George was not acting as a longtime friend when Peter asked him for his help. I wanted to tell our friend Peter that what he had heard from Jeff Coulson and Judge Brenan was only important if it was accurate, but he didn't take more than a breath before he addressed "another thing that didn't add up," Samuel Houten.

Peter posed a rhetorical question. "Anybody who knew Sam for any length of time knew he was emotionally unstable and jealous of his brother Vincent. How could he have convinced Christopher to murder his uncle? I can't imagine that he could." Peter Kunz was still questioning who might have had a strong enough motive to murder. It was the same line of pursuit that he took during his meeting with George Cavallas in George's office seven days ago.

"And then who killed Albert Thomas and Bert? And who drove into my car? You think Sammy could do all that?"

Audrey and I looked at each other and without saying a word asked each other, *Should we tell him or not?* Peter Kunz thought Bert was dead, and what he heard from his KC buddies as gospel was mostly inaccurate.

The information we knew to be accurate was not supposed to be shared. It was very confidential, but Peter was like us—a friend of Vincent's caught up in his murder. I felt that as far as the concerns that Peter raised, there were some loose ends to be sure, but Gerity and Peterson should be able to tie them up quickly with the cooperation of Bert Kelty.

Peter started to relay some additional information he had received when my wife made up our minds for us and interrupted him quite bluntly, "Peter all that is interesting but not very important. Peter, Bert Kelty is alive and coming in."

Peter Kunz incredulously asked, "Are you sure?"

Audrey firmly responded, "Chuck and Ed are arranging the conditions for his safety, but he definitely is coming in and intends to cooperate."

"Holy shit!"

CHAPTER FORTY-FOUR

As Detectives Gerity and Peterson had hoped, the security arrangements were acceptable to Angali and to his client, Albert Keltenski, a.k.a. Bert Kelty. With some minor adjustments to the immunity-from-prosecution agreement, all things were now in place for their informant to come in.

Bert Kelty had taken refuge in a run-down boarding house in Kansas City, Kansas. He was posing as a degenerate wino. Kansas City, Kansas, is the poor neighbor of its Missouri namesake just across the Missouri River. For authenticity and out of fear of detection, Bert had not bathed nor shaven for days. He was now eager to tell all he knew and face any consequences, but he also couldn't wait to get out of the rat hole he had selected for his temporary hideout.

The Kansas state police pulled up in front of the flophouse at 6:00 a.m. Saturday morning in an unmarked cruiser, to avoid drawing any unwanted attention. The hour was selected for the obvious reason that no one would be sober or out and about in that neighborhood that early on a Saturday morning. Bert was anxiously waiting. He quickly and nervously exited the boarding house and almost jumped into the back seat of the police vehicle as soon as he saw it arrive.

The transfer was uneventful. The police cruiser crossed the state line into Missouri and drove the extra twenty-five minutes to the secured safe house prepared by Officers Carlton and Wood.

Detectives Gerity and Peterson greeted the troopers and Bert Kelty when they reached the safe house. The detectives were now armed with the additional information they had received from the preliminary report of their forensic accountant, Fred Ryder. Both Chuck and Ed were anxious to begin an interrogation, but Bert had one more request: a shower and a clean change of clothing.

The forensic accountant hired by the Kansas City police organized-crime task force explained to Chuck Gerity what he characterized as a classic multilevel embezzlement scam.

The embezzlers had worked out arrangements with a select few Tri-State Tape suppliers. For the supplier to do business with Tri-State, that supplier would bill Tri-State their full wholesale price but then kick back the 15 percent discount that the company had earned for its good payment practices over the years.

Tri-State was paying top wholesale price, and its employees were reaping the benefits of the reputation Vincent Houten had spent his whole career developing. For the suppliers, they were guaranteeing the continuation of business and paying the same price for the product, only in two separate payment forms.

The second half of the scam was a bit bolder than a simple kickback arrangement. Purchases were made that were logged into the company inventory but were sold to some Tri-State retail customers at the wholesale price, the total proceeds going to the scammers. The cooperating auditors then inflated the periodic inventory report to conceal the lost/stolen supplies.

Those activities, according to Fred Ryder, had most likely been going on for years, certainly before the hiring of Bert Kelty. Fred informed the detectives that there were two additional twists that seemed to coincide with the Kelty hiring.

First, a local private shipping company replaced the use of UPS as the company's shipping source to its customers. Over the past three years, since the change introduced by Bert Kelty, the cost of shipping gradually increased until it eventually was double the previous UPS costs. The obvious question was who had an interest in the new shipping provider?

Secondly, an array of products began to be purchased that seemed to have nothing to do with the operation of Tri-State Tape. None of those mysterious products purchased appeared on the regular inventory report. That meant that they left Tri-State as soon as they arrived, never logged into the inventory control system.

A showered and shaven Bert Kelty exited the second floor bathroom, slowly walked down the stairway to be met by the detectives, and greeted with a cup of coffee and a box of Dunkin Donuts on the dining room table.

The safe house was a small two-story wood-framed building sparsely furnished and used as a hunting lodge for shooting pheasant and quail during the official season. It not being the hunting season, the lodge had been unused for the a few months. The surrounding fields that provided an ideal habitat for the birds also provided a perfect field of vision for the protecting officers.

The coffee and donuts were a very welcome sight to Bert.

CHAPTER FORTY-FIVE

The interview of Bert Kelty began quite affably and casually. Detective Gerity took the lead. "We want to thank you for agreeing to cooperate with this investigation. Are you now prepared to discuss what you know of the apparent embezzlement that went on in Tri-State Tape that has led to the murder of several people?"

Chuck Gerity was being excessively polite in his effort to relax Kelty. He also wanted to subtly impress upon Bert that even though he had an agreement not to be prosecuted for embezzlement, he was not immune to a charge of murder, and the murders were in fact a direct result of the embezzlement scam. There was a fine line between the two. Therefore the intentional inclusion of his remark "that led to the murder of several people."

Bert Kelty responded as if he understood the severity of the situation and wanted no ambiguity of his motive. "Detective, I am here to cooperate." After a pause of no more than a second, he forcefully added, "Fully cooperate."

Gerity wasted no time and asked, "Mr. Kelty, after you were hired as the general manager of Tri-State Tape, when did you become aware of a kickback scheme?"

"Detective, I was made aware of the kickback scheme before I was hired." Bert then offered, "And if you don't mind me anticipating your next question I was also aware of the inventory manipulation scheme before I was hired."

"We can with some degree of certainty surmise how you were informed, but for the record, please state who informed you and why." All roads led to George Cavallas, but Gerity needed it in the record.

Bert Kelty responded, "George Cavallas brought me in to manage Tri-State and continue the schemes he and Joan Olsen had been operating for the past few years. George explained how they worked, and I was to continue them. It was really child's play."

Chuck Gerity then asked, "If it was child's play, then why did he need to add you to the number of players?"

"Well, the number of players had expanded before he added me. Mr. Houten hired his nephew Christopher Mosley to work in shipping to give him a start after he had completed a drug rehab program. Christopher must have stumbled upon the inventory deal and told his other uncle, Sam Houten. Sam then wanted in, and now two became four: George, Joan, Christopher, and Sam."

Detective Gerity then, leading his informant, said, "The more hands in the cookie jar, the more the scam had to be expanded to satisfy the greedy. So four becomes five because of the need for someone to manage and diversify the program? Enter you."

"Exactly. I renegotiated some of the kickback arrangements and added a few new companies. To get new money for the group, I started the shipping company, which added a little extra money but took some time to develop. If I increased the cost of shipping too quickly, it would have been obvious to Mr. Houten or his accountants. The real improvement to our group was the product distribution scam."

Bert Kelty explained in detail. "I was approached by one of the suppliers that was involved in the kickback deal. He had developed a small direct sale business—knickknacks and kitchen accessories. He offered to have the products drop-shipped to Tri-State. We would use our shipping company to distribute them, only we would do that at Houten's expense.

"The scheme got better when I figured out how to have the product billed to Tri-State, and then this little direct sale business was operating at a zero-cost basis. The product hit the Tri-State loading dock and went directly into a Tri-State delivery van and then to the direct sales consumer. The purchases were booked as miscellaneous, and the product never showed up as inventory."

"What went wrong?"

Bert answered softly, almost reflectively. "Everything we did added expense to the company's cost of goods. No customer loyalty discount on purchases, lost inventory sold to customers at wholesale, increased cost of delivery, and then purchases that were unrelated to the business of Tri-State Tape. Those line items became more and more difficult to explain away."

"So then that is when Vincent Houten hired a forensic accountant?" Detective Gerity knew that George Cavallas claimed to have hired the accountant, a claim that would help to insulate him from the embezzlement investigation. Chuck wanted to hear Kelty tell his side without influencing him.

"Yes and no. Joan Olsen's role in our group was to keep Mr. Houten in the dark, give him only good news. Her talking points were that the increased expenses were necessary for the company to gain more market share." Bert elaborated, "It worked for a while, but for some reason, he lost trust in Joanie Olsen. He never made the connection between Joan and George, so when he decided he wanted a thorough financial review of his company, he consulted George."

Gerity asked, "So although it was Vincent Houten's decision to have the review, it was George Cavallas who selected who was to perform it."

"That's right, Detective, and I'm sure you can guess the guy was a plant. I worked with him to develop a sanitized report showing that the company was run expertly under my management and was poised to grow exponentially." Bert then speculated aloud. "The accountant must have uncovered something, something more than just our schemes, and maybe tried to blackmail George. Anyway, when he got whacked, I figured I was next."

"So you were afraid of George?"

"Yeah! George, Sammy, organized crime."

Ed Peterson, as the head of the organized-crime task force, said, "The Sacco family has said they were not involved in this. What do you know about that?"

"I never dealt with the Sacco family directly, but any kickback supplier or discounted purchaser who has taken a loan from them or got assistance with a labor negotiation or got help with a difficult building variance owes the family. If he doesn't pay the Sacco family, he gets his legs broken, and if I don't play along, well then, a guy with a broken leg comes to visit me."

Kelty reflected on this. "I never was sure that the Sacco family was involved, but I did feel and believed that there was someone involved with George and Joan that provided the necessary intimidation when needed. I reported to George when I got resistance from a supplier, and I never asked any questions about how the issue was resolved."

Gerity then directed questioning back to the financial schemes. "You suggested that Albert Thomas must have discovered something more financially significant. Any idea what George may have been involved in?"

"I was on top of everything that was happening on a day-to-day business basis, and I would have noticed if any other skimming was going on, and I believe that there wasn't. I've been thinking about it since Al Thomas was shot. The only thing I can guess is maybe there was something to do with the company pension plan. Mr. Houten started it when he purchased the company, and since it was building up over more than thirty years, it was quite substantial. Maybe you should look there."

Detective Gerity looked over the table at Detective Peterson. "I think it's time we issued arrest warrants for Joan Olsen and George Cavallas."

Without hesitation, Peterson replied, "I agree."

While Detective Ed Peterson was processing arrest warrants for George Cavallas and Joan Olsen, Detective Chuck Gerity contacted Fred Ryder, the forensic accountant. Upon the suggestion of Bert Kelty, Fred Ryder was instructed to begin a review of the Tri-State Tape retirement plan. He was now working overtime. It was past two on Saturday afternoon when he got his new orders, and he started immediately, as instructed.

At first blush, there did not appear to be any suspicious activity, and Mr. Ryder came to the conclusion that all seemed in order. As a trustee, George Cavallas did receive what seemed to be lucrative management fees for his service but nothing that appeared criminal.

In his effort to be thorough in his investigation, Mr. Ryder then went to the Tri-State offices and began reviewing the individual accounts in the employee confidential files. He didn't have to go beyond Vincent X. Houten's personal account. When he accessed his individual fund through the computer link to the investment company, Vincent's account showed a zero balance.

The Vincent X. Houten retirement account had named the Kansas City, Missouri, Charitable Foundation as its sole beneficiary. The foundation was established as Vincent's way of giving back to the city that gave him his opportunity. A two-minute Internet search revealed that the foundation was under the sole control of George Cavallas. More revealing and quite startling was the discovery that the Houten retirement account had, as legally required by the beneficiary assignment, transferred over eighteen million dollars into the foundation's accounts shortly after Vincent Houten's death.

It was 10:00 p.m. when Ryder was confident enough of what he had discovered to relay his findings. He called KC headquarters. "This is Fred Ryder. I need to talk to Detective Gerity right now."

CHAPTER FORTY-SIX

Audrey and I were glad to be back in our Palm Beach suite, as we often referred to our small condo, but we were also quite anxious to hear some news from KC. As soon as we woke, I followed my Palm Beach routine and walked to Green's Pharmacy to get the *New York Post* and the local *Shiny Sheet*. Thankfully, there were no new inaccurate news stories about the Houten murder.

We leisurely read the papers. I made a couple of my famous omelets, and then to pass the time, we spent most of the day lounging at the pool. We ordered a poolside lunch with a bottle of a light Beaujolais, but never strayed far from our phone in hopes of receiving a call from Detective Gerity after he and Detective Peterson completed their interview of Bert Kelty.

Detective Gerity called us about 3:30 p.m. As luck would have it, we had just reentered or apartment from our poolside escape. Without hesitation, Chuck informed us that he and Ed Peterson believed that they now had more than enough evidence to detain Joan Olsen and George Cavallas and in fact were in the process of issuing arrest warrants for both of them.

Audrey began the conversation. "Chuck, we all suspected that George and Joanie were involved in it all from the beginning to the end. I'm sure that Bert confirmed that to you and Ed, but what else did he reveal in the interrogation? There must be more."

Gerity was cautious in his response. "You said that George and Joan are 'involved in it all.' Well, Bert could not confirm that. He did confirm that they were up to their necks in embezzlement, and that's what we can and are issuing arrest warrants for."

Audrey persisted. "That's it? You brought in the only surviving co-conspirator involved in a plot that has resulted in multiple murders, and he can't help get you more than petty embezzlement?"

Detective Gerity calmly responded, "He has given us a lead on a more substantial motive for Vincent's murder and offered a possibility which may lead to answers for some of the questions that remain unresolved. His participation has been very beneficial."

I felt Audrey was frustrated and far too direct in questioning Chuck, so I intervened with a question politely framed. "Chuck, Audrey and I have a few questions that we can't figure out, but can you tell us what you and Ed find most disturbing? Maybe we have the same concerns. What facts don't add up for you?"

Chuck was polite but short. "Things are starting to happen fast. I can't be more specific than that. I will try to keep you in the loop as best as I can but no promises."

The conversation was over and Audrey and I were again left puzzled. I suggested that we shower freshen up and discuss the case over a cocktail. My wife unenthusiastically agreed. Our friend's murder investigation was getting exhausting. We were both finding it difficult to keep focused, but I knew we could not give up.

By 5:00 p.m. we were showered and dressed with cocktails in hand. I suggested that I get a pad of paper so we could write down our questions and concerns to better organize our thoughts. Audrey's response was "Boring, but go ahead if you insist."

The first question that I raised to start the exercise was whether Samuel Houten and Christopher Mosley were clever enough to put this all together.

Sam and Christopher certainly had motive to murder. The more I thought about it, the simpler it seemed to me. They were both named heirs to Vincent's estate, which meant millions to them. They were about to be caught embezzling from Vincent's company and lose it all, not to mention the possibility of a lengthy prison sentence. Sam hated his brother for his success, and just as he thought he was getting even by stealing from him, everything came undone. The only surprise was that Sam didn't kill Vincent himself.

Audrey had an additional insight. Although Sam and Christopher had a close relationship, she felt that it was unlikely that Christopher would act on Sammy's suggestion alone. But who could have been involved? Maybe George or Joanie, but certainly not Salvatore or Bert. Who else could be involved?

I was scribbling away. Audrey was now less bored, and the questions came rapidly. Who got Salvatore Liguria to give up Megan Kelly the night she was forced off the road in Wellington? Who even knew who Albert Thomas was before he was murdered? Who sideswiped Peter Kunz's car?

As Peter Kunz had surmised the day before in our apartment, Sammy couldn't have done all that. And someone had to have given Samuel Houten the heads-up that he was about to be arrested at the funeral luncheon."

Something was missing in the equation, a missing piece to the puzzle, a simple piece that could tie up the loose ends and expose the final picture. I looked down at my scribbled notes and thought, *what an elusive piece at that.*

Audrey and I were energized by our joint effort to review all that we could recall of the investigation but frustrated by all the questions that we could not answer. I said to my wife, "Audrey, let's go get some dinner."

We agreed that it would be a good thing to let off some steam, so we decided to go to the Breakers Hotel. It was only a few blocks' walk. We were certain to get lost in the crowd and most likely find a friendly bartender to help take our minds off the investigation. Hopefully, Chuck would satisfy our renewed interest and have something to tell us in the morning.

CHAPTER FORTY-SEVEN

Joanie Olsen was served and taken to Kansas police headquarters by four thirty central time on Saturday afternoon. She was charged with embezzlement and obstructing justice. It was not what the prosecutor ultimately wanted to charge her with, but it was a start.

Officers Wood and Carlton had no difficulty locating Mrs. Olsen. They drove directly to the Vincent Houten house on Ward Parkway and found her there in residence with her daughter, son, and their spouses.

As the officers presented Mrs. Olsen with the arrest warrant at the Houten estate, no one in the house appeared to be pleased, but no one seemed surprised. What was surprising was the matter-of-fact attitude of her children, as if they were expecting her arrest. Maybe they knew the score. Maybe they knew more than the police.

Serving George Cavallas was a different issue. George had been divorced and living alone for several years, and there was no one at his home when the Kansas City (Kansas) police approached his Mission Hills home.

Mission Hills was an exclusive upscale community just on the Kansas side of the Missouri-Kansas state line. The Kansas City (Missouri) police were then notified that Cavallas had not been located, and they were dispatched to George's law office in Kansas City, Missouri. Then, to be thorough, they also checked the Tri-State Tape office, which was also in Missouri, in an attempt to serve him with the newly issued arrest warrant, but all to no avail.

In desperation, Detective Chuck Gerity contacted the Missouri state police to search the Kansas City airport. Then he asked the Kansas City, Kansas, and Kansas City, Missouri, police forces to search the two main train depots and the numerous bus terminals in the immediate area. They had to assume that George Cavallas was fleeing, and time was on his side.

Detectives Gerity and Peterson spent two frustrating hours while the reports from the various police departments trickled in with no good news. At 7:45 p.m., the Missouri state police reported that they had found George Cavallas's car in the Kansas City International Airport parking garage. The parking ticket was stamped at 9:33 a.m. that morning. Their target had a ten-hour lead.

The state police and airport security would do a search of passenger lists for all departing flights that day, but Chuck and Ed knew that it was too late. George Cavallas was gone. The detectives were deflated, and as Ed Peterson started to pour two cups of coffee, Chuck Gerity stood up and said, "Forget the coffee. Let's get a drink. We have to do some thinking."

They went to the Peanut Bar and Grill, a small hole-in-the-wall bar and grill popular with the KCPD. It was early Saturday night, but the Peanut catered to a late night crowd so Chuck and Ed were able to get two stools at one end of the bar. They ordered their drinks—bourbon rocks for Ed, vodka tonic for Chuck. How Palm Beach.

They sipped the cocktails in silence for a few minutes, both deep in thought. Chuck broke the silence very bluntly. "We have an informant."

Detective Peterson hesitated before responding to Detective Gerity's suggestion that his task force had allowed an informant to penetrate its ranks. Detective Gerity had considered that possibility for some time. Too many things happened that required either perfect timing or very good luck for the suspects. The coincidences were adding up.

Detective Peterson took a large swallow of his bourbon. "I have to agree there is no way Cavallas could have gotten that much of a start unless someone told him that Kelty was brought in this morning." Slowly nodding his head, Detective Peterson softly added, "I think you're right, Chuck."

Chuck Gerity did not want to offend Peterson. He felt he had said enough, so he waited and allowed Ed to come to his own conclusion, a conclusion that they both knew was obvious. It was Peterson's crew that had let a mole in and therefore his failure. For Gerity to aggressively speculate about the leaks would have been rubbing it in Peterson's face.

Detective Peterson conceded, "Tonight, my light bulb went on. For Cavallas to be at the airport by nine thirty this morning, he had to know we got Kelty to the safe house at six thirty this morning. As soon as Cavallas knew Kelty was going to cooperate, he knew his cover was blown. Bert Kelty knew too much, and it was too late to take care of him like he most likely took care of Alfred Thomas. Someone had to inform Cavallas early this morning, and that gave him the three hours, from six thirty to nine thirty, to flee."

In that three-hour time frame, George Cavallas was able to book a flight, drive to the airport, park his car, then board his plane before anyone had a whisper of a chance to apprehend him.

With Detective Peterson's admission of a potential informant, Detective Gerity felt free to further speculate. "Ed, Samuel Houten had to know when it was time to get out of town."

Detective Peterson again acknowledged this. "Chuck, you and I were considering whether to arrest Sam at the repast or wait until we could arrest all three suspects at once. Who could have known that we had decided to arrest Samuel then and there?"

Together the detectives considered who could have known when Peter Kunz would be at police headquarters at the time his car was sideswiped. That appointment was scheduled less than an hour earlier.

Lastly, and probably more telling, they speculated that since neither Gerity nor Peterson knew who Alfred Thomas was before he was shot, who could have identified him and given a location to his murderer? Detective Peterson then asked, "How does that fit in?"

Chuck responded, "If we didn't know the accountant Alfred Thomas, then the mole didn't get that information from our investigation."

It was becoming more apparent to Detective Gerity that someone was and had been coordinating events surrounding the Vincent Houten murder and the subsequent efforts to cover it up. Those cover-up efforts involved the intimidation or elimination of many key witnesses. That person had to be inside the investigation circle and have direct contact to the Houten murder conspirators.

CHAPTER FORTY-EIGHT

Audrey and I must have let off a little more steam than we anticipated at the Breakers Hotel. We got to the Breakers Saturday night just before eight, and it was already hopping. A fun group from Illinois who were attending some kind of media conference decided to befriend us for some unknown reason, and the cocktails were flying. So Saturday night quickly became Sunday morning. Therefore Sunday day for Audrey and me started a little later and a little bit slower than usual.

Mercifully, the call from Detective Gerity that we had hoped we would receive did not come until close to eleven and after we had had our second cup of coffee. Thankfully, by that time, we were able to focus on the newest information he was about to relay to us. It was a short conversation, but unlike our last conversation or two, it was packed with detail.

Detective Gerity unemotionally informed Audrey and me that Joan Olsen was under arrest, and her preliminary bail hearing was scheduled for later today. He also told us that George Cavallas was able to elude arrest and that his car had been found at the

KC airport, which indicated he had fled, most likely to his native Venezuela where extradition was nearly impossible.

Chuck Gerity continued sharing, but out of sheer exhaustion, his voice faded to a whisper. Detective Gerity had been going at it hard for over a week. The last two days of one new development after another was taking its toll. "The charitable foundation Vincent Houten established and which was the designated beneficiary of his retirement account has been wiped out. Almost twenty million dollars."

I thought, *Wiped out? Vincent died ten days ago!* Audrey and I remained silent.

Chuck, without coaxing from my wife or me, offered further explanation. "Off the record, all eighteen point six million dollars of Mr. Houten's qualified retirement account were transferred to the Kansas City Charitable Foundation as the beneficiary designated by Vincent Houten." Vincent Houten had intended to establish a memorial legacy in his name and donated his retirement trust to be distributed for charitable causes in Kansas City. The sole trustee of the foundation was George Cavallas.

Since the retirement account had a designated beneficiary, the fund was obligated to pay out the proceeds as per the formal account contract, and this did not have the ten-day waiting period that was required to probate a will. A claim was legally processed, and the funds were forwarded to the Kansas City Charitable Foundation under Mr. Cavallas's control. As soon as those funds became available to the foundation, they were transferred to various foreign accounts.

I had only one question for Detective Gerity. "How the hell did George pull that off so quickly?"

Chuck answered, "Nate, all I can say is that it is simple in its complexity. But this is most likely what Vincent Houten accidently discovered that started the chain of events that ultimately got him murdered. He must have come across irregularities in the Tri-State pension fund."

Chuck Gerity and Ed Peterson were scrambling to follow up on all of the latest events. It was very considerate of Chuck to even call us, and we certainly appreciated it, but he had little time to chat. He had given us the abbreviated addition, but additional conversation had to be cut short.

Nursing our hangovers, Audrey and I didn't object to not being able to question the detective further. In time, I knew we all would catch up and be back on the same page. Chuck and Ed needed space and time, and Chuck had to save his energy. "I'll be in touch," the detective said and hung up.

Since Chuck and Ed came to the realization that an informant existed in their ranks, they concentrated solely on discovering who it might be. After their drink at the Peanut Bar and Grill, they returned to headquarters and began reviewing all electronic communications from the beginning of the case. They examined every email and every text message, starting with the most recent interaction involving Bert Kelty and his attorney and working back to Detective Gerity's first contact with KCPD.

The detectives were looking for a pattern of electronic communications that occurred prior to the events that they believed were leaked. If they could discover how the informant obtained (or at least how he distributed) the information, then finding the informant would become far easier. They worked through the night.

As the investigation proceeded, Gerity and Peterson were more convinced that the informant was in an inside, hands-on position. He was not a backroom tech-head with access to KCPD communications. The information that had been given to Sam Houten and George Cavallas and whoever else was relayed far too quickly.

CHAPTER FORTY-NINE

After our brief Sunday-morning conversation with Detective Gerity, Audrey and I struggled to make the noon mass at St. Edward's on time. The effect of the late night Breakers Hotel experience was wearing off. Our heads were feeling a bit better as we exited the church and began a leisurely stroll back to our condo for a Nathan brunch. I for one felt great comfort in the returning to a familiar routine in south Florida. It was a hectic week in KC to say the least, and I never would have imagined how much I missed our Palm Beach get-away.

We stopped at Green's Pharmacy on our way back to our apartment. Audrey waited outside while I entered Green's to buy the newspapers, *New York Post* and the *Shiny Sheet*. I said hello to Patrick Fell, who was a fellow winter parishioner and someone with whom I had regular friendly encounters. Patrick quietly said, "Nate, from what I have been reading, you have been up to your neck in this Houten murder. I'm glad to see you safely back in Palm Beach."

Although Patrick Fell's remark was meant for my ears only, the next person in the line to purchase newspapers overheard him.

The lady with a floppy sun hat and frayed lacy cover-up placed her hand on Patrick Fell's shoulder, pushing him gently to the side. Looking past Patrick directly at me, she loudly asked, "Are you Nathan Stevens? The friend of Vincent Houten?" The excitement in her voice took me by surprise. Why would that woman have such a keen interest in me?

I ignored the strange lady's question, handed the cashier a ten-dollar bill and waited for my change. The cashier seemed frozen and just stared at me.

I had seen a US senator from New York in Green's. I had seen more than one pop star in Green's. Rose Kennedy had breakfast every morning after mass in Green's, but I guess murder trumped celebrity. Acknowledging celebrity would simply expose you as a commoner. The intrigue of someone involved in a murder was obviously fair game.

There was a buzz of whispered conversation in the luncheonette area, then silence. The entire dining area stopped eating and turned to see who this person was and what this person looked like. I certainly didn't feel like a celebrity, more like a suspect. It wasn't a good feeling.

I certainly didn't wait to introduce myself to Green's breakfast crowd. I simply lowered my head and exited the pharmacy, ignoring the six dollars and fifty cents owed to me. Audrey was seated on the park-like bench in front of Green's, facing St. Edward's Church. I calmly took her hand and encouraged her to get up. Together, we strolled back to our apartment.

I didn't want to tell my wife about the Green's Pharmacy episode. It really wasn't a traumatic event for me, but she had been through enough traumatic events, and she didn't need to hear about another episode, regardless of how minor. It was just one more aggravating aspect of this whole mess that she shouldn't have to deal with.

As soon as Audrey and I returned to our condo, I began to prepare brunch: onion-and-cheese omelets, French toast, and bacon. While the ingredients were sautéing, I mixed two Bloody Marys. We toasted to our return to Palm Beach, and as the aroma of onions and bacon filled the air in the apartment, the phone rang. The shrill sound of our landline broke the serene atmosphere that we were both enjoying.

Our landline didn't have the caller ID function because we used it so infrequently. Therefore, not knowing who the caller was, we decided to ignore the ringing of our landline and focus on the original plan. I reasoned that if the call were of any importance, the caller would have our cell phone numbers or at least leave a voice message. The call would have to wait.

Audrey opened our sliding glass balcony door, and we planned to enjoy our brunch overlooking the Atlantic. Seated on our balcony overlooking the aqua-blue Atlantic, we began eating. She seemed very relaxed and even complimented the cuisine.

The food was good, the sky was clear, the breeze was soft, and my wife looked beautiful, but I couldn't put the unanswered call out of my mind. Curiosity got the best of me, and eventually I made an excuse to leave my wife for a brief minute and went to listen to the phone message on our bedroom phone set. I made sure I was out of earshot.

The caller was Robin White, the reporter from the *Palm Beach Daily News*, better known as the *Shiny Sheet*. Ms. White's message was brief. "I understand you are back in town. Please give me the courtesy of a return phone call."

When I returned to the balcony, Audrey immediately observed a change in my demeanor. "Nate, what is it?"

I wasn't sure how I should respond to Ms. White's request, and I didn't want to change the mood we were enjoying, so I tried to stall, "Absolutely nothing, dear. How is your omelet?"

Audrey pushed her plate toward the center of the table, leaned back in her seat, and unemotionally asked, "You're not going to play that game with me again, are you?"

I sat in silence for a minute to reflect. I realized she was quite right. I tried to protect her from knowing about my meeting with Pauli Ferguson and the Sacco family involvement, and that didn't work very well. So why did I feel that now that we had made it back to Palm Beach, things were different?

I felt that I owed my wife a sincere apology, and so I apologized. "Honey, I think that getting back to Palm Beach, settling into our apartment, and having such a good time last night at the Breakers made me feel like this bad dream was finally behind us. I didn't want that feeling to end for us so quickly."

Audrey offered her wisdom with a loving smile. "That's very sweet of you, Nate. However, considering all we have been through, we need to be open with each other if we are going to be of any further assistance in the investigation."

What could I say? "I agree with you wholeheartedly. Let's talk about how we should handle Robin White."

Audrey responded, "OK, but first tell me what happened in Green's pharmacy this morning?"

Damn, I couldn't even get away with that.

CHAPTER FIFTY

D etective Gerity hoped that the investigation to discover the informant in their ranks would uncover new information and go a long way to answer the question, "Who was involved in only embezzling Tri-State Tape, and who was involved in plotting Vincent Houten's murder?"

Systematically, he and Detective Peterson identified the key information that they believed was leaked. They then followed the textbook approach of analyzing the timeline of when the information was available to the investigation team and matched that time frame to the schedules of each individual in the team. Who had both access to the information and the opportunity to relay it?

After the detectives charted the events that they had identified as having most likely been carried out with the help of inside information, they created a chart that cross-referenced the schedules and the known whereabouts of every member of the murder task force. Someone in the know had passed on what he or she knew. There were a lot of coincidental events that could not be ignored.

Both Chuck Gerity and Ed Peterson agreed that no one was above suspicion. Therefore they carried out the investigation with no assistance from other task force members.

The first event they analyzed was their own meeting with Peter Kunz. That event stood out for a few reasons. It was an impromptu meeting and scheduled Tuesday morning, just an hour or two ahead of time. Someone was able to obtain that information and forward it to whomever decided it would be a good idea to scare Peter Kunz off the case by sideswiping his car in front of police headquarters, nearly killing him.

Additionally, who had driven the car that actually hit Peter's car? Christopher Mosley and Samuel Houten were already dead by then. Who was in a position to know the meeting was scheduled, and who was free in that short period of time to carry out the assault with no more than an hour or two?

The second suspicious event was on Thursday. While Chuck and Ed were putting together the pieces of the investigation, someone had enough information to accurately assume that Samuel Houten was about to be arrested. Whoever passed that information onto Samuel Houten caused him to panic, and his panicked reaction resulted in his death.

Lastly, George Cavallas could not have gotten the several-hour lead time he needed to flee the country without advance warning that Bert Kelty had made a deal and was about to testify.

Detective Gerity concentrated on the Palm Beach task force personnel. Information was being relayed to PB regularly, but the timeline made it unlikely that anyone in Palm Beach could have intentionally or inadvertently forward it to someone in KC with enough time to warn Sam, then Peter's attacker and finally George. Chuck concluded that it had to be a KC connection.

Detective Peterson focused on the KC organized-crime task force. His efforts quickly eliminated several individuals and reduced the number of possible suspects with access and opportunity to a single one.

The detectives had followed acceptable procedures, but the results were less than encouraging. Every road that the investigation took resulted in a dead end. When Chuck and Ed met to review each other's progress, Peterson concluded, "I don't have proof, but I believe it's J. C. Woods."

Gerity was visibly surprised. "Why Wood? He has impressed me as mostly reliable and a professional asset throughout this entire investigation."

"J. C. Wood has had my full confidence. He was privy to every step we took. Hell, he even screened my calls. He had both the information and the time to relay it to whomever he needed to. Nobody else had that much access."

Gerity said nothing. He just nodded slightly in agreement but thought to himself, *We must be missing something.*

CHAPTER FIFTY-ONE

Detective Chuck Gerity had been in Kansas City for ten days. He now was scheduled to return to Palm Beach on a 12:30 p.m. flight. In Palm Beach, he planned on wrapping up Salvatore Liguria's involvement and maybe paying a final visit to Megan Kelly. Gerity decided to leave the task of tying up loose ends in Kansas City to Detective Ed Peterson and his organized-crime task force. If necessary, he would return.

It was 9:15 a.m., and Detective Peterson had not arrived for a scheduled 8:30 a.m. final meeting with Detective Gerity before Gerity's return to South Florida. While waiting for his counterpart, Gerity passed the time patiently. He drank some coffee and enjoyed sugar donuts with the desk sergeant and a few other police officers as they passed through the station.

Detective Peterson entered the station slowly. His face was emotionless. He was deep in thought. He acknowledged Detective Gerity. "Chuck, something has come up." Detective Peterson then passed through the security door and headed down the corridor toward his office. Gerity followed closely behind. Peterson stopped at the doorway to his office, let Gerity enter, then closed the door behind them.

Without waiting to reach his seat, Peterson unemotionally stated, "I was summoned to the prosecutor's office. He told me that he wants this case wrapped up."

Detective Gerity was puzzled. He asked, "Ed, Vincent Houten was murdered two and a half weeks ago. Since then, there have been two more murders, a suicide, and what I would call two additional attempted murders. How fast does the prosecutor expect us to move? What's the rush?"

Detective Peterson told Detective Gerity that the message he had received not more than an hour before was clear. "The prosecutor said he got a request from the lieutenant governor's office. The governor himself wants this case off the front page. The prosecutor then said that the case looked closed to him. He said all the suspects are either dead or arrested, and the organized crime unit has more important investigations to pursue."

Detective Gerity responded, "That doesn't sound kosher to me. It sounds like someone wants us off this investigation to protect someone else. This is your town, Ed. What are you going to do?"

Detective Peterson laid out his plan for Detective Gerity. Peterson explained that he planned to immediately release a press statement that the KC police department was satisfied that the case involving Vincent Houten's murder and the subsequent criminal events that followed had been resolved. The statement would further mention that the Kansas City prosecutor's office would appeal to the Venezuelan government for the extradition of George Cavallas to face murder and embezzlement charges. Furthermore, the statement added, the prosecutor was diligently preparing the case to try Joan Olsen for charges including embezzlement and accomplice to murder.

Detective Peterson then asked Detective Gerity to release a separate statement, "Chuck, it would look more convincing if you could make a similar statement that would support the idea that this case is closed."

Chuck Gerity calmly asked, "So Ed, you're just going to close up shop?"

Detective Peterson reassured Detective Gerity, "Chuck, the prosecutor thinks that OCU should concentrate on organized crime. Anthony Angali may not be Mafia, but his activities, if we can prove them, certainly fit under the RICO justification."

Chuck Gerity got the message. "Great idea, Ed! Drop the investigation of Angali in the murder case but continue to investigate him for an organized pattern of embezzlement."

Anthony Angali was the center of everything. He connected the dots for Gerity and Peterson. Cavallas, Kelty, and the embezzlement scheme all pointed to him. But Chuck Gerity instinctively felt there was more. Something was still missing.

Detective Gerity had to agree that an indictment for embezzlement wasn't the outcome he would have hoped for, but at age seventy-five, Antony Angali, if convicted of embezzlement, would be put away for most of his remaining life.

Gerity's last request before he left for the airport was simple. "Keep me in the loop."

CHAPTER FIFTY-TWO

Detective Ed Peterson's press release was printed in the *Kansas City Star* exactly as submitted by him. Over morning coffee, Anthony Angali read the release carefully and was pleased with the content and the prominence the *Star* gave it. The press release and the statements of the Palm Beach task force assured Tony Angali that the Kansas City prosecutor was in agreement with the investigators. Case closed.

That was good news to Tony Angali. However, he understood that the greatest danger to him was Bert Kelty. As long as he was in protective custody, the possibility that Bert could break and give up Tony and his trail of embezzlement schemes was a very real possibility.

Bert Kelty was a risk not to be ignored. Tony's only option was to eliminate the danger. To get to Bert through the extensive security KCPD had arranged, and which he himself had approved, would be difficult. Tony Angali knew he would require some help. He had to engage his associates and call in a few IOUs.

Jefferson Coulson arrived home after another one of his afternoon cocktail rendezvous with some old and new trader acquaintances at the Capital Grill. He poured himself another bourbon and, glass in hand, began to doze off in his easy chair. His wife, Gloria, was not back from her own afternoon cocktail party with her girlfriends. The doorbell startled Jeff awake.

Jeff pulled his aching body out of his chair and lumbered toward the front door. Before he reached the door, the bell rang again, this time for several seconds. Someone was very impatient. Jefferson mumbled to himself, "Cool your jets, asshole."

When he opened his front door, Jeff was shocked to see Anthony Angali standing in front of him. "Tony, what a pleasant surprise." He also could not help but notice Tony's driver standing next to the car that they had just arrived in. The driver had a bulky build and was dressed in solid black. Jefferson was reluctant to jump to any conclusions, but he still felt that there was a message in the image. He would later put a name to the intimidating driver.

Anthony Angali asked in a low voice, "May I come in?"

"Of course, of course." Jefferson led Tony Angali to the den and offered him a seat across from his easy chair. He then offered Tony a cocktail, which he quickly refused. Jeff, his bourbon still in hand, sat back into his easy chair and asked, "To what do I owe the honor of this visit?"

Tony Angali leaned forward in his chair, looked Jeff straight in the eyes, and asked, "Jefferson, you called me last week about Bert Kelty. Looks like he's up to his ass in the Houten murder. What have you found out?"

Jefferson was still a little groggy but sharp enough to know not to reveal anything he knew about Bert or the investigation and certainly not to mention Judge Thomas Brennan. "I couldn't find out anything. Before I could get anywhere Kelty disappeared. The way corpse were turning up I thought Bert would be next." He then added, "From what I read the investigation is finished, and it looks like it's wrapped up."

Angali responded, "I read that myself, but there was no mention of Kelty."

Jefferson waited and said nothing. Tony would have to get to the purpose of his visit without Jeff helping him. The silence grew heavy.

Finally Anthony Angali offered, "I have reasons to find out more about Bert Kelty. I have clients who feel he robbed them." For emphasis, Tony said, "Serious clients." After another short pause, he added, "They want answers."

Playing dumb, Jeff asked Tony Angali a question. "I don't know how I can help. What do you want from me?"

"Coulson, you know everybody in this city. You have contacts in the PD and prosecutor's office. The contacts that I have I cannot access at this time. I'm sure you understand why." Angali's next words were not in the form of a request, "Ask around. See what you can find out."

Anthony Angali got up from his seat and started walking toward the front door. By the time Jefferson labored to gain his footing and reach the front door, Tony was already outside and halfway to his car. Angali stopped, turned, and informed Jeff Coulson, "I'll be in touch tomorrow" His message was clear: cooperate or else. And he meant now not later.

Jefferson was initially startled. It only took a few minutes before he started to feel anger. He said to himself, *I'm not going to let some Wop lawyer intimidate me.* His next action was to call Judge Brennan. They quickly agreed that they should talk to Detective Peterson.

Judge Brennan made the call to Detective Ed Peterson. It took only the fact that Anthony Angali visited Jefferson Coulson in Jeff's own home for Peterson to appreciate the seriousness of the information, "Judge we need to talk. Let's meet at the Peanut. Get hold of Jeff and let me know when you both can be there."

The Peanut Bar was Detective Peterson's choice because it was frequented by police officers and was also a regular watering hole of Jefferson Coulson. If Tony Angali went to the trouble of having Jefferson followed it would be difficult to see anything suspicious about Jeff and Peterson arriving at the Peanut separately. As for Judge Brennan, how could Tony Angali have any idea the judge had any involvement.

A quick shower to sober up a bit and Jefferson was able to arrive first. He pushed up to the bar and ordered a bourbon and soda. Detective Peterson arrived next and went directly to a rickety table against the window-less wall a good distance from the crowded bar. Jeff waited until Peterson ordered and was served his cocktail, then casually moved toward his table and took a seat. They exchanged pleasantries but waited till Judge Brennan arrived before discussing the issue that brought them together.

Judge Francis Brennan arrived thirty minutes after Ed Peterson and Jeff Coulson. The judge apologized and took a seat with the others but gave no explanation for his tardiness. The chatter at the crowed bar provided enough noise that the three were able to talk without fear of being over heard. The judge went directly to the point and asked Detective Peterson, "What evidence have you collected on Anthony Angali?"

Detective summarized, "Angali arranged the fake audit and the fact that it all coincides with Bert Kelty's testimony that it was done in several other businesses. That seems to me to be a pretty solid case, don't you think?"

Judge Brennan was not quick to respond. He collected his thoughts and then said, "Anthony Angali is a good attorney, but he will have even better representation, and they will make every effort to discredit Bert Kelty as a witness for the prosecution.

Frankly, that shouldn't be too hard to do. That is the weakness in your case."

Addressing the detective, Brennan spoke as a professor. "Ed, the other businesses that you have investigated and found to have been embezzled from are pertinent to the prosecution. They definitely show a pattern of criminality. But they are prosecutable on their own. Angali's defense will strongly object to their relevance in this case. They will take the position that they should be and have not been tried separately. It's a position that I would have to take seriously if it were in front of me in my court."

"So what do you see, Judge?"

"I see potential trouble." The judge explained the reason for his assessment, "If the defense thinks they have a strong case that your circumstantial evidence is inadmissible, they will defend and appeal if they are not initially successful. That would most likely take years. However, if the defense is not confident in their case, they will delay proceedings as long as possible and in the end attempt to make a plea arrangement and provide evidence about others who were involved. Bert most likely has information about many others involved. This defense strategy will also take years."

Judge Thomas Brennan's last comment was expressed in a matter-of-fact tone. "You should tighten up your case evidence, or I feel Anthony Angali will remain free for a long time."

Detective Peterson got up to leave. He leaned over the table and addressed Brennan and Coulson, "Thank you, Judge. You just told me what I should have already known. I have to develop a strategy to trap Angali, and I still have a lot of work to do." Without another word, Peterson walked out the rear exit of the Peanut.

Jefferson Coulson had finished his drink a few minutes before Detective Peterson left but waited till the conversation concluded before ordering another. He called to the waitress, whom he knew by her first name, and asked for his usual. Instinctively he knew the judge was up to something. Brennan knew or suspected something.

"OK, Tommy, why were you thirty minutes late?"

The judge sipped his beer and dismissed Jeff's suspicion by saying, "I had a few phone calls to make."

CHAPTER FIFTY-THREE

Attorney Angali, along with an accomplice, Carl Toscana, waited outside the Sheridan Plaza Hotel to observe the chaos about to be caused by the explosion of a strategically positioned car bomb. They detonated the bomb with the remote held in Carl's hand, and they heard the deafening sound of the explosion. The force of the explosion decimated the rear wall of the hotel parking garage. Vehicles in the garage were turned on their side by the force of the bomb.

Smoke from the explosion and fire from the cars became so heavy that the scene of the explosion was hardly visible. The dark smoke quickly became combined with the bitter smell of burning rubber tires. The prevailing breeze took the noxious plume of smoke directly toward the hotel, engulfing the entrance and subsequently penetrating the lobby.

The hotel patrons began to frantically run out of the main hotel entrance. Tony Angali and Carl Toscana had positioned themselves so they would have a clear view of the exits. They knew their plan had succeeded when they were able to identify the police

officers assigned to protect Bert Kelty among the civilians frantically leaving the hotel. As Angali had hoped, the police protection
unit determined that more than babysitting Bert Kelty, they were
needed more at the explosion site to help control the panic.

Tony Angali gave two instructions to his assistant, Carl Toscana.
The first was for Carl to remain outside the hotel's main entrance and
warn him if the police officers began to reenter the hotel. The second
was a bit more direct. "Shoot Bert Kelty if he makes it out past me."

Anthony Angali then quickly pushed past the occupants exiting the hotel. He entered the hotel lobby and made his way to the
stairwell. He climbed the stairs to the third floor where he had
been informed Kelty was being held. At seventy-five years old, even
though still fit, he had to wait a minute or two to catch his breath.
Timing however was essential.

Anthony could wait no longer. He cautiously opened the stairwell door to make sure that there were no police still stationed outside Bert's room. He then slowly moved down the hall to the hotel
room door. He was confident his information was good.

The knock sounded loudly in the hotel suite. After a few seconds, the knock sounded again. There was no response from inside the hotel room. Finally, Tony, mimicking a security guard,
loudly asked through the door, "Are you all right in there?" No
response. "Is everything all right in there?"

Tony Angali, finally hearing the door's lock being removed,
put his hand in his jacket pocket and took hold of his pistol. The
door opened, and Detective Gerity stood in the opening with gun
drawn. "Come in, Counselor. We have been expecting you."

Before entering, Tony surveyed the room. Bert Kelty was seated
in the desk chair at the far end of the room. Chuck Gerity was
standing in the doorway and holding a gun pointed directly at
him. Tony thought it best to release his hold on his gun and remove his hand from his pocket as casually as possible. Chuck took
a step back as an invitation for Tony to enter. But cautiously Tony

took only one step into the hotel room and remained just inside the doorway.

Tony looked at Bert Kelty and nonchalantly commented, "Hi, Bert. As your attorney, I would like to know how they are treating you."

Bert didn't look back at Tony but responded to Angali's comment. "Sorry, Tony. I can't do the time."

Tony then turned back to Detective Gerity and arrogantly said, "I don't think you have all your bases covered, Detective."

Gerity nodding his head slightly and after a brief pause said, "I'm pretty confident that I do."

The door to the hotel suite had remained opened and Detective Ed Peterson suddenly appeared in the doorway behind Tony Angali. Tony looked over his shoulder and then back to Detective Gerity. "Maybe you missed something. But as you can see, Detective, I have all of my bases covered."

From his position in the doorway just behind Tony Angali, Peterson was blocked from the aim of Gerity's gun. He casually asked, "Surprised to see you, Chuck. When did you get back from Palm Beach?" Before Gerity could respond, Ed Peterson turned and with his left hand, grabbed the hotel door, and violently slammed it shut. The unexpected maneuver, the noise from the slamming door, and the quickness of Peterson's action caused the intended distraction. Gerity was still holding his pistol on Tony, but he had let his arm lower while he was trying to look beyond Tony Angali to see Peterson's moves.

Peterson then forcefully shoved Tony Angali into Chuck Gerity. The aging Angali, propelled by the strength of the young Ed Peterson, served as a battering ram. Angali hit Gerity just below the chest with a thud. The air in Tony's lungs seemed to explode in his chest, his arms wrapped around Chuck Gerity in a natural reaction to a fall, then he became limp and slowly slid down Gerity's body to the floor.

Chuck Gerity was in an indefensible position. His arm holding his pistol was trapped against his body while Tony Angali was sliding down to the floor. With Tony's arms loosely wrapped around Chuck's body, the detective was trying to both regain his balance and free his gun arm.

Peterson lunged at Gerity before he could free himself from Angali. With the force created by his forward movement and the power of his two-handed shove into Chuck's chest, Detective Gerity had no chance. He was propelled backward. His pistol fell out of his hand and slid to the middle of the hotel room floor.

Ed Peterson was now in complete control. He drew his pistol as Chuck Gerity struggled to get up. He had only made it to his knees when Peterson pointed his gun at Gerity and said, "That's good enough. Stay right there." As for the seventy-five-year-old Tony Angali, he was in pain and lying on his back, gasping for air.

Gerity, still kneeling, bent over and placed his hands on the floor, waiting for the pain to subside and trying to grasp his breath. He then asked, "OK, Ed, what's next?"

While Tony Angali was still writing in pain, Peterson, without warning, fired two bullets into Tony's chest. The gunshot noise in the confinement of the hotel suite was deafening. Chuck and Bert were frozen. Peterson then reached into Tony's pocket and took his pistol. Then, as if nothing happened, Peterson asked Gerity, "What brought you back to KC?"

After a pause to collect himself, Chuck Gerity answered, "A few things didn't add up, so I thought I would come back to check them out."

Peterson, pointing his gun at Gerity, said, "Chuck, I'm curious. What things didn't add up?"

Detective Gerity tried to stall for time and deliberately began to explain what he figured out. "You tried to make J. C. Wood out to be the informant. But you had no proof, and I never thought

J. C. could have known about the meeting with Peter Kunz the morning his car was sideswiped. That raised my suspicions."

"There must be more. Please go on."

"OK. Since no one we investigated had timely access to all the information that was leaked, that left only you and me. I knew it wasn't me. Then I found it very interesting that Salvatore Liguria somehow knew your first name was Edmond and not Edward. I couldn't explain that. Can you?"

As Peterson raised his gun, he said to Gerity, "I don't think I'll have to."

Gerity, trying to distract Peterson, quickly said, "There's more. Aren't you curious?"

Peterson lowered his gun. "Yeah. I'm curious. Go on."

"Well, one Thomas Brennan, retired judge of the Missouri Superior Court, remembers a relationship between Angali and Kelty, a relationship that should have been disclosed while Tony was negotiating the immunity-from-prosecution agreement but was not. The judge also recalls a case or two where you, as lead investigator, sided with the defendant who coincidently was represented again by Tony Angali. To be honest, I haven't been able to get to that one yet. But I think that's enough."

"I'm impressed. The high-society Palm Beach detective who hasn't investigated more than one murder in twenty years put this all together, and you're right. You nailed it, but it all sounds very circumstantial, Chuck. Hard to prove, especially if there is no one to testify."

"One more thing, Ed. The prosecutor denies that he or anyone in his office told you to wrap up this case. You are now definitely in his crosshairs, and he will still be around to testify." Chuck Gerity could see that Ed Peterson was not happy with what he just heard. "OK, Edmond. How does this play out?"

"Pretty simple. First, Tony shoots you, and of course, Bert over there. I come to the scene and have no choice but to shoot Tony.

It's only a matter of mixing up the chronology. Then I'll just have to take my chances with the prosecutor." Peterson again raised his pistol.

"It's over, Ed. I have the whole conversation on tape. Put your gun down. It's over." The voice came from Peterson's left. It was J. C. Wood. Officer Wood had been stationed in the bathroom with a tape recorder running and his pistol trained on Peterson. Gerity was still looking down the barrel of Peterson's gun. Now Peterson was being covered by Wood's gun. It was a standoff.

The two detectives and Officer Wood were frozen for a second or two. Gerity thought this could end very badly and in that second or two decided to make the first move. He was waiting for the slightest distraction and then he would lunge at Peterson and try to grab his gun.

The distraction Detective Gerity was waiting for came but not as he imagined. Bert Kelty suddenly dove to the floor to get to Gerity's gun, which was lying on the floor a few feet in front of him. Detective Peterson instinctively turned and aimed at Kelty. Detective Gerity, still on his knees, raised his left leg, planted his left foot, and propelled himself toward Peterson.

When he attempted to get up from his knees, he found that they had become quite stiff. As he stumbled toward Peterson, he was able to only hug him around the waist, as Angali had done to him not ten minutes before. Peterson's pistol was thus restricted by Chuck's bear hug, causing the gunshot that was intended for Bert Kelty to enter the left side of Detective Gerity's abdomen. Gerity initially did not experience pain, but he knew that he had been shot.

Kelty retrieved Gerity's gun. He fumbled with the pistol as he tried to train it on Peterson. He was uncertain whether it had a bullet in the chamber, and if not, how to get one in there. Detective Gerity was still clinging to Peterson, and Peterson was struggling to free his gun arm. Peterson then grabbed Gerity's shoulder and, in a display of extraordinary strength, threw him across the floor toward his left and away from Kelty.

Peterson swung back to his right as Kelty was still nervously handling Gerity's gun. He aimed at Bert, and four shots rang out. *Pop. Pop. Pop. Pop.* J. C. Wood had waited until Detective Gerity was out of his line of fire, and when he had the chance, he ended the conflict. As Gerity surmised, J. C. was not the informant but the hero.

CHAPTER FIFTY-FOUR

R obin White, the Palm Beach *Shiny Sheet* reporter had left a voice message asking us for the courtesy of a return call. Audrey and I hadn't discussed whether we should return her call; Robin White and the *Shiny Sheet* were not our top priority. So when our phone rang the next afternoon, I definitely expected to hear Reporter White on the other end.

The call was instead from the PBPD. More accurately, it was from Detective Philip Morris. He politely asked if it would be convenient for him to come by and share some developments in the Houten case.

It struck me odd to be contacted for the first time in the investigation by anyone other than Detective Chuck Gerity. I asked, "Detective Morris, what's this about, and what's the urgency?"

Morris professionally answered, "Mr. Stevens, I prefer to discuss this with you and your wife in person. I'm sure the developments I mentioned will be of great interest to you. Is now a convenient time?"

As I hung up, Audrey asked, "Who was that, Nate?"

I answered, "Detective Morris. He is coming over with some information. I don't know what it's about, but I don't think it's good."

Detective Morris entered our condo not ten minutes after his phone call. He wasted little time with pleasantries. "I'm here to inform you that Detective Gerity has been shot. He is recovering in the Kansas City Medical Center as we speak."

"Detective, please have a seat." He accepted, and we sat around our dining table. Audrey asked, "Is he going to be all right?"

Morris assured us that he was expected to make a full recovery, but it would take some time. He added, "The bullet entered his lower left abdomen, damaging his colon but missing any other major organs."

I was shocked but also confused. I shook my head as I asked, "Detective, you said he is in the Kansas City Medical Center. How did he get there? He was here in Palm Beach when we talked to him not thirty-six hours ago."

Detective Morris clarified why Chuck had abruptly returned to KC. "Detective Gerity discovered some connections that appeared to break the case wide open. He needed to confirm his suspicions and did not want to have his travel plans known. Especially by Detective Peterson."

My wife and I almost simultaneously asked, "Peterson?"

Morris simply said, "It is all about Detective Peterson."

Detective Morris than freely reviewed the connections Gerity had discovered. He explained how in the search for an informant, Detective Gerity came to the conclusion that there was only he and Detective Peterson who could have all the information that had been leaked. Peterson attempted to distract Gerity by insisting J. C. Wood was the informant. That didn't make sense to Gerity and only confirmed his suspicions.

Detective Morris than explained how Judge Thomas Brennan also became suspicious after his friend Jefferson Coulson was pressed for information about Kelty by Anthony Angali. The judge was able to recall a past connection between Anthony Angali and Ed Peterson. The judge was also able to give a lead as to the identity of the chauffer Angali used in his attempt to intimidate Jefferson Coulson.

Morris added, "That lead has proven to be accurate. Without including Peterson in the investigation, Chuck was able to confirm the chauffer's name and get some background. He is Carl Toscano, a local thug associated with the Sacco family. For starters, he is being sought as an accomplice in the car bombing at the hotel."

All this new information was making my head spin. I was looking for a break. So before Detective Philip Morris could continue, I interrupted. "Philip, this is a lot to absorb. Can I offer you something? A soda, a cup of coffee, water, a cocktail?" The detective declined, but my wife and I thought it was a good idea—the cocktail suggestion, that is.

I could overhear the conversation between Audrey and Morris continuing while I poured the usual cocktails for my wife and me. I listened intently so as not to miss anything. I heard my wife ask Morris, "Why the special treatment? Why are you explaining all this to us?"

Morris paused and then replied, "Detective Gerity told me to give you full disclosure." He paused then added, "He said he owed it to you."

When I returned, Detective Morris summarized the struggle that had occurred in the hotel room after the bomb explosion that caused the distraction. He detailed the standoff in the hotel room that resulted in the shooting of Detective Gerity. It wasn't until then that we were aware that Anthony Angali and Ed Peterson had both been killed in the confrontation.

I thought, *Holy shit, a shootout at the OK Corral.*

Peterson had unilaterally reduced the protective detail assigned to Bert Kelty and transferred him from his ultraprotective hunting lodge to a far less defensible hotel in the KC Plaza under the guise that it was what the governor's office wanted. Gerity anticipated it and recruited J. C. Wood to successfully foil Peterson's plan.

Detective Philip Morris stood up from his chair in an obvious indication that he had delivered all the information he had or at least was instructed to deliver. Audrey and I quickly rose in response and enthusiastically shook his hand in sincere thanks for his open and through delivery of the details. It appeared that the case was finally closed.

Detective Morris humbly accepted our thanks and started walking toward the door. He paused and then turned to say, "I forgot to mention a detail that you may find interesting. Detective Peterson's first name is Edmond, and not Edward. Few people know that. According to Megan Kelly, Salvatore Liguria told her that a couple of guys named Anthony and Edmond in KC were clearing everything up. That was something that Detective Gerity found revealing."

Audrey and I returned to our seats at the dinning table. We sipped the cocktails that I had made a few minutes ago. Both of us were quiet, collecting our thoughts. I broke the silence. "Audrey, I think this is finally over. Peterson was the last piece of the puzzle. Who else could have convinced Christopher to kill his uncle? Not Sam, not Joanie, not George. That was the issue we could never accept."

Audrey reluctantly agreed. "Peterson was the hammer for Angali and for Cavallas. Carl Toscana, the bomber's assistant, was most likely the muscle. One or both must have been the one who pressured Christopher to murder Vincent." Hearing that from Audrey gave me the feeling of a great weight lifting off my shoulders. She really agreed. Boy, was I ready to move on.

I started toward our kitchen to freshen our drinks, but my wife just felt she could not give it up. Honestly, I wasn't quite ready to either. I listened to my wife list the unanswered issues that still troubled her.

Audrey asked, "Why did Tony Angali intimidate Jefferson Coulson for information on Bert Kelty when he was planning to kill Bert the next day?" I waited a second. Then she added, "And why did a seventy-five-year-old attorney decide it was a good idea to kill the witness by himself? And what's with Salvatore Liguria?"

The answers were fairly obvious to me, most of them anyway.

Anthony Angali was not interested in the additional information Jefferson Coulson could gather about Bert Kelty's background. Angali had everything on Bert that he needed. He worked with Bert. He intimidated Jeff only to find out who else might know, to find out who among Jeff's contacts could become a future hazard.

Tony Angali was making his list of whom he could trust and whom he had to deal with. If Jeff Coulson could provide inside information and where he got it, then Tony might have more work left for him to do, even after the elimination of Bert Kelty.

As to the question of why a seventy-five-year-old would personally be involved in the murder of a witness for the prosecution, the answer was also quite simple. Detective Peterson arranged the location and the plan of distraction and insisted that Angali be there so as to have all his ducks in the arranged barrel. Or was that fish in a row? Whatever.

I was satisfied and begged my wife to let it go. "Audrey, this is over. Everything is wrapped up with a nice tight bow. Please let it go?"

She looked into my eyes but said nothing. The longer she looked, the more I got the feeling that not only did she accept that the case was over, but that this could be an extremely romantic climax to the last two weeks.

The spell unfortunately was broken when Audrey said, "Nate, I still would like to hear what happened to Salvatore Liguria. I have known him a long time. And I'm curious about Carl Toscano as well. Where the hell did he come from?"

"Audrey, after all we have been through, I don't give a shit about Salvatore Liguria or Carl Toscana. I'm going to dress for dinner. I hope you will join me."

I started toward our dressing area frustrated with my wife's continued obsession with the Houten murder, and then my cell phone rang. I decided to answer. The voice that I heard was a familiar one, belonging to Pauli Ferguson. No one mentioned any names, and the phone conversation went on carefully.

Pauli began with a cordial greeting. "Glad to see you're back in Palm Beach, safe and sound. I was really worried about you."

"Thank you. I appreciate your concern."

"No big deal. I told you we hold you in high regard. Is there anything you need? I told you I would continue to look out for you."

"Well, there are only a couple of loose ends. Maybe you could give me some answers."

"Like what?"

"I believed you when you told me your family was not involved in this case, but at the last minute, Carl Toscana shows up. They say he is with your family."

"OK, take it easy, and I'll explain. Carl got his loyalty mixed up. He was more loyal to the attorney. He went to the attorney without our permission. That we will take care of."

Before I could ask another question, Pauli Ferguson shut down the conversation. "I told you when the family has to clean up, we clean up completely. Now, is there anything I can do for you personally?"

It just came to me in a flash. Without thinking it through, I asked, "Do you have any connections in Venezuela?"

Pauli waited a second or two and then said, "Maybe yes, maybe no. Why do you ask?"

"Well, it looks like everyone's accounted for in the Houten murder except for George Cavallas. The police think he's in Venezuela.

It burns my ass that he betrayed a longtime friend and client and is the only one that got to go free. The Venezuelan government isn't going to do anything, and they certainly won't extradite him, if they even bother to look for him."

"Agreed, but what's in it for me?"

"He took off with almost twenty million from the Houten foundation. Maybe you could get some of it back for your efforts."

"Twenty million?"

"Do you think you could help?"

"Maybe yes, maybe no." Pauli then said, "I'll make some inquiries."

I was pleased with myself that I gave him information that could get George Cavallas killed. It gave me a thrill that I didn't have to follow police and international protocol. I was feeling proud of myself that I was clever enough to think of a way to get to George. He was the worst of the bunch in my mind. Go to hell, George Cavallas.

"Nathan, I heard that conversation. You just gave information to the Mafia. Information that was confidential. You betrayed the trust that Chuck placed in us." Now almost screaming, Audrey asked, "Are you crazy?"

I smiled at her and answered, "Maybe yes, maybe no."

Made in the USA
Middletown, DE
13 February 2016